PARADISE JAZZ

BY KAT POMFRET

Kat Pomfret

SNOWBOOKS ~ LONDON

Proudly published by Snowbooks

120 Pentonville Road

London N1 9JN

Email: info@snowbooks.com

www.snowbooks.com

British Library Cataloguing in Publication

A catalogue record for this book is available from the British

Library

ISBN 1-905005-08-3

ACKNOWLEDGEMENTS

Kat Pomfret was awarded a Writer's Bursary from the
Arts Council England, East Midlands.

PARADISE JAZZ

You can be up to your boobies in white satin, with gardenias in your hair and no sugar cane for miles, but you can still be working on a plantation.

Georgetown lies thirty degrees north of the equator and ninety-eight degrees west of the Prime Meridian.

The distance from Georgetown to Washington is over 1,000 miles. The distance to the Texas state capital is twenty-three miles, as the crow flies.

The population of Georgetown is 29,000; the approximate number of families, in thousands, is six.

These are the things I know about Georgetown, Texas. It's this Georgetown, and not Georgetown South Carolina or Georgetown Washington that I am named for. I know also that even before my mother was born in Rock Street, Georgetown, Texas, USA, that the

Comanche, Apache and Kiowa lived there and that beneath the town are caverns containing soda straws, mastodons and dire wolves. I do not wish to know what a dire wolf is. I know I was conceived at a place called Booty's Crossing near the banks of a river whose name I have forgotten and there is a fire-fighting museum near the mall. This is so you get a sense of history. So you don't think I've sprung out of nowhere rootless and open-mouthed. I just remembered something else about Georgetown: something or someone is called Blue Hole.

This is no way to begin. But if it's background you're after, the history of our family is one great void. Before my grandma, who I guess must have cracked herself out of an egg, or been created from the Lord's own wishbone, there is nothing but soda straws and San Antonio. My world is a shrunken world. It is a world only of my mother, of Tantie (Tantie is my auntie who got pregnant four summers after my mother) and her husband, Jimmy, and, in the far and distant past of my childhood, Sanderson Miller. There are holes in this world the size of Africa, the shape of a father. There are things we talk about and things we don't talk about. Breaking this rule is like trying to walk on the ceiling: you're only going to get yourself hurt. We've got twenty years of roots here in England, ten back in Texas, and before that, nothing. The history of my family is blank as the desert horizon. The past is mile after mile of empty sand, with nothing to mark the end of one story and the beginning of another.

My growing up was poetic; the kind that everybody likes to read about but nobody wants to have. In print, my childhood was one gigantic laugh-out-loud Christmas TV spectacular (things are certainly funnier in the past tense than the present) but the truth is, for Mom, Tantie, Jimmy and me, life was like jambalaya; plenty of flavour and lots of good things but, looked at one way, nothing to hold it all together, and, looked at another, Lord, you try unpicking one thing from another. And the unravelling begins for the first time with a bowl of sugar doughnuts, begins over again with a first-class ticket for flight 181 and a bottle of Freixenet, then begins for real the night Sanderson Miller walked into Paradise Jazz and heard a soul-dark girl singing white-hot blues.

A bowl of sugar doughnuts

The most important moments of my life have been played out to a backbeat of chargrilled chicken skin, roasting chipotles and onions caramelising in the pan. At home, nothing was so bad it couldn't be soothed by a coming-together of starch, heat and sugar, or, for the worst occasions, Mom's special mashed potato – sweet potato, honey and cream folded into butternut squash. Nothing was so important that it demanded the grinding of the pepper mill or the pounding of the pestle and mortar stop for a moment. I can remember no heartache from my childhood without my mouth watering.

Other moms baked cakes. My friends had moms that made iced sponge drops, mini-Battenburgs and the angel twins – whip and delight – in assorted pastel colours. My mom didn't have time for that. If you couldn't boil it, fry it or grill it till it smoked then it wasn't worth eating. Doughnuts, fried banana (sometimes Mom'd drop a bit of rum in, just to see the yellow flesh dance in the flames), griddled pineapple and thick buckwheat pancakes, all eaten hot from the pan; these were the puddings I was brought up on. I never saw a potato sliced so thin, a sausage grilled so smart, not a lemon squeezed so dry as I did in Mom's kitchen. And it took a lot more than an onion to make Mom cry. Watching my mother make bread was like watching Mike Tyson going ten rounds in the ring, she rolled up her sleeves and gave that dough hell. No holds barred, certificate eighteen violence, that was Mom in the kitchen and man, did it taste good.

One day, Mom called me into the kitchen. "Let's make doughnuts," she said, but Mom had other holes than doughnut rings, other fillings than jam on her mind. She was going to talk the talk with me. It was my fifth birthday. I had no interest in babies and less in boys, but Mom had decided it was time and Muhammad Ali himself could not have made her change her mind. She flung a couple of handfuls of flour in the mixing bowl (Mom thought weighing scales were for wimps). "So," she said, "Ellie's mom got a new baby girl."

"Uh-huh," I said, scrubbing my hands up in the sink like Mom told me, "and Ellie got a new dumper truck." Toy cars were a deal more interest to me than babies.

"You know where she got it from?"

"Uh-huh," I said, drying my hands on Mom's skirts, gentle as I could so she didn't notice. "The toy department at the Co-op."

"What you talking about, lady-girl?" Mom sucked her teeth in a way I knew meant trouble was coming. "I mean the baby, not the dumper truck."

"Oh," I said, "the *baby*." I stood by my mother with my nose resting on the worktop. If I stretched up on tiptoe I was just tall enough to watch Mom up-end a bottle of milk into the flour, ker-splat! "From the baby department at the Co-op?" I said.

Mom got a whisk in her hand; over on the stovetop, on the ancient electric ring, a pan of sunflower oil was coming to the boil. She looked at me real close. "Are you sassing me, Georgie Easy?"

"No," I said, rolling my eyes at the vegetable audience.

"'Cause I won't stand sassing." Mom flicked the whisk from one hand to the other and lunged at the doughnut batter. It was Mom and the mixture in hand-to-dough combat. Mom had the advantage of surprise and, to be fair, the batter didn't put up much of a fight; it sent out a couple of dribbles, which Mom deflected with her flack apron. After Mom had got her breath back, she started over again. I knew she was telling me something she thought was important, 'cause normally her voice was like cracked pepper and now she tried to make it like sweet chilli sauce. "Shall I tell you where babies come from?" she said.

"Why you whispering?" I said. "Ain't nobody else here."

"Don't try me," she said.

I shrugged, "If you want," I said.

Mom lowered the balls into the boiling fat and as we watched them darken to a crisp gold, Mom spilled the beans on the whole deal in the kind of detail you'd expect from a woman who could skin a chicken with one wrist-flick. Mom told me how when a man and a lady decide they want a baby, the man puts Mr Major in Mrs Moo, and after a while a baby comes out.

We waited in silence for a moment. I listened to the bubbling oil. "Do the nurses watch?" I said.

"What nurses? Girl, what you thinking of?"

"In the hospital, when they go to make the baby, do the nurses watch?"

Ellie's mom and dad had gone to the hospital right before the baby was born. I thought it was an instant process.

"Lord, no," Mom said. "No and no. At least, not in the usual way of things."

"I still think it would be a lot easier to go to the baby department at the Co-op," I said. "Sounds like a whole load of trouble just to get a baby." What I was really thinking to myself was: there are some things Mom can't dust in icing sugar. The absence of a father had never troubled me before: some kids I knew had one, others two, and others none at all. Up to this point a father had been an accidental, like a bicycle or a pair of patent leather shoes. If what Mom said was true, and it was a pretty strange thing to invent, then there were consequences we needed to discuss.

Mom scooped up the hot doughnuts with a slotted spoon and licked her lips. Mission accomplished. She bombed them with sugar, but I wasn't so interested in the doughnuts any more. I was doing the maths. So I wasn't an immaculate conception. Somewhere out there was a Mr Major with my name on it. And that's where this story really begins. As Mom and me sat, with a bowl of sugar doughnuts between us, I made the worst mistake I could have done if I hoped to ever find my father: I asked my mother who he was.

Mom acted like she'd just bit down on a chilli. She stopped chewing, mouth open, eyes bulging, jam sliding down her chin, and stared at me. Then she sprang. "Get to your room."

"Mom!"

"Room. Now!"

I heard her cranking the telephone dial right round, breathing heavy as it span back on itself. Mom's usual reaction in any parenting crisis was to call my aunt (who gave her own baby away the week it was born), but as I heard her winding that dial, looping her finger around and around, it sounded like she wasn't too keen to hear my aunt's advice on this occasion. I pinned my ear to the wall and listened to my mother sob for twenty minutes. Then I heard her say, real soft, "No more Texas." When I licked the sugar from my lips, I tasted salt. They are the first tears I remember crying.

After my fifth birthday there were no more stories from back home, no mention of Grandma, whose mind left her body the day JFK was shot, and who lived for fifteen years on popcorn and powdered milk, or of Blue Hole, or of my baby cousin, Nina Ella. These people lived in my memory like the characters of a fairy tale: outlandish, indelible and beloved. Once I left the nursery, Mom never spoke of them again. Now, to misplace one relative might be considered bad luck, but to lose all of them? There were years I was convinced Mom was a criminal on the run from the FBI; later I decided she was an informer, given a new identity by the CIA, told to leave her old Texas life behind and flee to the welcoming shores of Rule Britannia. I have a good imagination. I have had to. I waited years for my mother's Big Revelation, ready to assure her I wouldn't blow her cover to the *News of the World* or the *National Enquirer* and every birthday hoping I'd be grown enough to be let in on the secret.

And so I grew up, Mom knitting a past, me trying to find the end of wool to unravel the whole concern. My first attempts, asking the men we knew – my headteacher, Jessica Wetherby's dad, Mr Dhir from the cash and carry – if they could be quite *but quite* sure they weren't my father, resulted in nothing other than the mortification of my mother, though this was some reward in itself. I decided, age eight, and inspired by Esther Rantzen, to adopt a hard-line approach to my mother's inexplicable cruelty, and I would stand with the phone in my hand, fingers hovering over the keys, threatening to dial Childline if my mother didn't tell me who my father was.

"Call 'em," Mom would say, peeling a banana, one eye on the TV.

"I'm dialling," I would say, my finger shaking, "see, I'm dialling." I never did.

I looked out for clues: my skin is coffee with and Mom's is coffee without. I also had reason to believe that my mom was open minded on this inter-racial business.

"Everybody mix-race," Mom said, "everybody mix up like Christmas pudding, trouble is some folks think they can pick out the raisins, pick out the bits they don't like, you know what I'm saying? I tell you what happens if they pick out all the raisin of the Christmas pudding, they lose all the flavour, sister, they lose all the flavour." Mom's politics were ahead of her time. When she tried her Christmas pudding metaphor on Mrs Wilkinson at the Post Office, Mrs Wilkinson puffed herself up, looked down her nose at Mom and said, "Christmas pudding is as English as you get. It's English through and through."

Mom just stood there and laughed her off the

pavement. The tears were rolling down her cheeks when she said:

Who put the fruit in your pudding, sister?
Who give you rum?
Who put the spice in your pudding, missus,
Where you think it come from?

Mom wasn't too popular with the neighbours. Mom says, when she arrived in '81 with money in her pocket in the middle of the strikes, the English took one look at her and said, *Get in line, lady, get in line.* The reason English people don't like immigrants, according to Mom, is not because they think we're dirty or stupid or cook funny food. These, after all, are essential English characteristics. It's much worse than that: they think we're queue jumpers. The way they think is this: until your ancestors have spent three hundred years shovelling shit, a hundred years shovelling coal and fifty years shovelling battered cod and onion rissoles, you haven't earned the right to anything. And when the neighbours found out Mom wasn't a refugee from a war-torn African state they'd never heard of, or some Caribbean paradise threatened by a freak tornado, but came from the richest corner of the globe, any pretence of sympathy dissolved. *Don't you miss sunshine?* they'd say. *Don't you miss cable? Don't you miss ribs?* Mom's disregard for good weather, good TV and good food was highly suspect. I had to agree.

By the time I reached twelve, Mom and I were engaged in guerrilla conflict. My birthday present that year was a diversionary tactic, *Finding Your Afro-American Ancestors: A Beginner's Guide*, a book which promised:

> *There has never been a better time to research your African American ancestors. Advances in technology have made it possible for a family historian to cover great distances in time and location. It is perfectly possible for the dedicated amateur to trace her roots right back to the West African coastal plains where her family came from.*

Mom and Tantie drew a distinction between Black History in the general (which was a good thing) and black history in the particular (which was a terrible thing and sure to end in no good). As long as I omitted the last twenty years, Mom and Tantie had nothing against this slave heritage, getting back to your roots thing. So essential was it, and so worried were they that I, one of only four black children in my school year, victim of the British education system and the media conspiracy that confined black faces to the sports pages, music charts and *Crimewatch*, would grow up alienated from my cultural heritage, that they would set me quizzes on it:

> On what date did Rosa Parks become a symbol of the civil rights movement for refusing to give up her seat on a bus?
> a) September 13, 1956
> b) December 1, 1955
> c) December 10, 1953

> Dr Daniel Hale Williams, a black surgeon, was the first to perform what type of operation?
> a) Lung transplant
> b) Open heart surgery
> c) Liver transplant

Most times out of ten these seemed to end in fights as Mom and Tantie could never agree on exactly what the right answer was. Still, none of these questions were as interesting to me as:

1. Who are we?
2. What did we do?
And
3. Why does nobody want to talk about it?

Mom and Tantie would rather I was focusing on the edifying distant past, poring through the 1850 census or Free Negroes 1860, scouring records from cemeteries, churches and courts, than asking them anything personal like exactly how many guys the two of them got through at Booty's Crossing. And for years whenever I questioned them the answer I got was always the same:

> Georgetown lies thirty degrees north of the equator and ninety-eight degrees west of the Prime Meridian.

> The distance from Georgetown to Washington is over 1,000 miles. The distance to the Texas State capital is twenty-three miles, as the crow flies.

> The population of Georgetown is 29,000; the approximate number of families, in thousands, is six.

Flight 181 and a bottle of Freixenet

There wasn't a place for a twenty-third birthday but
Zambezi, my aunt's café on the far side of town. There
was always something to celebrate at Zambezi. It was
always somebody's birthday or else somebody sat in the
window or under the stair had a piece of good news or else
it was Friday and we'd drink to the end of the week, or
Wednesdays, when we'd raise glasses to the middle of it.
In all events, there was always a reason to allow yourself
one more slice of chocolate pie, or a dash of rum in your
lemonade. You see, Mary had a sign hung by the coat-
peg at the bottom of the stairs, it read *leave your troubles at
the door*. "Trouble ain't welcome here," she always said.
Mary saw trouble as a downstairs, out-on-the-street type

thing and Zambezi, floating on the second floor of the city, its windows opening out on fresh air and the fields beyond, was above it. And though you knew whatever problem you came in with was waiting to be picked up along with your coat on the way out, for as long as you were in Zambezi you could clean forget about it.

When Mom and Tantie first arrived in England the idea was to run the joint together. It didn't work out. For Mom, cooking was about process; the thwack of the cleaver in her old wooden chop board, the rippling oil in the bottom of the pan. For Tantie, the end result was what counted every time. Mom and Tantie were the greatest cooks I knew, but they didn't even chop an onion the same way. When Mom put the butter knife in the jam, or mixed her chillies, or topped the banana pie with pineapple, Tantie would catch her out and shout her down. One day Tantie found Mom cooking dirty rice with the gizzards and livers in a single pot, and though gizzards and livers take the exact same twenty-five cooking minutes each, Tantie would no sooner put them together than substitute chitlins for maws; soon after, Mom took on the house they shared as bed and breakfast and Tantie moved into the flat above the café.

I got there just as the main food rush that night was

through: people were winding down, shaking out and rolling up. Tantie was clearing the tables, calling through to the kitchen, "Jimmy, is you peeling more onions?"

Jimmy gave up answering my Aunty Mary years before.

"Jimmy I says, is you peeling more onions? Hmmm? You too busy peeling to answer me, I suppose?"

"Hey," I said, "don't the poor man deserve a holiday? Jimmy's been peeling since breakfast, I bet."

Jimmy's bass voice came growling through the hatch. "Lord, Georgie, it's longer than that. I've been peeling since 1985. Since the day I met that woman, she's had me peeling, and if I'm not peeling, I'm chopping, and if I'm not chopping, I'm grating. It's a wonder I've any fingers left over. Prison has got nothing on your aunt." His face appeared through the hatch, cracked in a toothy grin, "Happy Birthday, Georgie."

"Prison don't iron your shirts, Jimmy T. Since when a man grudge his wife a little peeling, eh? And on Georgie's birthday."

The entertainment at Zambezi was as good as the food, and there wasn't a man sat to dinner didn't know the story behind it. Jimmy slipped a band of gold on Mary's finger back in '85. He loved her curves in all the right places (and though the curves were moving south, at least they were all moving south at the same rate), how she fried chicken (not *too* much chilli, *just* enough sugar), and the belief she had that he'd given up on, that it is possible to find good in this world and hold onto it. She loved his skinny up and down self (a woman needs something to feed up) and his soul ache. Tantie is a great admirer of a man with soul ache. But the main reason they got married is 'cause he was from Africa and she was from the US of A and Tantie always dreamed of one day going back to where it all began and Jimmy was determined to get as far away from that old hell hole as he could. Somewhere in the middle they met and they stuck.

About the same time Tantie persuaded the council to give out free contraceptives to underage girls, Jimmy was arrested in Kenya for leading a protest against state censorship. Tantie got to hear about the case (her hairdresser told her; there was an entire network of political agitators that side of the ring road) and Jimmy became her longest-running campaign. Two years of letter-writing, petition-gathering and placard-waving later, Jimmy rolled off flight BA 721 into Tantie's waiting arms. Three weeks later they were married. Now that may sound like a whirlwind romance, but, as Tantie said, her and Jimmy went back three lifetimes. Tantie is a great believer in reincarnation. Anyhow, that's how the story goes. Most of the time the history didn't come into it. They fought over the dishes, like every other couple you know. But if you ask me, that history was what gave it glue, what meant that if Tantie stopped looking good in a swimsuit and Jimmy forgot to take the bins out three weeks in a row, and Tantie caught religion and Jimmy finally unravelled like a great ball of string, they would always be together.

Tantie brought out fried chicken in chipotle sauce and with it a baked egg macaroni cheese, beet coleslaw, and red beans and rice. Tantie could fix you the best soul food this side of heaven, real belly poetry that mixed gumbo, Creole and Cajun with old as misery Afro-American cooking and gave hell to the politics of it all. Her banana pudding came with real Nilla wafers and the smoothest custard; her buttermilk pie had the best mallow meringue. Then there were her candied yams, served with toasted pecans and coconut cream, with bourbon for vanilla, or fruit puss with the softest biscuit dumplings.

"How's it going?" I said, plating up the rice, "had any victories?"

"Of course."

"Who was it this time? Oil company?"

"No," she said, "The government of – where was that place now, Jimmy?"

Jimmy shrugged, served himself his second lot of macaroni.

"I remember now – Pakistan."

That's the thing about my Aunt Mary. She left school at fifteen and she'd been frying chicken and chopping onions ever since, but she could take on governments. Don't get the wrong idea. She didn't go in for letter bombs or chaining herself to railings, nothing no way demeaning. She had no time for the Animal Liberation Front (as far as Tantie was concerned, God put animals on this earth for one purpose only and you're failing your duty as a Christian if you don't eat as many as you can). You wouldn't have seen Tantie standing outside an abortion clinic waving a placard; as far as Tantie was concerned, that was between you and your conscience. She just had a problem with the capitalist state. Or perhaps I should say, thinking of her now, telling Jimmy what for for not chopping enough onions and giving her sweetcorn relish when all she ever asked for was a bit of mustard, that capitalist states, multinational corporations,

tinpot dictatorships and the prime minister himself had
a problem in Tantie.

We'd started on the macaroni when in at the door,
with a birthday card and a bottle of Freixenet, came
Helena Jones.

Tantie said, "Girlie, we wasn't expecting you!"

"You didn't think I'd miss Georgie's birthday?" said
Helena, kissing me and pushing the booze at Jimmy.

"No," I said, "but –"

Jimmy got to his feet, bowed low. He smiled, "What
the ladies mean, my dear, is pull up and plate up while I
pour you a drink."

We none of us seemed to know just what to say after
that, and made a deal of being busy with scraping our
knives, and chewing and chinking our glasses until Tantie,
who never could deal with a silence said, "Leastways you
looking better than last time I saw you."

"You look great," I said.

It wasn't two weeks since Helena's mom passed.
Cancer. And the year before that, her dad, same thing. I
didn't know, thing that it is to say, whether I was pleased
to see her or not, for having a birthday seemed right then
a tactless thing to do; presents and cake, all that, of a
sudden seemed right inconsequential.

Helena said, "Is there any salsa, Mary? You know what a fan I am for your salsa. Especially with drumsticks. And as for you," and she squeezed my elbow, "birthday or not you ought to be ashamed of yourself: you can't turn twenty-three without a good tomato pickle, Georgie. I'd sooner go without cake."

She was the kind of person you felt lucky to know, but the kind that never would let you tell them that. Wasn't hardly a time I could remember her when she wasn't surrounded by sickness, and no matter the times I picked her up off the floor saying she couldn't stand it, she always did. But I worried about the girl; she was so used to getting by, to getting from sunrise to sunset and through long nights to the morning, I didn't know how she was going to start living.

Tantie seemed to have a pretty good idea. She popped the lid on a jar of salsa and said, "You coming on this march Saturday?"

Helena tucked her hair behind her ear and said she wasn't sure.

"What's the matter?" Tantie said, "You got something better to do? There's acres of rainforest being raped for peanuts, but if you've got something better to do —"

"Excuse me," Helena said, getting up, "I need the

bathroom." The floorboards squealed as she crossed the room.

"God, Tantie."

"What?"

"Not everybody is like you," I hissed.

"Don't I know it." Tantie cleared the plates as noisy as she could.

"Give the girl a break, can't you? You can't fight the world." I said, "You know, you can't fight the whole world?"

"Why not?"

"You just can't."

"What you mean is, I can't win so it's not worth trying. What happened if Martin Luther King said that? Eh? What happened if Ghandi say that? What happened if I say that and let your uncle Jimmy rot in jail or let your mom stay over in the United States of Shame and Disgrace letting that man do what he want with her? If that's the way you think, girl, you better get in your bed and don't bother getting out of it."

"What man?" I said.

"Never mind, that's not the point I'm making now. What I'm saying is, ain't no point getting up in the morning 'less you think you make a difference. It's better to boil than simmer, it's better to care too much than not to care at all. You can tell that to your mother."

Tantie hadn't spoken to my mother in three months, not since Mom bought a jar of Nescafé. This was what all their arguments were like: two proud old women who couldn't agree on the colour of the sky and didn't know how to compromise. They fought like sisters: eyes blazing and full of the righteousness of God. Some things would never change: Mary would always be one year older, Mom would always be one half inch taller. There was history. There was subtext. It spoke volumes. If anyone but my mom had bought that coffee, Tantie would've just kissed her teeth and muttered to herself, like I'd heard her do a hundred times. If anyone but Tantie had objected, my mom would have laughed in her face till the tears ran down her dress. But because it was each other, because they had shared the same womb, this was personal. For example, if Tantie shifted her bosom left to right, like she did when she was brooding over something, my mom would say later, "Did you see that woman? Think she the cat's pyjamas, heaving those great bosoms around like she the only woman in the world who's got them. She's the older one, of course she get them first, well she losing them to gravity first too."

My mom only had to call my aunt 'Mary', in a certain tone, for Mary to think she heard 'Hairy Mary', the song my mom used to sing about her in the bath about thirty years ago. This fight was not about Nescafé, just like their last fight wasn't about disposable cutlery, and their fight before that was not about trainers. All their fights were about the same thing: who's the prettiest, who's the smartest, who their mom loved most, and who loved her back. I had given up playing referee, 'cause they were scoring points I didn't even know about, committing fouls I didn't even see.

"Mom cares," I said, "but you know Mom, she's a realist."

"She says poor people can't afford principles. That's not realism, that's bullshit."

"She didn't mean it."

"I saw her raise that eyebrow. I know what that means." After forty years of fighting, Mom and Tantie didn't even need to open their mouths anymore; they could say it all with a look, a wink, a nod.

Helena came back through, fresh lipstick and red eyes, and Jimmy picked his Fender up and settled himself down into an old comfort riff he always seemed to fall into at times like this, keeping his eyes steady on the girl till he won a smile off her. Jimmy's guitar looked like it had been on more journeys than Jimmy; there were cigarette burns on the veneer, and it looked like someone had taken a knife to the moulding, but it played sweeter than a cherry.

"Paradise Jazz got a showcase next week," Tantie topped up Helena's glass with fizz, "Jimmy and Blooz Hot is on. You want me to get you a ticket?" Tantie always found apologies hard.

"Helena don't like the blues, remember," I said.

Helena looked at me, then looked at Jimmy, not daring to catch my aunt's eye. "I just prefer something a bit more upbeat, you know. I mean, all this griping. My woman's left me, my car don't go. You get enough of it."

Tantie looked like someone had stuck a firework in her soul-hole. "Well that's life, ain't it? Blues tell it the way it is, straight from the heart, with feeling, you know what I'm saying? With feeling. How that gonna bring you down? Long as a body can say what's on its mind, I think that's a mighty joyful thing. You say misery, that's one way of calling it, but the way I see it, what it's all about is that even when your woman leaves you, or your car don't go, you keep on singing. Ain't that right,

Jimmy, you keep on singing."

"When you put it that way —"

"That's the only way there is, sugar. Why you think blues players all live so long, hmm? John Lee Hooker, ninety years old, BB King and Nina Simone still blowing strong. I tell you why, 'cause they put it out there, 'stead of keeping it all in here," and Tantie thumped her great chest. "And if I ever met a body needed some bluesing, it's you, Helena Jones. The doctor ought to give you a blues prescription, is what." Even Tantie's condolences could feel like lectures.

Jimmy was blowing quotes left right by this point, slowly picking up the volume. Jimmy never said much, but when he played it was like a thousand words at once. Jimmy got the chops all right. He sounded like he'd been playing his whole life, like he was born and raised in the Delta and was just trying to work his finger-pickin' way back there. Truth is, Jimmy couldn't even hold a guitar right until four years ago. A customer came in, struck up, and Jimmy was hooked. The battered old axe he played he found in an ad in the *Evening News* but like I said, Jimmy had soul-ache and it came out of every pore. As he played on, Tantie got to her feet and started to shake herself in front of him, her feet slippery like a newborn on the floor as she slided and glided like a spirit thing, bogling, waist-winding, booty shaking. Tantie was not a young woman, but she said she had grown into her sex, and the way she moved herself could make the sun blush. Tantie was a mean blues singer herself. You ask me, Tantie had more rhythm in her left hip-bone than James Brown and P-funk altogether, but Jimmy didn't like Tantie singing, said it didn't do a man's heart no good to have his wife show him up like that in public. And on this, as if to make up for all the matters she paid him no notice on, Tantie let him have his way. Tantie used to sing the bars in Austin and Dallas, hitching a ride over to the big cities after her momma had gone to bed and coming back with the sunrise, breathing gin fumes. She'd got a big round voice that came at you like a curve ball, knocked you right off your feet. I would have loved to have had a voice like Tantie's, stead of like Mom's, like piss passing into a metal pan. Mom says Tantie could have done something with that voice, but as Tantie said, a good voice don't change the world. There's time for singing up in heaven.

Jimmy said, "Was that enough for you, ladies? I do hope so, because it was too much for me," and mopped his head with a big white hanky and laughed "Hee hee hee."

"Play some more, Jimmy," I said, "play one of the old songs. Give me some *Sweet Home Chicago*."

He rolled his eyes round in his head and looked at Tantie and said, "You know this girl never liked me, now she wants to kill me."

"Time for presents," Tantie said, and she brought out a hot rice pudding with baked mango coulis, toasted vanilla beans and a big jug of almond, banana and rum milkshake, and, just to reach the mark, a lemon cream pie she said needed using up. She'd got me a photo album and Jimmy gave me a camera. "Thought it about time we started a family photo album," Tantie said.

I took a photo of Tantie and Jimmy; Jimmy took a photo of Helena and me. It was another diversionary tactic.

Helena slid an envelope across the table to me. I've still got it – sky blue with clouds and a sheen to the print of it reminded me of sunshine. And that was Helena, didn't matter the day but she'd make an occasion of it. I gave her a sly look, but she wouldn't pass it back, just pulled her hair tight in a band: she had baby-like curls, fine and soft but thin with it and seemed whenever they was down she was wishing they was up and when they was up she was picking bits loose, always fixing it one way or the other, never happy with it and incapable of letting it be. I opened her card up, but this year there was more than a poem there; tucked inside was a ticket and my heart rose and sank real quick when I saw it.

"What you got girl?" Jimmy said.

"What's that there?" Tantie said, "A ticket?"

"Where you off to, Georgie?" said Jimmy.

I folded it out. "Flight 181," I said.

"Flight?" said Tantie.

"I got her a ticket to Dallas," Helena said.

It was just the kind of over the top thing you could expect from Helena these days. Time was you could count on the girl to keep me straight. Lately she was just heart over head every time.

"I wanted some good to come out of it. The money, I mean," she said. "I wanted, I thought in a way it would —"

I squeezed her knee under the table. Jimmy let out a low whistle. Tantie sat back in her chair, arms folded. "You can't go buying the girl a ticket."

"Tantie!"

"Why not?" Helena said. "It's her birthday."

"Why can't you get a record voucher, eh? Or bubblebath. The girl could do with bubblebath. What she want with a ticket to Dallas?" Tantie knew all too well Georgetown wasn't more than a bus ride from Dallas.

"Just a guess I took," Helena said. There was something between those two. They couldn't let each other be. Tantie was a doer and Helena was a thinker and I didn't know quite why it was but I think that the each of them found it harder to sleep at nights just knowing the other was alive.

"You should have checked," Tantie said.

"She's twenty-three."

"The day you have children is the day you tell other people how to bring up theirs."

"Listen to yourself," Helena said.

There was a silence could have curdled eggs. I had told Helena about Nina Ella, the baby my aunt gave away, but she had no business bringing her up right then. Nina Ella was way out of bounds and Jimmy intervened, "Why you always be stirring things up all the time? Girl was fine till you started in on her."

"She was not fine," Helena said.

"What business is it of yours if she fine or not fine?" Tantie said.

"I had the money," she said, "Georgie wanted the ticket."

Helena should have known nothing was ever that simple in our family.

Tantie turned on me. "Give it back, Georgie."

"Tantie."

"Give it back."

I thought about it. For twenty years, near as, I put up with the Authorised Version of the past. Mom and Tantie may have thought I was all played out with it, but I was counting my bars, waiting for the right time to pick up the tune, and here was Helena Jones standing in the wings waiting to bring me in. But talking about Georgetown was one thing; sure I'd threatened to go often enough, but if I went, then, in a sense, there was no coming back home again.

"Only a fool would fly to Texas," Tantie said.

I folded the ticket back in its envelope and tightened my fingers round it.

Tantie brought her hand down on the table. "Lord! Sanderson back in town and Georgie got a flight to Texas, that about all I need."

The rice pudding had grown a thick and wrinkled skin, the coulis congealed. I was beginning to think Jimmy may have put a little too much rum in the milkshake. "Sanderson Miller's back in town?" I said, my throat tight around his name.

Sanderson Miller was a hero round our way in the days when all you needed to be a hero was a Stag and sunshades. Sanderson had all that and more – a suede coat with a paisley lining that said *Made in New York* and a walk to think about long after he was gone. Sanderson could put a smile on a dead woman's lips; he could make your grandma come out in a sweat on Christmas Day. Sanderson was smooth as homicide.

Some towns have ghosts; we had Sanderson. He'd wait till just that time when everyone was shaking their heads saying, "This time that boy ain't never coming back," or, "He landed himself in some trouble this time, that's for sure," when he'd roll up with the windows down and the bass box shaking the windows. When Sanderson came to town bringing goodies from the furthest reaches of his international empire of funkdom, everything got hisself lively. He'd stand the men a couple of rounds and, fools that they were, they'd forget the trouble he'd left behind him six, nine, twelve months earlier and not notice the compliments he paid their pretty wives. The next morning you'd see the women whistling as they hung out the bedsheets and the men roll out of bed still drunk and calling for their eggs well done. It was the closest we got to carnival.

Sanderson smoked mean cigarettes he rolled himself, licking the paper with his old-dog tongue, tamping it down. He just had to reach for his tobacco to have ten men go for their lighter, just like he only had to lick his lips for women to give him their number. Dressed up in floral shirts and camel colour suits, he was the closest thing to a movie star I ever did see. Every kid round our way wanted a ride in his soul-black Dakota, and a couple of the older girls gave him what he was looking for on those leather seats. Or so the story goes. He was our own personal Stagolee: so bad the rain wouldn't rain on him, so bad the flies wouldn't land on him. But so good you didn't know what to do about it.

Mom and me had always been favourites of Sanderson on account of the American connection (though Sanderson, as he liked to proclaim, was a Northern nigger whose ancestors had known in which direction a good time lay) and on account of the fact that Mom was the only woman in town not trying to unfasten his pants. Sanderson always had a chocolate bar in his pocket when he came to call at our place, and he always called me Georgetown, real solemn, not George or Georgie like all the other grown-ups I knew. Mom said she never could understand how he was always coming across so many pretty scarves just about the time he came to visit. He was the only man she let call her Agie, and the only man I ever heard try. Still, Mom didn't let me take candy off him. Mom said, "A man don't give nothing away without he want something in return." (Mom could find a moral for most occasions.) Sanderson just used to wink at me like we were the only two people in the world and slip the Hershey's under the cushion for me to find later.

Above all these things, Sanderson was a brother, and he didn't stand for no mistaking of that fact. I remember the Lady Di street party we held in '81, the terrace decked out in red, white and blue, the kids eating cheese and pineapple hedgehogs, jelly and Neapolitan ice-cream and Mom's contribution: home-made ground beefburgers. This NF guy who lived two streets away didn't seemed too pleased his son was sat next to me, was giving it all the 'ain't no black in the union jack' business. Sanderson looked at him, not bothering to take the cigarette from his teeth, not needing to raise his voice a beat above breathing volume, and said, "But there sure is a cunt in the National Front." From that day, whether Sanderson happened to be in town or out of it, Mom and me got less trouble from the neighbours.

All that changed when I got to twelve. Mom caught

him making out with a girl two years up from me at school and chased him out and his Columbian Gold after him. After that he didn't stop by this way any more, and I guess we all thought Sanderson had used the last of his nine lives. The thought of Sanderson back in town, sat there with his arm wrapped round some blonde honey, just about made my heart beat backwards.

Tantie's voice was soft as a prayer, "Trouble comes around fast enough, Georgie. Don't go looking for it."

Jimmy sat, eyes down, revolving his plectrum around his two thumbs.

Though Mom and Sanderson had been friendly, Tantie had always been twitchy at the mention of his name, which I put down to the fact that Sanderson had a soul so black it could blind a girl. Something about her reaction that night, her eyes like a little lost child, made me turn my ideas round. Mom's familiarity and Tantie's anger with Sanderson came from the same place: he had something on them, and maybe that something was something worth knowing.

"What you think gonna happen?" I said.

"The man's loose, damn it. His pants is loose fitting, his morals is loose as a bad tooth and his mouth, well, that's the loosest of all."

I knew Tantie too well. I knew the last thing she said was the first thing on her mind. "Ain't Sanderson's job to keep Mom's secrets," I said, "and it ain't yours either."

Jimmy sat, not even blinking, turning that old pick around and around those tired old onion-chopping, gut-plucking fingers. I stuffed the ticket tight jam in my back pocket and angled my chin at my aunt the way I'd seen her do at my mom. If anyone knew who my daddy was, it was Sanderson. And it didn't take me a moment to figure out how to get the truth out of him. Sanderson kept the key to his soul where most men do, and I'd done some growing since Sanderson Miller was last in town.

Tantie looked at me and said to Helena, "Girl, you see what you started now?"

Sanderson Miller at Paradise Jazz

Sanderson should never have been in Paradise. Even if he was at home there like a snake in Eden, even if the town was waiting on him like the second coming, even if he'd forgotten he was banned twenty times over and that Paradise Jazz was two streets up from Zambezi; even if all these things were true, Sanderson should have picked another night for his homecoming. You see, though no one could ever have stopped what was meant to be, I can't help but think that maybe if the moon had been fatter in the sky, or the stars spread out in a different arrangement when Sanderson Miller first heard and saw a soul-dark girl singing light-as-death blues, then this story might have had a happier ending.

A Delta man had set Paradise up, a man by the name of Earl Skinner, back in '81, but after a couple few years the call of Orleans got too strong and he sold it on for the price of a plane ticket and a case of whisky. Paradise was bought and sold maybe ten times in the next fourteen years, by men Mom says knew nothing of music but the sound of money. Then, in '95, Son Son, a God-loving man who would have been a preacher if blowing cornet could save souls, bought Paradise with the compensation money he got when he lost his leg. You won't find it in the guidebooks, and, being a cellar bar, you could walk over it a dozen times never knowing it was there. But once you've been there's no leaving it behind. Paradise sucked up sorts from that world part like a black hole, 'cause for twenty miles all around was a zone of total snoozation, and the cats there, black or white, lapped up all that Son Son could feed them like it was cream, and the consequence of this was there were two kinds of customer at Son Son's: first-timers and every-timers.

The every-timers were ugly as minor seventh – their skins smoked like crocodile hide, their voices cracked like a broken bottle, their eyes as yellow as their teeth. There wasn't a vice in existence didn't have its corner in Paradise and it just about broke Son Son's heart. "The blues is the devil's music, all right," he'd say, "it's his invitation and his calling card." Some nights he'd threaten us, "I'm turning this place straight, you hear? No blues, no jazz, just good *Christian* music from now on." Nobody ever thought he would. Paradise Jazz trailed behind itself a tail as long and smoky as the devil's, knotted with enough kinks and coils to trip you up. But it seems to me that talking 'bout what's bad and good, right and wrong had no business with Paradise. Paradise was the kind of place where black and white mixed like salt and pepper, cream and cardamom; it settled itself in the space in between one thing and another, the place where myths became legends and legends took off their coats and played the kind of blues to leave blisters on your soul, lesions on your karma. I'm talking 'bout people like Byther Smith and Taj Mahal; even John Lee had dusted his broom in Paradise back in the day, and some might say it was out of place in that little northern town, but what do they know? There's no legislating for what might happen when a person catches rhythms like they got at Paradise. Probable or not, outside of London, I'd say Son Son had the best venue and the choosiest crowd, and it beat like a heart; only thing keeping that cold place breathing.

Paradise had its prophet healer in Son Son's nephew,

Bo. With a lemon slice and a fistful of crushed ice, Bo, who'd inherited the family love of the Lord, would use his own mixological talents to minister to the sickest of souls. Bo offered spiritual remedy (gin, vodka, whisky; Bo knew there were many paths to enlightenment) and could do things with a cocktail shaker that tasted almost like salvation. For the lustful man he filled the driest martini. Slow as regret the morning after he'd pour vermouth, then pour it out again, letting the fumes hang in the air like a bad conscience ought to.

For the gluttonous man, Bo prescribed a Paradise special: the 666. Just watching him layering liqueurs like a coronary, six of whisky cream, six of chocolate, six of amarula, was a lesson. Envy was dealt a potion shaken and strained through the finest mesh, one part lime juice, one part Elixir du Dr Roux and one part dry vermouth. It tasted good as sin, fine enough to make you count your own blessings 'stead of eyeing someone else's.

Bo didn't need to ask your trouble to know the penance. He read souls easy as cream. The jealous woman was served a syrup of beckerovka, gomme and lime, the liquor given a final twist with a serrated lemon slice and left to stand for six minutes dead. It brought on a passion flush to work against the green-eye. Pride was blue champagne – the fizz poured in tight on top of vodka, blue Curaçao and maraschino and served in equal measures to every man stood at the bar. Anger, a barbed wire slash of the shortest vodka martini with a bloodspill of Pernod and Chambord, to make a man consider the consequences.

Sloth was counteracted by *crème de cacao blanc*, *crème de banane* and coconut milk, a soporific blending guaranteed to give you nightmares, while a single shot of Goldwasser at the bottom of a hi-ball saw to Avarice: impossible to drink, the measure stuck to the sides of the glass, glittered darkly and left the drinker dry. Bo could attend to every one of the seven deadlies and any combination of them you care to imagine. You can bet he kept a drink in mind for me: he called it magnolia blossom – pure gin, lemon juice, grenadine and cream – the colour of angel hair, he said, to teach a woman how to keep away from breaking a poor man's heart.

Son Son had organised his first amateur showcase that night. Jimmy and his Blooz Hot band were first up, then Little Sista, some out-of-towner white boys with keyboards, then Pa Roper on harp with His Jazz Masters, who'd come up two hundred miles, such was the draw of Paradise. Though Son Son knew too much about the relation of blues and the human heart to try anything as contrary as a blues competition, everybody knew Son Son was looking for a house band and Jimmy had got himself a bad case of nerves from meditating on the fact of it. Tantie said she couldn't get a day's work out of him the week beforehand, he just shuffled round the house blowing harmonica and passing wind. As we sat stage-back, wedged between the cashews and the empty bottles in the store cupboard Son Son liked to call a dressing room, Jimmy licked a Rizla with the tip of his tongue, tamped the cigarette together and stuck it between his teeth. He took a deep breath. "Remind me why I'm doing this, Georgie."

"You'll kill 'em," I said.

"It might be the other way round," he sucked on the end of his roll-up. Jimmy doesn't smoke, never has, and he never lights up, but something about the sprinkle, roll, tamp, suck ritual is kind of comforting to him.

"Anyhow," I said, "seems to me you're not the one should be worrying. All you got to do is play; it's Bob what's got to sing to them."

Jimmy looked at me. He rolled his eyes like a shaman. "Don't you know? Bob locked himself in the toilet half an hour ago. I do not think he is coming out."

Tantie and Mom came waltzing over, friendly so you would think they had never blinked out of time with another in their lives. Mom's skirt was shorter than a good time, her lips redder than a fond memory. Mom and Tantie were right at home in Paradise, VIPs as the only authentic Americans in town. They'd been in England nearly twenty years; you'd have expected their consonants to harden and their righteousness to soften on a diet of milk tea and sponge puddings, but instead of going native, falling in with the blue rinses and roast lamb, they'd given mouth-to-mouth to a town in its death throes, fitted it with a pacemaker that beat to bluegrass and not just stood it on its feet but shown it how to dance. In moving here, they'd made a Texas of their own, with soulfood and chicken wings, and the blues and the jazz and their own personal sunshine with a canned laughter soundtrack and their own backing band. There was something in my mother and her sister independent of time and place, rising above it, something inside that would always work itself out. Texas ain't a place, it's a state of mind, I knew that before I could count to ten, and I'd inherited the boots, the hat and the attitude, mongrel thing that I was. Mom and Mary rubbed up the town like chilli rub on a spare rib, but they were adamant about one thing: they were never going back. "What's that you saying about Bob?" Tantie said.

Jimmy looked up at her mournfully. "Get a dying man a drink?" he said, "I'm about to seize up with thirst here."

Tantie shifted her bosoms around while she thought about it. "One lemonade, coming up."

"You couldn't put a little whisky in that could you girl?"

Tantie shook her head as she headed to the bar. "I could now, course I *could*."

Diddy came waddling through, out of breath and patting the top of his head like he did when he got like this, jumpy as a spit on a hot skillet. Diddy always made me smile. I guess he must have weighed about twenty stone, and just breathing must have come a struggle, but I never saw him out of the Blooz Hot standard issue black waistcoat, pants and jacket (with a black tie too, real sophisticate, that was the image Blooz Hot liked to cultivate, and as Jimmy said, if a man is going to get shot down, he may as well be buried in his finery). Diddy looked like a Prohibition gangster, like Al Pacino in *The Untouchables*, only a thousand Pukka Pies later, or that Howling Wolf line 'bout being built for comfort, not built for speed. "Brother, are we in trouble," he said.

Jimmy didn't even turn round. "What's with you, man, can't you see I'm focusing?"

"Well you want to quit focusing and start praying, 'cause man I'm telling you, those guys, that Little Sista, I heard 'em in warm-up and they are shit hot. Shit, I tell you man, hot."

Jimmy shook his head slowly and said, "Now that is something like demeaning."

"You're not going to lose to no Little Sista," I said. "Those guys are extra virgin; you're twenty-year malt."

Diddy shrugged, "I'd say if anything comes with age it's the blues. Still, maybe someone wants to teach me a lesson otherwise."

Tantie came back with a straight-up lemonade and a sorry looking Bob, "You ask me, that's an evil-sounding blues Little Sista have got themselves there."

Nobody looked at her. We all knew Tantie and we all knew she meant it was a white sounding blues, but Bob's mom was white and, besides my own less than pure-bred situation, it didn't ever seem right respectable to me to say a thing like that. Jimmy shrugged at Bob, but Tantie mistook our silence. "You see, Bob, white blues, it just ain't got no depth to the groove, you hear what

I'm saying? No colour to the sound and the rhythm's too blind to hold on to."

"Woman, you pick your moments, anybody ever tell you that? You pick your moments." Diddy was twisting his tie around his finger like a first-day schoolboy.

"See, life is like an onion – first time you cut it, it makes you cry. But keep the heat low and steady and all that anger turn sweet like some kind of miracle. That's what the blues does – turns sorrow to caramel, and that's the trouble with eskimo blues, it's too raw or else burnt up to crisp; they ain't found the sugar in their onion yet."

Son Son's head appeared round the storeroom door just in time. "Fellas, you're up." Diddy and Jimmy grabbed their instruments, Bob gave a deep swallow, and they headed for the stage.

Now Blooz Hot generally favoured an uplifting blues, almost ragtime, but they started with a Delta song, *Hard Time Killin' Floor Blues* – Bob with an angelic falsetto that defied his size and Jimmy with a neat guitar backup. I guess they knew the competition were both good times bluesmen, and they wanted to give something a little different, or maybe they wanted to take us down so they could bring us up some. Anyway, there was a sorrow in those falling notes of Bob's you could feel in your bones, took you back to a time when heartbreak was an everyday thing and singing about it was as natural as breathing out. It was almost too much to hear them play a song like that straight up. The crowd didn't know what to do with it, half-sober as they were. Truth was, I wasn't the only one with an eye out for Sanderson. The women all had their hair fresh done and the men looked sharp enough to cut. Two hundred eyes levelled at the door every time it swung open and Bo had a martini glass about to crack with frosting, but Sanderson, who we expected though we knew it was the last place he ought to be, was keeping us all waiting.

The boys followed up with a solid dance-style *Baby Don't Go,* Bob giving a mean harp solo with a Sonny Boy feel; Jimmy took it up a notch with a blazing *Shake That Thing.* Diddy caught on, and Bob gave a bit of old-fashioned scat make your grandma smile. By the time they hit on *Give Your Woman What She Wants*, which Jimmy said was Tantie's all-time favourite song, Jimmy was funking out the finger picking, Diddy was shaking that thang like three hundred pounds of heavenly joy, and for a while the three of them were freaking out up there. They were the bluest men in the whole damn town, and there wasn't any doubt in my mind Tantie was going to be finding a new vegetable peeler Saturday nights.

I squeezed Tantie's elbow. Tantie smiled a little to herself, "They's not as bad as they could have been."

After *Give Your Woman* they took a breather. Diddy kept a bass line going, *dum-dum-be-dum*, just letting his fingers play over those strings like he didn't even know he was doing it, like he could keep on playing till the end of the earth regardless. Bob let out a long moan seemed like someone left the window open on his soul. "O-o-oh Brother!"

"What's the matter, man?" Jimmy said, licking sweat from his upper lip and looking almost all his sixty years. This was not in the carefully scripted and well-rehearsed catalogue of improvisations they had been practising.

Bob shook his head, his cheek flesh wobbling. He raised his eyes to the ceiling, turned his palms to heaven, and said again, "O-o-oh, Brother."

"Tell me what it is, man," Diddy said, looking to Jimmy for reassurance.

Bob let his shoulders hang down, his head sunk on his chest and he breathed heavy as he said one final time, "O-o-oh, Brother." He stood tall. "It's my woman."

Mom leant over to me. She smelled of Bacardi. "Bob sure is a fine looking man," she said.

"What your woman done, Brother?" Jimmy said, smiling now they were catching up on him.

"She told me to get me a J-O-B."

"Why she say that, Brother?"

"She says she want a B-M-W."

Jimmy and Diddy raised their eyebrows and shook their heads at one another. "And what you say to her?"

"I told her, Sister, you *got* a B-M-W, you got a Black Man Working for you. Ain't that enough?"

They dropped straight into *Boogie Chillen* to close, hot enough for people to forget they ever heard the name Sanderson Miller.

Later, while the boys downed straight whisky chasers (skipping the beer to get quicker to the point), Little Sista took to the stage, and they didn't let nobody down, but like I said, hearing them after hearing my uncle Jimmy was like following rum with moonshine, and I headed to the bar. "You drinking, Tantie?" I said. "Malibu, yeah?" But Tantie looked in need of something much stronger.

"What's the matter?" I said.

"Nothing," she said. "Nothing at all."

I followed her eyes and ran bang smack into Sanderson. I shook on the spot at the sight of him. In his long leather coat and his wool hat, he was still a fine man. Sure Sanderson was old now, with a bad conscience eating away at him, or so it should have been. Never mind that, I looked at Sanderson Miller, and I was eight years old with buckteeth, making daisy chains, waiting for him to roll his fine self out of bed so I could show him what I made. I looked at Sanderson Miller, and I felt the blood flow thick through me the way it forgot to in this old place.

While I was meditating on the beauty of the badness of the man, damn but I'd let Tantie get in there first, before even the men he owed money to with thirteen years interest and the girls gone to fat on a long promise. Tantie and Sanderson had tucked themselves in a corner. They looked like they were chatting casual as spilt milk, but I could see Sanderson flipping his cigarette lighter round in his left hand, and Tantie's right foot was tapping a flamenco on the floor. All of a once, Tantie came storming past me, almost knocked the glass clean out of my hand.

"Hey!" I said. "What's the hurry, Sister?"

"Stay away from that man, you hear?"

Course, I ain't never been capable of that. Don't know a woman who was and soon as I could see Tantie rewarding my uncle with kisses, I worked my way over.

"Sanderson Miller," I said, when I saw him jangling the change in his pocket, "old dog got himself a new bone."

And he smiled and one of his tooths was gold now, I could see. "Looking good, Sister, looking good."

"Doing myself just fine," I said.

"That's what I see. Real fine, Georgetown, real fine."

"What brings you back home?"

"Oh," he said, "The wind, and you know, it ain't no use fighting the wind, now is it?"

"You just missed Mom," I said. She had last been seen two songs into the Little Sista set, leading a dazed-looking Bob to the rehearsal rooms, though Mom wasn't short of practice.

He nodded.

"You is calling on her, isn't you?"

Sanderson took a long draw on his cigar. He was flirting past me at some girl on the other side of the room, like an old pro, keeping his hand in; glad to reassure hisself he hadn't lost the touch.

"She ain't mad at you, still, if that what you thinking, even though it been years, and you ain't even called, and seeing as how you and she were such good friends, but she ain't still mad. You can call in."

"Run along now, sugar," Sanderson said.

"Sanderson —"

Sanderson could kill a smile quicker than a brawl. "Run along, Georgetown."

I slouched to the bar. Diddy took pity and bought me a rum and coke, must have been a double 'cause about that time the world took on a mighty strange shape. I floated by Sanderson again, hips swaying, body trying to say what my mouth wouldn't but there was every kind of offer on the table for Sanderson that night. I don't think he noticed me till I stumbled into one of his shoeshine boys and then he looked at me not much impressed, like you might regard a dog trying to dance on its back legs. Mom hadn't surfaced, and Tantie said I was best off stopping with her and Jimmy that night. Pa Roper played — Bo Diddley stuff, nothing out of place, but rocking it too much altogether, and Blooz Hot seemed a sure thing. We waited for Son Son to tell us what we thought we knew when Bo came up on stage and said we had a fourth performer. People were grumbling when a girl, sheened like bloodstone, smoothed like onyx, bright like black star sapphire, a girl curved like a guitar and tight as an E string, with no band and no backing, got up to sing.

Her voice cut through that thick air like oxygen and

one by one people pressed up to the stage. Here was someone had what we needed and was giving it out like it was candy. There was every gradation of sweetness in that voice, from the thick syrup of the cane to the sharp sugar kick of a sherbet, and whereas the trouble with a sweet voice, too often, is that it gives you nothing to hold onto, this voice had grit to it. It didn't so much slide over you as peel the skin from your back. And the songs she sang, low down dirty blues with jassed breathing, the old Ma Rainey and Lucille Bogan tracks in a way to put the original clean out of your mind. This girl gave some smoke.

Pretty soon she had the whole room going: the beer in Pa Roper's glass, the second hand on Bo's old wrist-watch, the blood in my veins, or so it felt, all shaking in time with her boogie and then, just as she got everything bubbling nicely, just as the steam was starting to rise, and I saw the guys loosening their ties, the ladies kicking off their shoes and saying you never so old, so drunk or so out of love you can't stand one last shimmy, she cut it dead, not three songs into her set. Course this was a ploy we'd seen before, ain't nothing like an encore to prove a point, but the place was up and angry at her and seemed like the anger pleased her more than the applause, 'cause it wasn't till someone made a name for her that she started over again, and this time with the Nina Simone track, *Three Women*, and she was another singer again. Mom, charmed out like a snake by the song, her cheeks flushed, a hicky on her neck, said, "That's a voice to make you homesick."

"Hmmm, girl, I could be in Orleans right now," Tantie said.

Mom shook her head, "Not Orleans, I mean *home*sick."

"That voice got to take you back further than 1970, Mary," Bob said.

It was an old voice all right, and as she got herself warm, she got ugly, there was a growl at the bottom of her purr and she moved from loud to soft, high pitch to low in a way made you dizzy. Most singers like to cook it up a little, steam it or smoke it, and it's the way of the cooking, the heat of it and the flavour that makes a song; this kid served it up raw, and taking no more pleasure in it than a whore does, 'cause while the rest of the room hotfooted it, she stood there still as deep water and cold with it, seemed like more we loved her, stiffer she stood, and you would have thought it a sermon she was preaching, so stern she was with it.

But Mom was time travelling. "Right," she said to Bob, "You're right, that voice a whole lot older than anything I heard, like being in the room with – well I don't know."

Jimmy was rolling a cigarette "It's got a pedigree all right, stretch all the way back to Eden and the first bite of that apple, no kind of a voice for a girl to be messing with."

In the wash of her rhythm you could hear the Atlantic Ocean crashing on the Ivory Coast, in her vibrato there was the death rattle of the free-born slave and the cry of the war-rape baby. That voice, that voice gave you soulhunger, sent you back to where you came from and further back and to go with that, the worst case of vertigo: I didn't know where I was or who, and we argued whether you'd call it jazz stressed over blues or blues-drenched jazz, Diddy maintaining it had a biting, hard-driving street flavour you could cut yourself on, till Jimmy said, "Hell, woman, ain't no name for it. Only truth is, that girl sings."

Bob said then, his eyebrow cocked, "Anybody else thinking of Robert Johnson?"

"Tsch!" Tantie scolded, but everybody knew to get a sound that good, if she ain't quite sold her soul to the devil, she must have done him a mighty fine favour. Diddy came over with his wife, Talitha, a plump brunette. "You know who that is?"

We shook our heads.

Diddy trembled where he stood, his toes and fingers curling, "Look at the girl. Don't she remind you of nobody?"

We stared. Tantie squinted her eyes.

"Lord!" Mom let her hands loose of Bob and dropped them dead to her sides.

Diddy nodded.

"It can't be," Mom said, "Arii Cook's girl."

"Arii Cook?" Bob said.

"Less talking, more looking, if you please," Tantie said, nodding in the girl's direction. "Damn it if she ain't the picture of her, only a shade or few darker."

"I tell you it's her," Diddy said. "Aurelie Morea."

People around us started talking and looking at the girl in a new way. It wasn't the grease and glitter of fame that impressed them: we'd had bigger names than Arii at Paradise and she'd been no singer, anyhow, just some B-movie star, some ex-beauty queen, who'd washed up here for a night, after her Hollywood days were over. There was no kind of deal about that. It was this: not twelve hours after Arii Cook left the mic here, they found her, full of pills and coke and not a breath left in her. It ought to have been the last place her daughter would show.

"Reckon she's come to lay some ghosts to rest," Bob said.

"Or raise them." Jimmy shook his head.

And while the rest of them swapped notions on what happened to Arii Cook, suicide or what hell else it could have been, and what her daughter meant by showing up here twenty years after the fact, I turned my eyes to the back of the room. Sanderson and his cronies were playing poker in the shadows, and I saw the game had stopped. One of the players was sat with his head in his hands; I guess Sanderson had cleaned him out already. The other two had swivelled their hips round in Aurelie's direction, they were stroking their thighs. But Sanderson – and this was a sight I never thought I would see – Sanderson was on his feet, his hands dangling down by his side. Sanderson's mouth was hanging open, and if I didn't know better I would have said, on the self-same night I made up to seduce the man, that Sanderson Miller, for the first time in his life, had fallen in love.

Aurelie

When I sing at Paradise Jazz, I go in disguise,

wear sunshades to protect the world from my eyes,

hide my irises lest anyone be mesmerised.

I'm ready

to ditch the backing band

the *do-wop-be-bops* and *sha-la-las* of ma and pa

and take it solo from the top.

So stop your guitar strings

let the drums hold off.

I don't want none of you breathing

less it's nice and soft and in my time:

I'm singing

and you're hearing me

I'm singing and you're listening.

Is it crazy talk? Let me translate for you.

Take my hand and let me relocate you:

floor to ceiling, left to

right, black to white.

Let me dizzy you with

my stride, my bounce, my vamp.

I got a backward bop, I got scat,

a bag of tricks and I know where it's at.

I'm singing

and as for you, you're hearing me

as for you: you're listening.

I start with a harmony

then surf in on the melody

running over tabletops

getting people wet.

I hypnotise you, numb you, lull and lullaby you.

You don't smoke

you don't drink

you leave your women be.

Next to me

ain't a thing worth nothing and I'll turn you

straight

better than religion,

faster than a jail sentence

surer than love.

And when the police come knocking

they won't pin a thing on me,

when trouble's sniffing it's clear to see:

I'm not guilty.

I'm just a voice

singing in the bewilderness: it's you what's dancing

blowing on the breeze: and you're weeping.

The hematite girl

Merg was being precarious up a ladder. Pinking shears in one hand, staple gun in the other, he attacked the walls with the competition entries, leaving Prit Stick trails on the coving. "Hold the ladder straight," he told me.

"I am."

"It's wobbling."

"*You're* wobbling," I said. At the museum, everything did. It wasn't just the exhibits that were antiques: the ladder, the electrics, even Merg – it was all decidedly antediluvian.

The walls obliterated, Merg caught his breath at ground level. The blancmange mould pictures hung at twenty degrees to the horizontal and the margarine tub of Copydex had stuck itself to Merg's cardigan sleeve. He looked at me like he might check a larding needle for rust, "How are you?"

"I'm fine," I said. It had to be the seventeenth time he'd asked me.

"You *look* fine."

"Well then."

"But you know what they say about looks." Proverbs had the weight of Talmudic law with Merg. "Looks can be deceiving," he said.

"I'm fine."

Merg wrestled the ladder back to its place and nodded, which meant nothing. It was a nervous twitch he had, was all, you were a fool if you thought it meant he agreed. "You can have more time off."

"And do what?" I said.

"Get away," he said, his own anaemic face tinged blue.

"And see who and go where? And anyway," I pinched his bony old elbow, "who would hold the ladder?"

Merg pressed his spectacles into his face. "I'd manage."

"Manage to break your neck, most like. I'm fine, like I said, except for I'm parched, and no one's as much as boiled a kettle since I got back."

So Merg made the tea (milk first), I washed the mugs, and we both made a sham of the usual routine. It was a Thursday morning, so as Merg did a stock take of historic novelties and re-ordered King Henry VIII non-rubber erasers, I spread out newspaper, sipped my PG Tips and shuffled copper coins into piles.

It wasn't such a bad job. The collection, I admit it, the sugar ladles and potato ricers, the jelly bags and cake hoops, wasn't exactly Jorvik, you know, it wasn't Madame Tussauds, but it had a certain kitsch appeal, even if eighteenth century kitchen artefacts weren't your usual. Our prize exhibit was a butter mould cut like a Friesian cow, complete with udders. People came from miles for that one, they seriously did. Even the *Rough Guide* had given us a good write-up; Merg still kept the review, highlighted in turquoise, behind a Perspex frame on the outside wall. "An eccentric little museum," it said. We fitted right in. Our town was just like every other small town you ever saw, full of inbreds and stuck two centuries back with its teashops and souvenir outlets. There was the river with its imported swans and the fuchsias bred to peak the week of Britain in Bloom and a shabby castle that every Viking, Protestant and revolting handloom worker for centuries had tried to raze and which was now sinking slowly into the soft alluvial soil of the floodplain.

At eleven o'clock, Merg put his favourite show on and I Mr Muscled the cabinets clean of grease and snot as Merg conducted the big band classics of Frankie and Sammy with a skewer. Then at twelve there was a blast of Bacharach, and Merg, when he thought I wasn't looking, danced like a man with time to make up, spinning on his heel on the cracked linoleum, his old shoes squeaking and his hip clicking. Merg had survived two ulcers, a stroke and emphysema; he was stuck to life like a stamp to an old love letter. He didn't just work in a museum; he lived in his own personal time capsule. The Great Ideas of the Twentieth Century had marched right past his front door and in this lack of knowledge, and the accumulated detritus of generations past, Merg found bliss. I watched him then, reflected in the cabinets, jigging like a cricket, his waist independent of his hips, his knees moving unconnected to his feet, hands pantomiming the actions, mouthing all the words to *Do you know the way to San José?* It was a good day back; it was a day like most others – a day with no visitors to get in our way.

After more tea and Hobnobs, Merg heaved out the

Brother, folded his ring-bound back on itself and, in the back boiler cupboard he liked to think of as an office, began to type up exhibition notices for the dairy scoops we'd moved out of archive; I went through our visitor book, Sno-paking out inappropriate remarks.

It was four o'clock before we had a visitor. Merg swore — "fiddle-faddle" — and we exchanged looks as the electric buzzer sounded alarm, but it was only Jenny Finch and a box of vanilla slices from Greggs. Jenny was large-bosomed and defiantly blonde, plump and succulent with blue eyes, dimples and an aura of milk and strawberries. Jenny ran the town library; she and Merg had been courting fifteen years, since '83 when Jenny moved up from Cornwall, and everyone knew Merg only had to say the word, and Jenny would have slipped on his ring, but he didn't, and Jenny grew older and plumper and blonder, with a tough and stringy affection for Merg, her love gristled like game that's been hung too long.

Jenny always bought the afternoon cakes, and she brought the gossip too. For, working in the library, and then being treasurer of the local Historical Society, she got to hear things first. She never remembered the juicy stuff, though; to Jenny there really was nothing more interesting than whose library book was overdue and who'd been where on holiday. That afternoon, though, all she wanted to talk about, or not talk about, in a deafening whisper, was my mum. "How are you, my lamb?" she moued.

"She's fine," said Merg.

Jenny looked unconvinced, "Do you think so, Merg Merton? And you being an expert on the female disposition, I suppose. She looks peaky."

"Peaky?"

"She's not been eating. Look, dear," she raised the volume, "I brought you a fondant fancy for your tea."

"What does the girl want with a —"

"Pink or orange, my lamb, take whichsomever one you like, only leave me the chocolate."

"God," muttered Merg, his regular catchphrase, "give me strength with this woman."

I wrapped the fancy in kitchen roll. What would they say, I thought, if they knew, when my mother died, the first thing I thought of was shoes, size five, three inch heels, in bright red patent leather? There we were, the three of us, sat around the bed, at the end of it all, and the tears were falling down and pooling on the kinked linoleum, but I wasn't thinking of Mum, not the pain, not the things left unsaid or all she was missing out on; for the first time in two years I was thinking about me. At the same time as something black and hard and heavy hung in my gut – something I knew couldn't but tear on its way out – something else, sweet as sherbet, some dizzy light dandelion seed, rose up inside me. Dad got ill, the first time, when I was fourteen. I was twenty-five when my mother died. I looked after my parents as soon as they stopped looking after me and my memories of growing up were of parties I didn't go to, boys I didn't see, worries I saved them. But now there was no need for sensible shoes. There was no one to keep happy, no one to worry about, only me; and I felt free. There, I felt free.

The museum lay in a quiet, out-of-the-way location, our entrance branching off one of the vennels that riddled Castle Hill. It suited Merg and me; we could come to work and forget about the world outside. We didn't trouble to lock the door while we scoffed, so there we were, Jenny and I on the old plastic chairs, Merg perched on a footstool, eating our cakes and Jenny, smelling barely of port, barely of warm milk just before it turns, and overwhelmingly of French perfume, maintaining a continuous monologue in her West Country burr that was like being slowly smothered in clotted cream, when there was the sudden squeal of the door hinge, the electric buzz of the bell, and all of a sudden the warmth of the late summer day was in the room and a throaty laugh ran through the place. On the doormat, by the fish kettles, stood a girl like a wild thing, her hair spilling like lava over her shoulders, her hematite skin shining in the last sun, all breath and sweat, her blackness bristling in that northern town like a cat preparing for a fight. She grinned at me and pressed her finger to her lips.

Through the panelled windows of the door, we watched. I heard footsteps hard on the cobbles and a moment later a herd of men hit the top of the hill, three wide in the passageway, arms pumping, breathless and huge cameras bouncing on their stomachs. Not one of them looked through the gap in the brickwork that opened into our courtyard. Once they'd passed, the girl opened the door and stepped out onto the flagstones. Just then a trailing paparazzo peaked the hill. He stopped, she froze. The camera bulb flashed. The girl smiled, and she disappeared, just for a moment, in the light, as the walls were bathed in colour. And then she was gone.

It was so quiet you could hear the building breathe, joists and beams conversing, beetles and mice in the skirting and the ticking of woodworm, the gutter dripping on the flat roof over the porch. You could hear, too, almost, the smells that rose up from the drains clogging beneath our foundations, and, through the wall from next door, curry sauce, fish, lard and vinegar. I looked at the spot on the floor Merg had missed with the mop, the walls mummified in layers of viscous white with the cupboards hanging off them, the warp of the ceiling that hung belly-low in the middle and my own reflection in the glass cabinets, there in my cardigan, my glasses on, not blonde, not brunette, not fat, not thin, not tall, not short, not anything. And I felt right then like some beetle that's spent its life beneath a rock and caught for the first time a glimpse of sun.

"You know who that is," Jenny said, knowing we didn't, enjoying our confusion, "Aurelie Morea."

Merg blinked.

"Jack Morea's little girl."

Merg blinked again; I hadn't seen him this shook up since someone accused him of buying his Suffolk egg cup from Ikea. "What's she doing here?"

Jenny raised her eyebrows. Even Merg knew that about a million years ago when Aurelie was a baby, her mother overdosed in the Royal County Hotel, not a quarter mile away. "She's at the university," Jenny said, "staying at the County, would you believe it."

"Oh now," said Merg, which was his strongest term of disapproval.

"Well maybe it's a good thing, poor thing, brought up with a madman and some peculiar strange notions I'm sure. At least she's got the money now, just turned twenty-one, see, well, she can do as she pleases, can't she?" Jenny peeled back the paper casing from a second cake. "Did you ever see anything like it, though? I reckon she's touched, but then, with a mother like that –" Jenny sank her teeth into her pastry layers, careful not to smudge her lipstick on the icing, "Not to say, a father like *that*."

"Like what?" I said. "He was a philosopher, wasn't he?"

"Oh, Helena, you don't believe all that nonsense."

I shrugged. The man had been a recluse for almost as long as I could remember. If I thought about him at all it was as some crazed genius, sitting in some rocking chair, *Ride of the Valkyries* on the phonograph and a white beard down to his knees as he wrote.

"Of course she doesn't believe in all that. She's a sensible girl."

Merg was right: I was sensible, on the outside. On the

outside I was as sensible as a Post Office savings account and double-gusseted knickers. But what if, once you got past all the Green Cross Code and cod liver oil of my childhood, there wasn't a glittering dark seam of something far from sensible, and when Merg said then, "What would Helena Jones want with philosophy?" I said, "What else is there? Love and politics and truth," and then, as Merg folded his paper, "there's a world out there," I said, surprising myself, "a world."

What a thing to say. I'd attached myself, limpet-like, to the rusted, crusted barnacle of that town for the whole of my twenty-five years. If there was a world, well, I knew nothing of it, for my experience was not practical but theoretical, and even then it wasn't horizontal (borders and boundaries, places and people) but vertical – stretching back through smallpox and damsels-in-distress, Corn Laws, barons and bastard sons, back, right back, to the primordial soup.

And then I said, "Everyone has to believe in something." And although a minute ago I'd barely heard of the man, a new possibility burned in me; it ripped, it caught like brandy. "I'm going to read that book. *Theory of Soul*, wasn't it? I'm going to see for myself." The stool I was on rocked on the uneven floor from one corner leg to the other.

"Dear," said Jenny, "the man was a charlatan."

Merg frowned, "It just doesn't make sense, those symbols, I mean not now, not –"

"Nothing makes sense, though, does it, Merg? Not any of it. So why not Jack Morea. Why not?"

"I'm only saying –"

"Well don't," I said, "just don't bother. What would you know about anything anyway?"

We regarded one another through the scalded pause. Merg's eyes fell as he said, "Take the rest of the afternoon off, eh, Helena. If you like. You must be tired, first day back and all that. Get home early. Have a nice warm bath."

"Yes," I said, the throb of rebellion quietening, my adrenalin congealing in my veins, "yes, I think I will," and, Merg and Jenny shaking their heads, I hit the door.

In the hollows of those hallowed halls
within the library walls
on the shelves where Saints Paul and Augustine debated
on the paper-pulp pages where Pythagoras postulated
something happens.

I hit like a sonic boom.

Look!
Here's a cleft to cling to,
a crevice, a breathing space
in the dry desert of knowledge

I unearth a mirage.

Look!
Between two words or betwixt
the lines of a couplet on a page
in the centre of the letter o
or the midway of a question mark and its
dot, at the breach between fact
and fiction or the fissure where art and science
don't
quite
meet, beyond the outer edges of truth where neither statistics nor hypothesis
reach
in the canvas-white cleave between two brush strokes
or the rests in a musical score
is an area ungoverned by binary law
and I claim it for my own
demolishing reputations (my father's first)
abolishing credence, the old enslavements
half-black, half-white, half truth, half-trash,
the tutors can't plug the leak in their watertight proofs where I seep in
and soul?
I know what it is.
It is beautyartchaos and it lives

in the holes in arguments

where the drumskin of knowledge is wearing thin

and magic glances through.

Not a crazy idea

Aunt Gelda and Troy sat in front of the TV, eating Fray Bentos and crinkle cuts. This was how I'd left the two of them four days before, in a swamp of shagpile and velvet, in Gelda's shabby bungalow, nestled in the crotch of a grubby cul-de-sac, getting high on the combined odours of pot pourri, cat, Febreze, Anaïs Anaïs and wee. "The house is a mess," I said.

"So's your hair," Troy said, without taking his eyes from the TV.

Gelda said, "Nobody ever died of mess." Gelda's theory of immortality also decreed that nobody ever died of not paying a gas bill on time, nobody ever died of going to the supermarket in her dressing gown and nobody ever died from not taking her betablockers. Beautiful and eccentric, Gelda was one ugly, freakish accident waiting to happen.

"You could trip over something," I said, picking up kitten-heel shoes and copies of *Vogue*, disentangling frosted martini glasses and support tights. All our meetings began this way. "The dust," I said, "your asthma. What's in the pie?"

No one said anything.

Aunt Gelda (actually, Great Aunt Gelda and so Gag for short) was by far the most glamorous person in the family. As children, Troy and I had watched awe-struck as she took to the cobbled city streets in foxfur, false lashes and ferocious heels, terrifying the single men of the town. It was difficult to believe her a blood relation. Now pushing eighty, (and still a size twelve, she would want me to tell you, and most of her own teeth) she was stylishly attractive in a ghoulish, Vivienne Westwood-on-a-state-pension kind of a way. Her long white hair hung down past her waist when it wasn't pinned in braids on the top of her head and she still had her nails done at Top-to-Toe Beauty on Thursday afternoons.

Gelda had entertained troops in the World War, though how, and whether the MoD knew about it, was anyone's guess. Her sister (my grandmother) and later her niece (my mother) had persuaded her to a precarious sobriety ever since, through well-administered financial bribes but after fifty years of doily crocheting, scone baking and preserving, and with a small no-strings legacy of her own, she'd announced, at Dad's funeral, that she wanted to see the world. Gelda had an insatiable urge for travel. She didn't care for bridge and daiquiris, mini-golf, all-you-can-eat paella buffets or origami lessons by the pool. For Gag, whose ideas of foreign travel were formed in the war, going abroad meant danger, it meant adventure, and, most importantly, it meant men.

"Guess what," I said.

They looked at me. "You're getting married," Gelda said.

"What?" I said. "No."

"Shit," said Troy, "you're pregnant."

"Yeah right," I said.

"What then?" Both of them looked dubious that any lesser piece of news could be interesting enough to warrant missing *You've Been Framed*.

"Guess who I saw at the museum this week."

"You mean you actually had a visitor?" said Troy.

"Does this mean you'll get a pay rise?" said Gelda.

"Does that mean they're going to let you stay?"

There were rumours that The Museum of Eighteenth Century Kitchen Objects was under review; the council would get more in rent from a coffee bar, what with our prime location in the central groin of town, than they ever could from raiding the donations box. The letters page of *The Gazette* was hot with talk of cultural relevance, of funding priorities and the justification of a twelve percent rise in the council tax. Merg had nightmares of the exhibits tarnishing in the latte steam, me putting double choc-chip muffins in poly bags, him grating cinnamon on the mocha.

I ignored them. "Aurelie Morea," I said, "you know, Arii Cook and Jack Morea's daughter." I thought this was pretty impressive news. The last famous person any of us had seen in the flesh was Princess Michael of Kent when she opened the cancer wing at the hospital and patted Dad's head, and that was back in 1983, but all they said was, "Jack Morea," and "Fancy that." And they went back to watching TV.

I went through to the kitchen and gathered together the dishes that looked closest to growing mould. I tried to hear what they were saying but could make out only the canned laughter of the TV show and one of them passing wind. It was four weeks since we'd buried Mum. Not that the euphemism quite worked because there she was, still at home, on a shelf, next to Dad and Gran and Granddad and some great uncle I'd never even met. Despite all my deathbed thoughts of *carpe diem*, best of a bad etcetera, there I was still carrying on the old routines; my bread and margarine life went on, only instead of doing Mum's washing-up, I was doing Gag's.

I picked soggy cornflakes from the plughole. When people heard about Mum they said sorry, then they said aren't you good, or brave, or kind, as if that were some kind of consolation, or it would get me anywhere. I wasn't good because what good is goodness in the end? Where does it get you?

I washed the sink of grease, then I ran the water, piling the crockery in. I watched the bubbles rise and I plunged my hands in and held them there. The water scalded, so hot it felt cold but I didn't move. Already I could see without scrubbing how the caked-on grease lifted away. It was effortless, the hot water and bubbles conspiring to make dirty plates new, and in a moment what is crusted and morbid is brand sparkling clean, glistening on the draining board, ready to start over. And it's easy, easier than letting them be and letting them stand, watching the mould grow over, the leftovers blacken in the damp and corrupt, being reminded all the time. I wasn't good, just too lazy to be anything else. And exhausted.

We'd made jokes about it because at the bottom of it all was something so horrible it didn't bear considering and our laughter distracted us from the sound of my father coughing, the smell of my mother's sick in her hair, waking at four in the morning because someone needs fetching or carrying or soothing or lying to, someone wants to hear that everything is going to be all right, and I want to lie to them. I am good at lying: we pretend at four in the morning, in the dark, in whispers, that the cancer won't find us, and we eat cookies and drink Ovaltine and laugh about nothing at all, laugh until it hurts. After a while there are no more tears to cry. But even then cancer is greedy – my mother's right breast wasn't enough for it, nor was any part of her; it laid its hand on me, though the doctors knew nothing of it, came out through her body and into me, covered and smothered me, wrapped itself around me so tightly I'd never be free.

The night Mum died, I drank till I passed out – gatecrashed some twenty-first at the rowing club, drank pints of sweet cider and danced to the band. Because I could. Because I had to do something. And then I spent two weeks crying in bed. And then I saw Aurelie. I saw Aurelie, free and beautiful and black and shining, and for a moment, looking at her, I forgot about myself.

I'd waited till Friday, when Jenny took her perm to the hairdressers, and I went to the library for *The Theory of Soul*. I scanned the philosophy shelves, the self-help shelves. I went to the microfiche and found the title and filled in the request form, and I waited while the librarian went to fetch it and stamped it out, and I took it in my hands. I ran my palm against the dust-jacket, covered in floral psychedelia. I hugged it to my chest and hurried home where I propped it up against the salt and pepper while I ate my crispy pancakes that night. And I didn't get up until I'd read the book through, and the surprise I got, the delight: it was like putting my hand in my old jeans pocket and discovering that all the time, without ever suspecting it, I'd had a fifty-pound note stashed away there. Jack Morea had got in my head and looked at the world and written it down and it all made sense, for the first time: I was so grateful, it felt like love.

Theory of Soul came out at a happier moment, it seemed to me, in a flower-power, free-love moment when people thought the world was about to crack open like a walnut. Men had just walked on the moon, a President had been shot dead on live TV, so when Jack Morea said he'd identified the forty-one constituent parts of the human soul, people who thought they were on their way to being someone started dropping Jack's name like acid, wearing T-shirts of his most popular quotes, including the equation, which nobody understood. There's even a photo somewhere of Jim Morrison with *whoever said "to err is human" made a big mistake* on his chest, and after that, Jack just had to eat bad shellfish and the whole world got the shits. He started work on a sequel and he married a movie star. Then along came Aurelie and the breakdown and the full-page ad in *The Times*. And as quickly as he came, he was gone, and it's funny how people who'll buy your book when you're on the front of *Newsweek* don't rate it so much after you've been on the front of *National Enquirer*.

I ran a wet cloth over the surfaces. I hung the teatowel on the plastic hook behind the washing machine. I checked the milk was still good and threw out a greening crust of Hovis. I took a fresh loaf from the freezer. I thought about what I might have been doing if Mum and Dad hadn't gotten ill; dancing in some Ibizan bar, my sun-streaked hair snaking round me, perhaps. I loosened the lid on a new jar of marmalade ready for Gag's breakfast; I did all these things like a clockwork girl whose parts only moved in certain ways but I knew, like the book said, that if it wasn't for circumstance, bad luck, chance and the melanoma time-bomb, all that, I'd have been a different girl, one who didn't live on tiptoe.

I grabbed Gag's ostrich feather duster and ran it over the hall. The house was an eclectic combo of art deco, bohemia and baroque. Gag had chandeliers hanging from her low ceiling, and gold cherubs on the wall. Every drawer, every shelf, every surface was trashed with boxes and bags of sweetened rose, lemon and peppermint lumps. I dusted my way back through to the lounge. "I'm reading his book," I said.

"Whose?"

"Jack Morea's. I'm reading *The Theory of Soul*."

"I didn't know you were interested in philosophy," Gelda said.

"Well I am."

"Did I know that?" Gelda lived in dread of Alzheimer's. She made us test her at intervals for early signs of dementia by quizzing her on her religious beliefs and political allegiances. Do you believe in the death penalty? Under what circumstances would you vote Liberal Democrat?

"I don't go on about it," I said.

"Philosophy," Gelda said, philosophically, "is so bourgeois." She'd always thought of herself as a Trotskyite, confusing eccentricity with political commitment. She and Troy drifted back to ITV.

"It was quite famous in the seventies, wasn't it?"

"So was Jimmy Osmond."

"I thought it might be good for me, you know the counsellor said I should –"

Gelda did her Jewish grandmother bit, "What d'you want us to say, Helena? Hmmm? You want me to burst a vessel every time you visit the library?"

"What is it with you?" Troy said, nudging the volume down and sprawling out on the floral sofa, "are you hung on the guy?"

"He's about seventy."

"So you have noticed."

"Newsflash, Troy. Not everything in the world is about sex."

"Then what is it about?"

"It's about ideas and stuff," I said, "philosophy."

"Yeah right."

I threw a cushion over at Troy. He threw it back.

"I don't expect you to understand philosophy, Troy. I

don't even expect you to be able to spell it."

"Call me a doctor," said Troy, monotone, "I'm bleeding."

Troy and I had always behaved as if any display of affection was akin to incest. Even in the womb we'd jostled for a space of our own, Troy not wanting me to cramp his style, me not wanting to be caught in his downwind; we'd raced each other out, five weeks early, me trailing my big brother from the start. Ever since, he'd taken the greatest pleasure in doing, saying and being the opposite of whatever I did, said or was. I told myself regularly that Troy didn't really despise me, my friends, my clothes, my values and that, somewhere, beneath that shaggy haircut and oversized sweatshirt, Troy actually thought I was a tolerable member of the species. By this point in our lives, though, the role-playing was non-negotiable.

"Why *Theory of Soul*?" Gelda said, "I've dozens of old *Cosmos* with quizzes just the same."

I shrugged. Mum and Dad, Troy, Gran and Granddad, all anyone in my family had ever wanted was to be normal, to blend into the knit-one-pearl-one, magnolia-coloured dado-rail, BHS back-to-school extravaganza world of suburbia. *Theory of Soul* promised something that

was not petrified, nor railed off, not housed behind glass
and coated in dust. Anything exciting in our town had
happened so many centuries ago that you couldn't help
but feel insignificant. The very gargoyles despised us.
Theory of Soul hit like a sonic boom, rustled the unruffled
opinions of the dead like autumn leaves underfoot. It
squeezed between the tightly bound pages of the library
shelves and wrestled monumental Truth to the ground,
kicked its shins, bloodied its prose. Authority ruptured
like a bust spleen, kaleidoscoping a thousand fractured
worlds. I read it and my lumpen heart palpitated.

Gelda shook her head, "I worry about you."

"You don't need to."

"All these ideas." Gag was fond of reminding me that
the Second World War, the Spanish Inquisition and bell-
bottoms had all started with an idea. Ideas, for Gag, were
dangerous, unpredictable things.

"He's the one you should be worried about," I said,
kicking Troy. What did Troy want from life? Beer. And
MTV. He'd be a hedonist, only he hadn't the backbone
to commit to a single philosophy.

"Leave him alone," Gag patted his leg.

"Is he ever going to get a job?"

"I've got a job," Troy said, "I'm a student."

Troy, after failing sociology and tourism, was in the third year of a cultural studies degree.

"You're twenty-five, Troy," I said. "Grow up, can't you?"

"Troy's fine," Gelda said.

"That depends on your definition of fine."

"Well," said Gelda, "he's happy."

Troy and Gelda exchanged a much-rehearsed raising of eyebrows and smiled at me with a cruel sympathy. "Did you finish the washing up, dear?"

Troy turned the TV volume up to seventeen.

In the South the past

He introduced himself straight off, solemn as an undertaker, before we'd even left the queue of bug-yellow cabs at Fort Worth terminal B. "My name is Primrose Seaman." Primrose had a resemblance to a certain other brother I knew back home, but he was softer than Sanderson, like Sanderson dipped in warm milk and sprinkled in cinnamon, a mustard-coloured individual without the smooth mahogany of Mr Miller, but with something of the same indisputable pride in the manner of his being that made me feel right away at home. "Now we're acquainted," he said, and smiled. There can't have been a tooth left in his head.

We joined the highway, Primrose coasting in the far lane, me checking the time of my Greyhound.

Everything was smooth to plan. I was sure of myself as a swallow migrating for the winter, as easy as salmon swimming upstream. The sky was a perfect wash of azure under the smooth bubble of heaven, my mind the same cerulean gleam. I studied Primrose's reflection in the side-mirror.

"I guess you're thinking it's an unusual name."

"What?" I said.

"Primrose." He guessed wrong. Thing was, way he said it, it sounded the most natural name in the world, and to fit with him like a ball and a glove on a tight catch. I had been wondering how he lost his teeth, but I said, since it seemed to be expected, and I didn't want to disappoint, "It sure is an unusual name."

Primrose looked at me in the mirror like he was expecting me to throw him a stick. He frowned a little, his skin pleating itself, and said, "I suppose you're wondering how I came upon it." Without pausing for breath he told me, "My mom called me Primrose. She called me Primrose 'cause it's a great way to get to know people. I tell 'em my name is Primrose, they ask me why for, and before you know it, you got yourself a conversation going." He beat a rumba on the leather wheel with his long fingers. "Mom reckoned a person called Primrose would never be too lonely and on the whole, I find that to be the case with my own self." His voice rose and fell like a songbird, climbing and swooping over words in a way could mesmerise a girl, giving a melodious, cantabile effect a long way from the tight vowels and sharp consonants of Rule Britannia and his toothlessness whistled like a currant cake hissing on the griddle, giving a shrillness to his speech as his breath fought its way past his gums, (but tuneful with it, always tuneful).

"It's a good reason for a name," I said.

"You ever meet another Primrose Seaman?"

"I never have."

"I didn't think so. I never heard of another Primrose Seaman in the world. It's a responsibility. I get up in the morning, I look myself in the mirror and I say, Primrose Seaman, you're the only one of you the world has got, the only one, so don't go making a mess of things. I find that a reassuring thing on the whole. For myself, personally. A reassuring thing."

We had hit interstate. If everyone in Texas was friendly as Primrose, I would find my father quick as bruising. I considered whether I could manoeuvre the silence round into a question, but Primrose got to the pause before me.

"I once saw – you get CBS in England?"

"No."

"I once saw a programme on CBS, about a fella called –" he slapped his chops together, folding his forehead, "well, I forget the fella's name right now, but that ain't the point of the thing. The point of the thing is that this fella, I mean the one on CBS, he had an idea to find out every other fella with the same name as him, whatever that was, I don't remember. Anyways, he looked them out on the internet and flew states over states to try to get them all together, for the Millennium, see. What do you think of that now? Would you want to do that?"

"I guess I never really thought about it."

"If I ever heard of another Primrose Seaman, I don't know what I'd do." Primrose had freckles scattered like blessings all over his nose, and long, soft lashes, would feel like angel kisses on his cheeks. "I'd just as soon not know about it."

"You never got laughed at?" I said, "I mean Primrose being an unusual name and all."

Primrose laid his head to the side. "You know, I suppose I'm the kind of a fella just doesn't get laughed at." I could believe it. He must have been six-three or so, and back at the airport he'd lifted my case like a bag of apples, "I always saw it as a positive. Back in Georgetown a man was looking for positives. A man was fine-tuned to the tracking down of the things. I once saw a programme – you get Fox in England?"

"You're from Georgetown?" I said, "Georgetown, Texas?"

Primrose's lips relaxed themselves into an easy smile of assent. "The only one there is."

I silently apologised to God that I had ever doubted his existence, for here was a miracle flavoursome enough to convert a confirmed denier.

"You get Fox in England?"

"What?" I said, for Primrose's mind was as limber as his voice. "Oh," I said. "Some of it."

"Did you ever see a programme about positive thinking?"

"I saw Oprah."

"Oprah!" He bunched his lips tight and twitched the bud of his mouth from one side of his face to the other. I guessed he did not share my mom's enthusiasm. Mom and Tantie were always on the lookout for Black Role Models. This was my mom's way of ensuring I didn't grow up to be a drug dealer, prostitute, or McDonald's employee. I saw Desmond Tutu and Maya Angelou when they came to London. Nelson Mandela I met about three times; I could just about pass a freaking A-level in South African history with a specialist subject of Nelson Mandela's childhood, youth and political awakening. Oprah was Mom's favourite. Mom made me sit through every episode ever made, and she would interrupt about eight times every second to say, "And she was raped all those times, don't forget," just to make it clear to me that I wasn't going to be able to use this product of a broken home thing as any kind of excuse for my own failure to forge an international media career.

"Anyways, I saw this one guy," Primrose said, impervious to my reverie, "he was an expert in positive thinking. He said something I thought was a mighty powerful thing. He said, ain't nothing you can change but your attitude, and there ain't nothing you can't change by changing your attitude. What do you think about that then? Myself, I meditate on that. Meditate on it. And I find it on the whole to be true."

"I never thought of it."

Primrose kept a steady sixty-five on the interstate. The road was clear. I scanned the horizon for something I might remember; a landmark, the fall of the rays through the dusting of clouds. "It's warm," I said.

"Warm? You think so?" Primrose allowed himself the possibility, "I guess so. For October, it's warm. For October I find it to be most unusual warm. But you haven't told me your name. I mean, now that we're acquainted."

"Mom called me Georgetown."

"No shit." He laughed, his tongue resting on his bottom gum. He laughed for about half a mile, all past the dirty underskirts of Dallas city limits, through the approach to the scrapers tall enough to trouble clouds, until we got almost to the heart of the place and the traffic started to clot. "No shit. She from Georgetown?"

"Yes."

"This Georgetown?" Primrose's voice was climbing octaves, his body twitching round in the seat with excitement.

"Yes."

"Man!"

I was a little unsettled by this reaction. No one in England ever behaved like that, but then, Mom said, in England they are used to black folks having strange names and most times people called me George, forgetting it wasn't ever short for Georgina, Georgette, Georgia. Whatever.

"I guess you must have reminded her of home. I guess you must have. Is that right? Did I guess your story?"

"I never knew the story."

"You should ask her. Everybody got to know their story. Your momma still alive?"

I nodded.

"You should ask her just as soon as you can. What your momma's name? Maybe I know her."

"Agatha. Agatha Easy."

"Agatha Easy?" He turned round in his seat, drifting a half-lane, "Agatha Easy's your momma?"

"You know her?"

He indicated, pulled over to pass a truck, checked his mirror, pulled back in. I could see the back of his neck goosebump.

"You knew my mom? Primrose?"

"Went to school with her. Same grade and all. Agatha Easy. Pretty girl, Agatha. But she left school, you know I think it was to look after her momma. You know about all that?"

"I know Grandma went crazy the day JFK got shot. I know she lived off popcorn and powdered milk."

Primrose dipped his head left-right. "I'm sorry," he said.

Neither of us spoke for maybe a couple of miles. Primrose kept checking me in the rear view with a shy smile. I never knew Mom hadn't seen school through. The row she gave me when I left at sixteen, you'd have thought my mom was a doctorate at the least. Knowing it now felt kind of bad, not so much because I thought Mom gave up on account of me (which had to be the real reason she left, my grandma got sick when Mom was still a girl), or because I never thanked her for it, but because I'd never taken the trouble to ask. I guessed there must have been aspects of the past that Mom wouldn't have minded discussing, but these weren't the same things that interested me.

"It's a small world," I said, though truth is I was not surprised. If my father himself had been waiting at the airport, arms outstretched, singing, "Welcome home baby, welcome back home," I would not have raised one eyebrow.

"Is it? I never have flown. Never have."

"I mean," my tongue had grown so unwieldy in my mouth, "you knowing my mom. You knowing my mom, I mean it's possible that – I wonder if you know my daddy too?"

Primrose's foot must have slipped on the gas pedal.

We pitched forward. "You don't know?"

I shook my head.

"I mean your mother and me," Primrose developed an interest in the radio. He punched the pre-sets and jacked the dial until his voice lost itself in the smother of rhythm and blues. "I knew her and all, but, we wasn't intimate, you know, that kind of detail —" Primrose was jerking his head side to side. He let out a breath it sounded like he'd been holding his whole life, "Truth was, I never knew she'd had a kid. I never knew it until today."

"But Georgetown is a small place, right?"

"Don't even tell me you've flown over here to find your father. Don't even tell me that."

"Well I have."

"Well I don't even want to know about that." He punched the steering wheel and swung his head. "You know, you did a crazy thing flying in to Dallas with an idea like that on mind."

"There are crazier things," I said.

"No," he said, "there ain't. That notion you've got, it's the crazy of crazies, the big mother crazy of all."

We must have been almost at the bus terminal. I caught flickers of the city, fat businessmen, Chilli's Too, Auntie Ann's hand-rolled pretzels. The traffic thickened again, congealing at red lights, then trickling slowly into

Dallas. I rolled my window. It was afternoon already and the Greyhound was a three-hour ride. I'd be lucky to get a nose round Georgetown before sundown.

"So who's looking after your mother?"

"What?"

"I said, while you over here trying to kiss feet that kicked you, who's looking after your momma back home?"

I shrugged, "She can look after herself." I began to consider the possibility that Primrose may not have known my mother. No one who has spent more than a minute in her company can doubt her awesome self-sufficiency.

"And who looking after you? Lord, girl, let me tell you, a father you got to look for ain't worth finding," Primrose pulled over sharp as we got to the terminus, hit the breaks, killed the engine. "And he ain't worth the price of an airplane ticket for sure. That's forty dollars, honey."

***

I checked my bags at a small hotel in downtown then headed for the Great American High Street of 1997; it was bright like a clean face, its perfect round cobbles like fresh-baked bread-rolls. Oak and pecan trees dribbled sap on the sidewalk, their leaves crisping on the branch and winging through the air like confetti. Plump acorn buds scattered across the path, a crop of schoolkids sucked cup-ice and jumped rope.

Had a little kitty car 1968
Took it round the cor-ner
Policeman stopped me put me in jail
All I'd had was a ginger ale
Go Polly, the Wolly, Patch, Pepper!

I dipped in and out of the old storefronts that lined the boulevard, (*neat*, I said to myself, picking up the lingo like a headcold, *neat*), glad of their striped awnings arching over me like palm leaves, picking up gifts for the folks back home: a jar of lemon sauce for Tantie (though I knew fine well she'd tell me she could have made it better herself), a bottle of bourbon for Jimmy and for Helena a book of Civil War recipes. I held out on a gift for Mom. For now. I felt dry and dusty after thirteen hours of air-conditioning but in Georgetown everyone shimmered. They glistened with perspiration, they shone with self-satisfaction, they gleamed with cocoa butter and coconut hair oil. Round-hipped, large-breasted women danced down the way with their arms wrapped round men skinny as dingos. Puddles of old women sat laughing on benches, pools of girls stood on street corners, drenching onlookers with the fullness of their smiles, the easy liquidity of their eyes. And the flesh of those people! It came in caramel, amber, toffee, coffee, latte, amaretto, terracotta. I must have been living in black and white the twenty-four years before I visited Georgetown.

The day ripened as I walked, the heat of late afternoon mellowing to the balm of early evening with the sun like a fat baby rocking itself to sleep in the sky. Cars coasted round town, the girls and boys checking each other, the music weaving in and out of the dusk, knitting a blanket of night. I had always wondered why Mom had called me after a place she couldn't wait to get away from. Now I wondered why she had left at all. I walked my homestreets, breathing the air of a succulent evening until the moon rose in the port-coloured sky like a white lady climbing out of her bath. I went back to the hotel, glad at last to be sleeping in the same town as my father.

***

The one thing Mom missed about the US, and just about the one thing her and Tantie were guaranteed to agree upon, was hot dogs. Though Mom didn't get a pang from depriving me from my father or any notion of home, I knew she thought she'd failed as a mother in some regard by denying me the pleasure of an all-American (about as Southern as sunburn) hotdog. I ordered myself a jumbo from a seller on the corner of Rock Street and while the guy fried me some slices, I asked him all casual, like I'd asked twenty people already that morning without getting a positive, if he remembered Agatha Easy, used to live in Rock Street maybe twenty years back. It was a long shot all right, but then I had spent a lifetime standing way back from the line trying to hit a target I could not even see.

He didn't look up from his onions, and his voice was flat as old beer. "She left town." He handed me my dog. "Three dollars."

"You remember her?"

He spat on the sidewalk, scratched his nose. "No." He eyed the sky.

I took a bite, nearly scalded my tongue. I walked my sneakers facing back toward town ('cause I'd got the stride going now; like sugar to onions to bring out the sweetness, all I needed to bring me out my sass was a little American air).

"Not for three dollars I don't."

I looked at him through one eye, then another, took a napkin, sucked ketchup off one finger.

"What about Mary Easy?" I said, hoping that, if I had to haggle, there might be some kind of bulk discount.

His face cracked like a chick hatching out of an egg. "Mary Easy? I sure do. I sure do. That girl could sing – more than sing, if you know what I mean. I mean, that girl could *whistle*. You want mustard with that dog?" The hot-dog man started talking real fast, his hands scooping shapes in the air, his hotdogs burning on the grill. I tried to match up the twinkle in his eye with my twelve-stone nappy-haired aunt. I was not at all sure that it wasn't a case of mistaken identity. "I took you for a journalist. I did. But you're a friend, right?"

I nodded carefully.

"How's she doing?"

"Good," I said.

"She ever do anything with that voice?"

"She got married."

"Married," he wiped the back of his hand across his forehead. "Well. I tell you what," he said, grabbing a napkin, "give her my number, will you? Tell her to give me a call now, you hear? Case things don't work out with that husband of hers."

By noon I was convinced that Mom's dark hints about the place were shadows of nothing but her own mind. I was like a card returned to its deck, held upright by my brothers and sisters on every side, walking down the street two inches taller than I'd been before. That afternoon, not having much luck with the old neighbours – all kids my age with kids their own or old folks with memory as strange to them as youth – I trailed the municipal cemeteries looking for Grandma's grave. I found it squatting in the damp of a yard thick with dead. There were other Easys there, but no relation of mine or hers, I guessed, since they were not grouped like a family, giving shelter to one another, but scattered away in odd corners as if they'd settled themselves just as far away from each other as could be, as if they couldn't stand to be sharing the same soil, or they thought they'd find a better class of maggot in their own patch. The graves on either side of my grandma had the names and fancy stones of strangers. I pulled up the long grass from the root of the tombstone and scraped off the moss with my fingernail. The town had two words for my grandma's fifty years: Celandine Easy. That was it. There was no date, no dearly beloved, nothing to link her to those still living or those gone before. Mom never came back for the funeral. She told me, "Your grandma died long since, honey. She died the day JFK got shot and there's nothing and no one to go back for now." "Except for Grandma's sake," I said, "except for it being the right and obvious right thing to do." Mom peeled potatoes.

I moved some flowers, good coloured ones, the best I could find, from one grave to hers, and then I struck up with a song, about the only decent sort of a song I knew.

This is what I want to do, sweetheart
This is what I want to do
It's just to lay down my head
Just to lay down here with you

Someone started whistling along with me, a half-key out and two beats behind. I turned round to cuss him and saw an old white guy sat on a shaded bench, eating an ice-cream, a frozen lolly dripping on his shorts. "It's one hot day," he said.

"Hot enough, for sure," I said.

"That's some accent you got there. You Canadian?"

"American," I said. "I just been – I just been away a while is all."

"We just moved back," he said, "me and Margaret." He jerked his head at a red-faced woman making her way over from the church. "Now we've retired, we decided there's no place like Georgetown. Crazy as. We spent twenty years trying to save up enough cash to get out of here. Now we can live anywhere we want, and here we are."

I took a place next to him on the bench. "It changed much?"

"No," he said. He thought, biting the end of his ice-cream cone. "Well, I guess, some of the buildings and all, but the people? You'll never change the people, and what is a place without people? You know?" He looked at me, "You've got mustard on your shorts."

"It's a friendly place then."

"Sure. Don't signify what you read in the papers. These days everybody get along with everybody in Georgetown. Black, white, Indian, whatever. And you know why? Ain't a man in town without a bit of nigger in him." He laughed. His breath smelled of pear drops.

"Did you ever know a family called Easy?" I said. "Back in the days, I mean. Used to live on Rock Street."

"Back in the days," he ran his tongue down the lolly stick to catch the drips. His wife hollered over the dead, "You leave that Zester alone, Jack. That's my Zester now, y'hear?"

He shook his head. "There used to be a family called themselves Easys, over on Rock Street."

"Did you know Agatha Easy?"

"Skinny girl," he said.

"Not skinny," I said, "More kind of rounded."

"Skinny," he insisted.

"There was probably more than one Agatha Easy," I said.

He crunched on the cone with his gums. "I only remember the one."

"What about Mary Easy?"

A smile came like a snake slithering through long grass and he said, "Mary Easy. There's a name that booms like a thunderclap. You hear it, and you expect to get wet, you know what I mean?" He laughed under his breath, like he didn't want to share the joke with me. "You see her, tell her Sham was asking after her."

"I'll ask her if she remembers you," I said, not even wanting to wonder why he called himself one thing and his wife called him Jack.

"Oh, she'll remember," he winked as his wife stopped by us, out of breath and hips the size of Alabama.

"Let's get, Jack. This heat is – well, I'm just beat," she gave me a smile, but one that had been used so it was all stretched out of shape and stale and barely recognisable as a smile at all.

Jack took to his feet and offered her the lolly. She twisted her face at the sugary stick. He shrugged and bit into it himself.

"Hey," I said, "what about Georgetown Easy?"

The woman looked closely into me, like she was reading a map to somewhere she had forgotten ever existed. "Come on Jack," she said.

Jack stopped. "But there wasn't no Georgetown Easy. There was Celandine, and the girls, and –"

The woman fixed me with her eye and tugged at her husband's sleeve. "I'm telling you," he said "there wasn't no such person." And all the folks I met that day, the pastor, the barmen, the doctor, black, white, man, woman, none of them remembered me. "Georgetown?" they said. "A baby called Georgetown?" They scratched their heads and shook themselves like a dog with the fleas, as if the bare thought of it itched at them, as if the very idea of a baby called for a town was as dumb to them as it was to me. "Nope. You must be mistook." I walked back heavy to the hotel that night, my skin blistering in the heat, my brain swelling like sourdough.

Ain't even the past

The clerk at the Records Office of the County Clerk smiled at me. "Birth or death?" she said.

"Birth."

"Too bad," she said, "death is cheaper."

The office in the Courthouse was a haze of bad language, boredom mixing with hope and curdling with frustration. Like everything else in the town, the records office had an antique feel to it I found reassuring. The wood panelling and cobwebbed chandeliers, the black and white photographs of unamused men shouted of unarguable authenticity, officialdom and authority.

"How much is birth?"

"Eleven dollars. Fill the form and bring it back to me."

I stared at the form: "I don't have all these details."

"What you missing, honey?"

"Father's name."

"OK," she smiled at me with sympathy, "we don't need that."

"And driver's license."

"You ain't got your license?"

"I've been living in England."

"England!" she said, "I thought that was a mighty strange accent you got yourself. Just as cute as —" she laughed; it sounded like a car starting on a cold day, "as cute as I don't know what!" She twisted her bra strap. "Well listen, if you're born overseas we can't help you, sugar. You got to write to the state department, up in Washington. They keep a track of all those up there, see."

"I was born in Texas," I said. "We just moved on afterward."

Under her lips, her tongued worked over her teeth. She smiled conspiratorially, "You put down what you can, all right?" I wrote down Mom's name, my birth date, my name.

She took my form and went backroom. "Wait here," she said.

I took a look around me, at the people standing in line and kicking at nothing on the carpet, hands in their pockets and mind on their shoes. I caught the eye of one young guy, young black guy, in jeans and bad attitude, and he looked back at me. Well what you looking at, I thought? Me and my Topshop jeans, me and my face don't fit here no more than it fits back – I couldn't think back home – back in England? Well look away; I ain't got nothing to be ashamed of. He looked at me and I could tell by the jut of his jaw he was just gonna go on looking at me till I looked away, only I wasn't going to look away, I wouldn't. I got as much right, I thought, as you have to look, and I pinned him there so he was the first to break the stare.

When the clerk came back her kindness had evaporated like alcohol from an unstopped whisky bottle, leaving nothing but a sour taste. She said, "You sure you got this right, honey?"

I nodded.

"Only we don't have no one by this name." She lifted her lips away from her teeth. "Georgetown – that's your real name? That's not a nickname, is it?"

"I don't think so."

"Well is it or ain't it?"

I shrugged. "Funny kind of nickname," I said.

"You must have been born out of state." She raised her eyes at the woman waiting next behind me. She motioned me to move aside.

"Can't you just search out-of-state records?" I said.

"We only have Texas records here. You'll have to go to the state where you born." I could see her nose curling. I felt anger blistering. I refused to be shamed into leaving.

"Look," I said, "there must be a mistake. I got my passport. See. From the US government and it says right here. Name; *Georgetown Easy*. Date of Birth; *July 13th, 1975*. Birthplace; *Georgetown, Texas*."

The clerk looked at the photo and stared back at me, her nose approaching mine, and I explained that the photo was taken a while back, back when I got the passport for a school trip, years ago but at the same time as I said all this, memories were hatching inside me like blowfly, breaking out like a plague of the things. At the same time I was assuring the clerk that I must have been born in Georgetown, Texas, USA, I realised that I couldn't have been, that the one solid as bone, true as blood thing I knew about myself was a lie (if the Williamson County Record Office say you don't exist, don't matter how much the ache in your heart or the throb in your head might suggest otherwise, you are insubstantial as candy floss). My passport wasn't proof of anything, any more than one lie can make another true.

"Wait here, please," she said, and she flashed me a 1,000-Watt, electric-chair smile.

My brain frazzled as it all came together, Mom's insistence we couldn't afford that school trip, and, when Helena persuaded her parents to put up the cash, that I was too young to travel. Then her sudden capitulation and the proffering of a passport I swear I never filled in no application for.

I saw the clerk talking to a fat white man in shirt and braces in the office back. He nodded his head heavily and looked right at me, right *through* me to the chain of deals that had got me in this mess and that I was silently calculating for the first time (Mom to Sanderson, Sanderson to the Washington division of his empire, because just as trouble ends in regret, so it begins with a man like Sanderson Miller with a kick in his step and a gleam in his eye and no more respect for the law than for the men whose wives he's entertaining). "Shit," I said. (None of us are eloquent under that kind of stress.) "Shit." I pushed my way past the queue, an avalanche of arms and stomachs, and out of the hall, out into the lobby, out past the receptionist, legs pumping, mouth dry, out into the white hot hole of the street. At midday, mid-October 1999, I was born an orphan in High Street Georgetown, Texas, USA.

I stuck my arm out into the road and pulled a cab out of nowhere in my first piece of luck since landing. I stepped in calm and told the driver to take me to the hotel. I was praying, praying real hard, that the kind-eyed clerk wouldn't call immigration.

The driver checked me in the mirror. "Don't I know you somewhere?" he said.

I started. "What's the odds?" I said.

"Maybe I know your sister."

"I ain't got a sister," I said, straight back.

"Where you from? England? You on vacation?"

I nodded.

"On your self?"

"Uh-huh," I said, "on myself. To this place. Don't make no sense to me either."

"Baby, it make all the sense in the world," he said. "You're lovesick."

"Who've I got to be lovesick for?"

"Fine looking woman like you got men she don't

even know about to be lovesick for. But you looking for someone special, I can see that."

"I ain't lovesick."

I considered: I could turn myself in, let my mother and Sanderson swing for their sin and maybe in the course of it uncover what they were so determined I'd never find out. I had a vague idea to call Helena. But Helena would play it down the line for sure, stick to the rules. This was a complicated thing that was beyond Helena's realm.

"Georgetown ain't such a great place for a vacation," the taxi driver said, "That's to say, living here's bad enough."

"Well I guess that's what my mom thought," I said, "she was quick enough to get out."

"Was she? Good for her. Good for her, I say. Getting out ain't nothing but a daydream for most folks. We're just drop in the middle of Texas, nowhere to go and two hundred miles to get there."

"Two hundred miles ain't so far," I said, thinking, since my flight left in the morning anyhow, that maybe we should just drive to Fort Worth right then and I could check in before anyone had time to raise the alarm.

"It depends what you find when you get there. Right here we got New Mexico to the West, Oklahoma to the north, let's see, you got Arkansas at north-east, Louisiana at east and Mexico at south." He looked at me as if he'd just delivered the punchline to the world's greatest joke. "To get anywhere worth going takes money, and there ain't an honest way to get that kind of money together."

"Don't see anything bad about the place," though I was finding it hard to put my hand to the enthusiasm I'd had when I landed.

"Sure, if you don't mind folks knowing your business, but if you want to keep a secret, Georgetown's a hellish place to be. Same old faces, same old troubles your life long. Trouble is we ain't got nothing. Orleans got jazz and the Delta got the blues; by the time we got ourselves together there wasn't nothing left over for Georgetown. Hell, we ain't even got a name of our own – you know how many Georgetowns there is?"

"Six," I said, "maybe seven."

"At the least, and we the smallest of they all. Say, you don't look so good."

"I'm fine."

"Sure you are – English chicks are always fine. One arm hanging off, bullet wound to the head and English chicks always fine. Still, you don't look so good."

My guts were burning, my throat tight like neat

whisky. But it was more than physical. There was something inside that didn't have a name and couldn't be tied down to a left or a right side, a particular organ, an estimated location. I kept playing the evidence round in my mind – 33, 45, 78 RPM, trying to find a way where the facts of the matter could be added, subtracted or otherwise mathematicised to produce some other answer. What explanation could there be for why, before we got to England, there was no trace of me? And then the craziest thing happened, right then in the back of the cab, crazy like snow in the middle of July. I started to cry and all the time I was crying I was apologising to the cab driver like a real lily-assed English chick.

"I get lots of it," he shrugged, "I get it all the time. I got one old girl does it regular. That's what you get in this job. Drunks and old folks and girls with broken hearts."

"I ain't –" My head was grinding. My tongue was thick in my mouth and something was rising up out of me. "Can you drop me here?"

I went back to my room. I lay on the bed, on the chintzy bedspread, on the pink poly coverlet. I opened Jimmy's bourbon, looked for a toothbrush mug, drank from the bottle. I came to Georgetown to find my father and lost my mother; my mom was not my mom, my aunt was not my aunt and my homecoming was going nowhere. As for me, I was not Georgetown. I was maybe *Philadelphia* or *Wichita* or *Atlanta,* and what did any of it matter anyway? Stories like mine were as common as clap, everyday as rape. There were hundreds of girls with stories like mine, with daddies that didn't want them and skin the colour of confusion.

***

My flight left at eleven the next morning. I got up at five and called a cab to take me over to the Greyhound. I was almost at the depot before I remembered Blue Hole, but as soon as it came to me I had to go back. The driver swore I was crazy but he turned right round and left the engine running while I walked up to the water edge. I'd imagined Blue Hole often enough, a bluer than blue space so deep it gave you vertigo, and I'd visioned my father stalking the shallows, knee deep, chest deep, waiting for me to get back to him. I stared down into it and saw nothing but my reflection, unsteady on the surface. The heat of the day hadn't picked up. Winter was whipping round the park, trying to make up for lost time, tarnishing the last leaves, withering the green. A bird called out across the hollow. Mom will be at home right now, I thought, most likely baking the hell out of an innocent sweet potato, waiting for me to call her and tell her that her cover was blown. Mom knows she cannot hope to get away with this. I took a moment to consider the most exquisite way to confront my mother (I thought of her, from this time on, in inverted commas – 'mother' – alleged, perjured, reputed, disputed matriarch that she was). Let her wait, I thought; let her sweat herself till she's tender and ready to fall apart, till she's so cooked in her own juices it don't even need a knife to cut her, or a fork to hold her right where you want her. Then I thought, the thing about Blue Hole is, the thing about it is, it isn't really blue. Blue is the colour of the unclouded sky stretching out before you, a hopeful tone that lifts your eyes and your spirits with them, the colour of summer and heaven and something that won't get dragged back down to earth. And this? It's just a trick of the light is all, a mirage, sky reflected in plain old water and a foolish feeling. It ain't even blue.

Mothballs

"Liquorice and blackcurrant?" Gelda held out a battered enamel snuff tin with a swimsuited Betty Grable on the lid. This was war booty, won in a bet, the story went, in the blacked-out back room of a side-street café in Pigalle between rounds of strip poker. It came out on long car journeys and other you-never-know scenarios stuffed with comfits, spare knicker elastic and twenty-pence pieces.

"No thanks," I said. I didn't want a sweet. I didn't want Gag to be there at all, but Half-Moon Coppice was off the same junction as MacArthur Glen and Gag had a fifty-quid note trying to hokey-cokey out of her purse.

"You can't get Jimmy Choos at MacArthur Glen," I

told her, for the eighteenth time, hoping, as I bombed up the slip-road, that she might yet change her mind and I could drop her at the slot-machines at the Welcome Break and pick her up when I had done.

"They're a designer outlet, aren't they?" Gag said, twitching in her seat to the rhythms of bossanova. "This is a good one," she said. That's the thing with people who listen to Radio 2. They can't just listen to it. They have to be telling you every five minutes how deeply wonderful it is.

"Are you going to wait in the car?"

"I'll have to try them on."

"At the wood."

"Oh no. I want to meet him. I've never met a madman before. Men with shell shock and syphilis, yes, but never a mad philosopher. You don't get many of those."

"Jack Morea won't be there. He lives on Harris, you know, in the Hebrides. I mean he doesn't live in the woods, does he? He's not a – leave the wing mirror, Christ – he doesn't live in some wood."

Gag examined her manicure, bored of the topic. "I wish Troy was here."

I said nothing.

"Shame he had classes."

"Oh," I said, "tragic."

Gag snapped her snuff tin shut and stuffed it in her bag, "Why are you always so unpleasant to him?"

"Everyone's got a hobby."

"Well he's sensitive."

"Like a bad tooth."

"Listen to you, answer to everything." Gag rested her foot on the dashboard and painted over the chips in her toenails with Morello Cherry, "You should talk to him."

"And say what?"

"You've got to make the effort, Helena, or what will happen once I've gone?"

"Don't say things like that."

"Why not?"

"Just don't."

"It won't be long now. I'm quite looking forward to it. The weather's lovely this time of year, once you get north of Marrakech."

"Marrakech?"

We'd come to the exit roundabout, a real eight-laner, lorries to my left, lorries to my right. "Or Nice. You know I can't think which one I prefer. Of course my Arabic's quite rudimentary but then —"

"You can't afford another holiday."

"I've my lab money."

Someone with Gelda's taste wouldn't last a week on a giro. For years she'd been hiring her body out to medical research at twenty quid a throw. Electrodes wired to her forehead, her wrists, and places an old lady shouldn't allow interference, Gag did her stuff in the psych lab, picking red triangles from blue squares as they flashed up on her VDU, trying to nail as many as she could in each ten-minute round and keep her high score ahead of the rest. It was some kind of experiment into ageing and the brain, reflexes, shape recognition, all that. There were whole rows, whole roomfuls of wrinklies, Gag said, shunning the pensioner's matinee at the Odeon to test their wits against an ancient Amstrad. Troy reckoned they were putting drugs in the biscuits – Aricipet in the custard creams and Cognex in the bourbons. He thought the whole blue triangle escapade was a diversion. I'd made him promise not to tell Gag, who thought she was part of some Nobel Prize-destined effort to cure Alzheimer's.

"Anyway, it's not a holiday," said Gag, "I'm relocating."

"Relocate? Gag," I flexed my fingers back on the wheel and enjoyed the crack of knuckle, "you can't *move* to Morocco."

"Why not?"

"For a million reasons. You don't know anyone."

"I make friends easy. I've been before you know; I wasn't in the country an hour before I had a proposal of marriage. It was the hair, you see. Well," Gag smiled, and ran a hand down her neck, "not just the hair." Gag allowed herself a moment, flexed her foot, stretched out her pink, pink toes on the dashboard. "But maybe you're right, maybe it's Nice; after all the language helps. Let's see, *Je voudrais une bouteille du vin rouge*," Gag swung the rear-view round for full preening benefit.

I snapped it back round and swerved a half-lane as I did.

"Oh!" Gelda pressed her palms together and hopped in her seat, "I adore this song."

It was a Beach Boys track.

"You know what this reminds me of?"

It was *Good Vibrations*.

"I don't want to know."

"Montmartre."

Gelda had got her self stuck in a moment just south of VE day, just north of Paris, and never had found her way back to the future. Every pretty girl she saw, every good looking man, more than that: onion soup, black pepper, soft cheese, spring mists, tulips, *everything* reminded Gag of Paris. Even Brian Wilson.

Gag was nineteen when the war broke out, and first thing she did, the week she heard, she thumbed a ride on a tuna schooner over to Calais. She was there when the tanks rolled into Paris and, the way she tells it, blonde in the days when being blonde meant something. Gag had been beautiful, in the way that old people always are in their stories of youth, but with Gag you could believe it, for she still had good grey eyes and fine bones and a nose that flirted with the world whether she would or she wouldn't.

Gag was mid-flow, "You know the world was black and white then, it really was, not just the pictures, the world. All the smoke you see, the smog and then the dirt I suppose and the clothes all brown and greys, you know I don't think I saw turquoise till I was thirty, or fuchsia, can you imagine? Of course they were all quite in love with me, pour souls, and – well, it's not the kind of story I should tell you, I suppose."

My mother, who trembled at anything more exotic than a satsuma, had always hated Gag's stories. Gag just had to say, "I remember," just had to say, "pass the Beaujolais," to have my mother change the subject. I supposed that was why, in the last few weeks, without Mum to interrupt, Gag had been telling us more than ever.

"I could do without this, you know, after everything," I said, "you fending off fakirs in Marrakech."

"You needn't carry on, Helena. Everyone retires."

"You can't retire," I said, as we moved onto the dual carriageway, "you don't do anything." You couldn't retire from being a lush and a flirt. "Who'll look after you?"

"Who looks after me now?" Gag said.

"I do."

"You," Gag said, "don't care if I go barefoot."

Someone in the right hand-lane was making a dickhead sign at me. With a real effort I eased off the gas. "We'll talk about it," I said. "Later."

"You won't change my mind."

"It's not that simple, is it, Gag? You can't just up and move, there's legislation, legalities, all kinds of —"

"Oh," said Gag, "those."

"You can't just pack up and —"

"It's the EU, isn't it though? We're all Europeans now."

Christ. "Morocco isn't in the EU. For God's sake, Gag, it's another bloody *continent*."

"It's in *Lonely Planet Mediterranean Europe*," Gag insisted, "and your inter-rail pass is valid, Troy said so, so –"

"What does Troy know? He's an expert on his own arse is all Troy knows."

"Helena!"

I came off the dual carriageway and followed signs for the B7008. We were almost at Half-Moon but instead of feeling any sense of inner calm all I could think of was Gag in some *Hideous Kinky* type bind and me a thousand miles away. "Where will you live? Thinking of pitching a bivouac in the souk? I mean, what will you live on?"

"My dear, I've packed up for the continent before now with nothing more than a corkscrew and a white bikini and got by perfectly well. I still have many talents, you know." I stalled then, as the light turned green and I shuffled gearstick, break and gas. "You know your problem, Helena?"

You, I thought, *right now, with your shoe fetish and your insistence on force-feeding me Jimmy Young and turning today into a family trauma as if my whole life hadn't been one long one.*

"You know your problem?" Gag said, loving the rhetoric of it all. "You think too much."

"Right," I said.

"You should learn to be more *laissez-faire*. You know, *que sera sera*."

I stopped the engine. We were there, or at least we should have been. We were at Half-Moon Coppice only Half-Moon Coppice wasn't there. There was a row of people carriers, toddlers wrestling with young mums in spiked heels and denim and a tangle of trolleys, but no sign of a tree. At some point between Jack Morea's visit and mine, Half-Moon Coppice had become a supermarket, an extra value one with neon signage and a burger van in the car park.

Of course, I thought. Of course it has. What had I thought, that I could drive back to the past, catch the M1 two junctions and arrive back at five years old with everything in front of me? I felt like those kids, the ones who try to get back into Narnia and run up against the cheap wood and mothballs of a wardrobe. There wasn't a way to get from where I was to where I wanted to be. I was stuck, with the museum, the mouldering house, Gag and Troy and their perpetual crises.

Gag, meanwhile, gave a purr of delight, "Arthur Macglen it is then, Helena. And we've plenty of time for lunch."

For most of man's history, we have understood that the individual's success has been dependent on the success of his group, the tribe he belonged to. Actually the success of the group – and I mean especially the family – is always at the expense of the individual.

Jack Morea, *The Theory of Soul*

Playing metaphysicals

The Chubby Clam had taken a perfectly good pub, scooped out its insides and filled it with tat: bits of driftwood that I knew for old skirting boards, shards of Blue Nun bottles that had done the rinse cycle in a Zanussi and what looked like crispy seaweed from the Peking Monk. Still, Gelda liked it (the waiters wore tight trousers and they did liqueur coffees), and Troy did too (the chips came in a crunchy coating), and week after week in a charade of family unity we'd come here, ever since Mum, and dine among gravy, lemon detergent and stale sweat to the strains of Paul Young and grizzling kids.

Gelda sipped sherry in geranium lipstick and a mauve

poncho. She was flying out to Mexico that evening (no mention of Morocco, not for two weeks, but I knew better than to think that conversation was over), and had dressed for the occasion. A plastic sombrero was folded into her hand luggage. "Why Mexico?" I asked, still hoping I'd persuade her to somewhere safer, Malta, the Canaries or Southend-on-Sea.

"I've always liked Aztecs," Gelda said.

"Yes," I said, "and tequila."

The waiters brought our food, beef dinners for Gag and Troy, vegetable wellington for me. I waited till Troy had his fork loaded up, roast potato speared through a chunk of beef, carrot balanced on the end and the whole smothered in mint and apple and redcurrant sauces and gravy, an effortless feat of engineering. "I saw an estate agent," I said.

Troy spoke through his mouthful, "No."

"Troy," I said. I knew his lines before he said them.

"I said no," Troy said.

"Let's talk about it," I said, "at least."

"I won't sign the papers. I won't sign them, Helena, and you can't do it without me. You can't sell it. Can she, Gag?"

"Hmmmm?" Gag had been admiring the cut of the

waiter's trousers. "The law," she said, without meaning much by it, "is an ass."

"We can't just pretend nothing's happened," I said.

There's denial and then there's retardation. Troy still hadn't accepted Mum and Dad were ill and took any reference to their death as a personal affront. He seemed to believe they were just on some very long holiday someplace with bad telecommunications links, so trying to talk about what happened next was like trying to paint the Sistine Chapel when you hadn't worked out how to take the lid off your Crayolas.

Troy chewed and cut, scooped and swallowed. I kicked him under the table, felt stupid when he didn't kick me back. "It freaks me out living there, Troy, all their things."

When we were little I would build Lego towers, Troy would knock them down; I'd bake fairy cakes, Troy would eat them before they'd cooled enough to ice. It was a law of the universe: for every action of mine, there was an equal and opposite reaction from Troy. Fighting with Troy was genetically illogical; I may as well stick pins in myself, but we did it all the same. Evenly matched, neither one of us had a reason to make allowances. There's a scar on my stomach I owe to Troy and a place on his skull where the hair won't grow. Other kids used to bet marbles on who'd win; five cat's eyes said Helena, three Dutch oilys, Troy. Brothers and sisters grow out of that, they're supposed to. But it seemed a shame. At least when we fought we used to connect, with our fists in each other's hair, kicking and biting; there was respect. Something better than all of this.

I'd have liked to have been Troy, to sometimes have been the one with the wisecracks and the right pair of trainers. But then who would have been me? Someone needed to be down-to-earth, and the wilder he got the more sensible I became, and the worst of it was he blamed me for it. Now all that had changed. Ever since Mum and Dad had died, Troy, who'd spent most of his life, most of their lives, giving them grey hairs, started acting like the perfect son. Troy was mourner-in-chief, black jeans and sweatshirt; it was him put Mum on the shelf, in the showiest urn; it was me had to face her every day, first thing before breakfast, when I got in. Troy would check for dust when he came round.

There was no one to impress. No one to award points or keep peace, but we didn't know how else to be and there were old scores to settle. When Dad got sick again, the second, the final time, it was me that moved back in, and when Mum got ill, I stayed. I got the steady job. I never let them worry. As for Troy, all the time Dad was ill, the iller he got, the harder Troy partied. He put himself in hospital one time: he needed his stomach pumped he'd drunk so much, and there was me, wheeling Mum from Cancer to Casualty and stopping to buy him deodorant in the foyer.

"Troy," said Gag, "tell Helena about that nice girl you introduced me to at The King William."

Troy mumbled something and loaded up another mouthful.

"Such a pretty thing, what was her name, Troy? Something French, wasn't it?"

Troy smirked into his cheesy topping.

"Not Aurelie," I said.

Troy speared one of Gag's roast potatoes.

"Yeah right," I said, "like she'd even look at you."

"She did more than look."

I pushed my plate away. Troy had always had, as he put it, a way with women. ("What way?" I'd asked once. "Any way I want," he'd said.) I think he appealed to women's nurturing side. They saw him, and, convinced there was something human beneath the dirt, they wanted to take him home, bathe him, cut his hair and burn his clothes. He was a one-man archaeology project, a Stig-of-the-dump with a six-pack.

Troy revolved his fork round his fingers like a drummer in a rock band, spattering the ceiling and a young family behind him with flecks of cold gravy. Troy *was* a drummer in a rock band, a college four-piece called Pupas that played Foo Fighters covers for beer money at eighteenths and twenty-firsts and was trailed by a blubbery mass of fourteen-year-old would-be groupies that left Troy and his mates in terror.

"Aurelie Morea. Well, you're not the first," I said, "or the tenth."

"So what? Not everyone's living in the nineteenth century."

"Troy —" Gag interrupted feebly.

"You're pathetic," I said.

"Helena —"

"Maybe I'm in love; did you think about that?" Troy looked as if he'd opened his mouth to belch and Verdi's *Requiem* had come out.

"When have you ever been in love?" Troy's girlfriends followed one another like a scratch follows an itch.

"H," he said, warming to the idea, "it isn't the kind of thing you need to practise, you know."

Troy's retarded state was a constant reproach. It was obvious that I'd deprived him of vital nutrients in the womb; oxygen, perhaps.

A waitress came and took our plates, dropping Troy's gravied knife in my lap as she swivelled to allow him a flash of cleavage.

"I just think —" I began.

"I don't care what you think." Troy downed his Guinness and smacked out a belch.

"Did I tell you about the time I met Edith Piaf?" Gag said, having eaten all her meat and rearranged the vegetables on her plate.

"I'm not sure." All Gag's stories blended into one and I was busy glaring at Troy.

"In the laundrette? Edith Piaf couldn't walk down the street in those days, couldn't go for her hair set, but there she was, collecting her smalls, and wouldn't you know it, you never would guess, but —"

There was a bar at The Chubby Clam still; the old bar, from The Woodsman, before the makeover. You could look across the ball pool and see into it; over the corridor with its Ikea seascapes, past the quiz machines, through the double doors, old men in flat caps still supped warm pints and dogs dozed on the stone floor and scratched fleas. The oaken chairs and tables, the cardboard beermats and the suedette cushions were covered by a thick film of beer and covered by the ground remains of scratchings, nuts and pie-crust. The whole room had a nicotine-yellow tinge and a stout-brown stain, the same sepia tint of fond memories. A fire crackled in the grate, I knew its tattoo of cracking knuckles and the smell of charred treacle it gave off in place of heat. We used to go there with Dad. He'd buy us shandy, real shandy, bitter and lemonade, and Troy and I would roll around declaring ourselves drunk, and scoff prawn cocktail crisps from plastic packets, bright orange and sugar-sharp on the tongue and, now I think of it, carcinogenic most likely. We used to go there, and now we sit here, where everything is spic and span, kitsch and clean, and I don't know why. I don't know if I'm the only one it bothers – the only one who even remembers.

The waitress came back with a coffee for Gag that smelled of Tia Maria.

"They don't let drunks fly, you know," I said to her, wondering how many times we'd need to stop on the way to the airport.

"Get us some fags from duty free, will you?" Troy said.

"I was thinking of a holiday myself," I said, "next month."

They both looked at me.

"Who'll drive me to my manicure?"

"I'd go while you're away, that weekend you're in Barcelona."

"Who'll feed the cat?"

"Troy can."

"I'm too irresponsible."

"It's a cat, Troy, you open a tin."

"What kind of holiday?" Gag narrowed her eyes.

"It's a retreat. I found it on the internet."

"A cult," said Gag. "How exciting,"

"It isn't a cult, it's run by someone who used to work with Jack Morea."

"Do you think you'll have to shave your head?"

"It isn't a cult," I said.

Troy interrupted, "What do you think Mum and Dad would make of all this?" He wore mint sauce on his sweatshirt.

"I'm not playing metaphysicals with you, Troy," I said. "We can't spend the rest of our lives trying to guess what Mum and Dad would have thought; we'd go crazy."

"What colour is the sky on your planet, H? We don't

need to guess what they'd have thought. They thought he was a flake. The whole world does."

The whole world might. The man hadn't written anything in years. He'd never got over what happened to Arii Cook, never got over the guilt of it all; he was stuck on his island, half-crazy with grief. Maybe he was a flake. But what Gag and Troy didn't get, never would, was the romance, the hopeless, depthless poetry of the man. And all the gossip, the mystery of he was and what he'd done, just impressed me the more. Everyone wants to believe in magic – everyone dreams of that slipper-fitting, wand-waving, prince-kissing moment, and Jack Morea made it sound like more than a fairy tale. Doctor Morea promised that one chiropractic twist with which all the mess in my life, the bits and pieces, the failures might be aligned.

And without the book, what else was there? The lavender baths the counsellor recommended? The herbal teas and scented candles? *Theory of Soul* made sense when nothing else did. I kept it with me, spotted with ink stains and coffee cup marks, stamped out each week by Jenny with a sigh that grew louder, more pressing each time. I carried it round like an asthma inhaler. I read it over, curled up on the sofa, by the light of the fire, or in bed, my light burning into the night. I read it at work while Merg scoured auction catalogues; I read it long after I must have known every word by heart.

"Jenny Finch told me what it says, you know. One of these books about how your parents are to blame for everything."

I swirled the melting ice round in my empty glass. What was the point of even trying to explain it to Troy? "It's about how to find yourself."

"I wouldn't bother if I were you."

"Pass me a plaster, my sides have split."

"It's not their fault, your sad little life, your sad little job. No one asked you to play the little martyr. Florence Nightingale. You make me sick."

"Let's change the subject," Gelda said. I saw her hand shake as she lifted her glass.

"Fine," said Troy, "let's change it to puddings. I'm going for treacle sponge with a side order of Mississippi mud pie."

Gelda went to the bar to order and Troy looked at me, skinned over as cold custard. "It was your choice, Helena."

"Feed the cat."

Troy rocked back on his chair again. He knew I

wasn't going anywhere. "It was your choice, what you did, nobody asked you. All of it."

***

Gelda and I sat in the landside McDonald's. Gelda picked at her nuggets. "I wish you'd just say it," I said.

"Why do I need to say it," Gelda spooned the cherry from her butterscotch sundae, "when you already know? What you mean is, shouldn't I give you the chance to change my mind." Gelda sucked her spoon and looked at me. "Jack Morea is a fool," she said.

"People didn't always think that, did they? Back in the seventies."

"When everyone was doped to their kidneys, you mean."

"So you never believed in the theories? Is that what you're saying?"

"It was a phase, that's all, a craze, hysteria, or history, one or the other, if there's a difference. Gurus came cheap back then, came along oftener than buses. When you get to my age, well, you realise there are no answers."

For all her stories of Left Bank and *la resistance*, Gag wasn't any better than the rest of them. Actually, I thought, she was worse. The others didn't know any better. Gag, according to her stories, had seen poetry, beauty, truth; she'd got out, and she'd come back, jacked it all in for roast dinners, brass bands, double-glazing. "You think you're so out there, don't you, Gag? Well," I searched around for words to napalm my great aunt's sense of complacency, "you're about as anarchist as fish paste, as loft insulation."

"I remember when loft insulation was revolutionary," Gag said.

"So the whole world fell for it, but Gelda Geller never was fooled, is that the line?"

"Oh I fell for it, of course I did. We all did, but then —"

"What?"

"Well, we looked around us. All these formulas," Gag released a toasted almond from her dentures, "these principles. You can't have a theory on life."

"You have to. You have to, or what do you do?" The table-clearer eyed us warily over the chicken nuggets, swabbing at the ketchup and empty paper packets.

"You experiment." Gag slipped a mayo sachet in her handbag. "I haven't believed in anything at all since I saw that Roswell documentary. Yes, in vapour rub and clean underwear and in washing behind your ears, in cabbage water and the benefits of a really good orgasm. Anything more than that," Gelda sniffed, "gives me nosebleed."

She smiled, "Can you fetch my carry-on, dear? I think we're boarding."

As we hugged goodbye, Gag patted my shoulder, her hand soft, "I worry, that's all. You're like the man whose house is burning down and all he can think of is his fish fingers defrosting in the ice-box."

"What man?" I said.

"Priorities, dear. It's a lot to cope with, I know, but you're not helping yourself. Psychobabble, that's what they're calling it these days you know. If you lived to two hundred then maybe these kinds of questions would be worth considering, but let me tell you the next fifty years are all you've got, and they're going to go like that," Gag never could click her fingers, and never would give up trying, "like that, and you don't want to waste them playing cat's cradle with theoreticals."

"Are you trying to make me feel better?" I said.

"Of course not," Gag looked offended, "just remember we are human beings, not human thinkings. Go out with Georgetown. Meet some boys. I don't know."

"Have you got your medicine?"

"Don't fuss. Chairman Meow's off Whiskas, by the way, so you'll have to –"

"Now who's fussing?"

Gelda's name came over the tannoy. "Last call flight MJ127."

"Morea had this idea of an alternate self," I said.

Gag grimaced.

"Like this person that we're born to become, but, somehow, things that happen to us, life experience, it takes us away from being this person, forces us to be someone else. Gag, I keep thinking that somewhere there's this version of me who's, I don't know, riding camels or –"

I looked at Gag. I expected her to tell me that camels were very uncomfortable, but she came up to me and put her arms around me. She held me so tight it hurt.

I kissed her goodbye, "I just want to know the truth," I said, "know who I am, who I'm supposed to be, because I don't."

"Of course," said Gag, "but you're looking in the wrong place."

"But –"

"The truth is like your G-spot, Helena. It may take some patience, but you'll certainly know when you've found it." She turned and trotted off to the gate, then, over her shoulder, eyelashes batting beneath that pink sombrero, said, "And it won't be in a philosophy book."

I never hurt nobody but myself,
and that's nobody's business but my own.

Two inches short of the perfect fit

I had returned to a frenzy of interior design, a barrage of paintpots and pelmets, a filling of gaps and crevices, the carpet and skirting for the first time coming snugly together, the coving describing an arc of perfection, a halo to the angelic harmony of my mother's decoration. I waited until I had a witness (Jimmy, an alibi and a guarantee, five rungs up the ladder, paste brush in hand, trying to get Mom's *Pretty Primrose* border to hang halfway straight over her embossed *Via Sienna* wallpaper) before I told my mom what I knew.

"Promise me. Promise me, Georgie that you won't tell Aunt Mary," her eyes were on Jimmy.

"Is that all you have to say for yourself?"

"What else do you want me to say?" Mom busied herself with the bottom of the ladder.

"How about an apology?"

"What have I got to be sorry for? You think I lied to you?" She looked like her conscience was clear as clarified butter. "Sit down, calm down," she said, "I'll cook you mash potato."

"I'm not six years old."

"What?" Mom said, "You too old for mash potato?"

I knew if I let Mom get a saucepan in her hand, if we moved from the lounge to the kitchen, onto her territory, then she had won. Mom had been peeling, grating, frying and boiling her way out of conversations the last twenty years. The reason she fed me so well is 'cause you couldn't talk back when your mouth was full. Once we got into the kitchen, Mom would start being Mom, and I would be the little kid, watching wide-eyed as Mom laid down the law. It was the same with Bob. He'd been staying over more and more often, ever since the showcase, and Mom just kept feeding him up and feeding him up, and I knew she hoped one day he'd get so big he wouldn't fit out the door. "Can't we for once in the hell get a take away?" I said.

Mom beheld me with eyes mean like a cheese grater.

"You don't like my cooking?"

"Mom!"

"You want to cook? Hmmm?" Mom worked her turkey neck thing she thought said all about her ghetto upbringing, but I knew she got from Oprah. "Miss Thing, you want to rough up your hands peeling potatoes and scrubbing pans? 'Cause if that's what you want to do, ain't nobody here going to stop you."

"We were talking about my apparent non-existence."

"Are you sassing me? 'Cause I won't stand sassing, Georgie Easy."

"Mom, I'm telling you, I'm *asking* why the County Clerk don't even –"

"You believe a total stranger?" Mom's voice was somewhere up near the ceiling rose. She had a supersonic disbelief. "I never told you a lie my entire life. Jimmy, are you sure you ain't got too much paste on that paper, 'cause I can see it bumping from down here, looks like I got moles in my walls."

When we first moved into Flass Lane, back when Tantie lived with us and the plan was to open as a B&B for parents visiting their kids at uni, the whole place needed decorating. I think the sight of it, carpets worn bare and wallpaper greening with mould, must have been my first memory. Flass Lane was a real nice street; a find, as Tantie put it, with nice girls and boys to play with, Mom thought, spoilt lumps of things that they were, and for neighbours we had on one side of us a teacher and on the other a nurse; Mom picked it up for nothing on account of the work needed doing. Mom may not have known much about DIY, but she was a woman of ingenuity. Her boyfriends those first months were all men of trade: a plumber, an electrician and a carpenter, big-handed, big-hearted men. That first year was a blur of sawdust, mouse droppings and cockroaches, and the only price was one it didn't cost Mom nothing to pay. There was an uneven love walled into the foundations of that house, stitched into its fabric and coursing through the piping. Now, as revenge for my Texas trip, Mom had decided to ensure my sticky fingerprints were removed, my grip on the place loosened, my skin, my hair, my dirt excavated. The front room was the last corner of empire for Mom to quell.

"I could go to the police," I said.

Mom shrugged, "You're the one with a fake passport."

"And you're the one responsible."

"If you want to take that chance –" I could see Mom's

tongue working in her cheek pocket. Jimmy's face was stiff with discomfort. I watched him up and down those paint-splattered steps (the ladder the only homely thing left), up and down, sure-footed, heavy-hearted, and felt a strength rise in me.

I walked over to the phone. I picked up the receiver. Jimmy stopped his brushing and turned to look at me while Mom stared resolutely at the other wall, either trying to prove her indifference or spotting brush hairs in the eggshell finish on the radiator. I dialled, got as far as the second nine when Mom threw her hands up. "OK, OK. If you want to blackmail your own mother."

"So why ain't I registered?" I still held the receiver in my hand.

"Never got round to it."

"It's the law."

"Hah! Plenty of things is the law."

"Yeah," I said, "like not faking passports."

"I never faked a passport in my life!" And Mom's rage was so big in that claustrophobic room, the furnishing encroaching on all sides, rug upon carpet, over underlay, layers of lining paper, wallpaper and border, that I wondered indeed if she was right. Surrounded by the twisting vines of Laura Ashley, the truth was incredible to me. "Jimmy, do you hear the things she's saying? Did you ever hear a girl talk to her mother like that?"

"So you *are* my mother, then?"

Jimmy took a Stanley knife down and cut a piece of border soft as birthday cake.

"Lord, Georgie," Mom said, "a passport, a registration form. These are little things between a mother and a daughter. There is more important things. Ain't there? More important than paper."

Mom's words may have been conciliatory, but she had adopted her confrontation pose – arms folded high under her chest, stout legs thrust apart. I was standing the exact same way. I had always admired the sight of my mother going into battle: giving the neighbours all flavours of damnation, telling my teachers what they needed to be told. But I never did think I'd see her and me squaring up to a fight. Though part of me was terrified, I knew too that what I'd been doing all those years was learning, like a cub watching the lioness hunt, and I was ready for my first taste of blood. If there was anything I could have done to get the truth from my mother – if screaming myself white would have made a difference, if violence or the threat of it would have met my ends, believe me, there was nothing so low I wouldn't have bent down to do it.

We stood there sulking for a while, both trying to think of something clever to say. We had not made a whole success of this mother daughter thing. Sure we got on tuneful enough for as long as I played in her key, but sometimes I felt my mother didn't want a daughter, she wanted a doughboy, something could be rolled and reshaped and sweetened to please. After a while Mom's varicose veins got the better of her and she sat down. Mom served up her sweet chilli sauce voice, "What happened back in Texas, that's my life, see. My life, not yours, not your business to go snooping around in. Everybody allowed their secrets, or ain't I allowed a life of my own?"

I was not about to fall for the vocal trick that hadn't fooled me at five years old. "It's my life too," I said, gruff as coconut shell.

"Just 'cause I'm your mother don't mean you got rights over me. Do you see me asking about every guy you sleep with?"

"Mom!"

"No. Because I mind my own, and it's only a shame there ain't more like me," Mom was pouting and playing with her hair. Her legs were twitching and her eyes kept flicking to the kitchen door. "Are you sure you don't want me to fix you a little snack, eh, Georgie?"

Other people comfort ate. My mom comfort cooked. I shook my head.

Then she said, in the same breath, "Your daddy ain't nothing to you. What difference you think it going to make? You think you can ring him up, and he'll come running? Well, it ain't going to happen."

"We got a problem, Agatha," Jimmy said then.

"Too right," I said. "Too right."

"No, I mean," Jimmy pointed to the wall. There was a gap of petunia blue where the border didn't quite reach.

"Damn," Mom said.

"Shame," said Jimmy.

"Another roll would have done it."

"Half a roll, even."

"Just two inches short of the perfect fit."

Jimmy looked at us, beat. "Ladies," he said, "I think I'll be moving on here."

"Jimmy, you couldn't do me a quick rub down on the woodwork through the hall, could you?"

Jimmy shook his head weightily. "I don't think so," he said. "I think not tonight."

"Or move the chest back into the bedroom, almost felled myself this morning."

"Maybe another night, Agatha," and he gave a sham cough as an alibi.

I tried to catch his eye as he walked out, tools in hand, back stooped, tried to tell him I didn't want to be left alone with Mom, because I didn't trust myself any more than I trusted her, but he mustn't have seen me; he can't have done.

Mom sat back in her big chair. After five minutes her face was softening into sleep.

"You're my mother – you ain't God, you know." I said.

"As far as you are concerned, I am Jesus, God and the holy spirit. You know, Aurelie says you're lucky not knowing your father. Did you consider that? She says she wish she didn't know hers, the way he treat her."

"She don't mind taking his money though, does she now?"

"She needs it."

"Like a shark needs more teeth."

"She does. She's studying."

"Studying Sanderson Miller's ceiling."

"They ain't sleeping together."

"Whatever."

"Sanderson told me. Says he's waiting."

"Since when did Sanderson wait for even a bus?"

"Well I don't know what you got against the girl."

"Don't you now," I said. Mom and Tantie and Jimmy and Sanderson were all falling over Aurelie. Son Son, Bo and the Paradise every-timers too. Sure, the girl had a fine enough outside, that I could understand, but it wasn't the outside folks were interested in; even the men wanted more than that, wanted the inside, the liquid honey centre. And the testimony! Grown men told me they heard the sound of their mother's lullaby in her song, and hard-faced women whispered that her voice was the sound of their unborn babies crying from the other side. Journalists across from London to write her up would find themselves unable to form their thoughts into words, ending up scribbling, doodling, spilling shapeless ink. Myself, I didn't believe any of it. Some people put too much store by a face that's inherited and a body that won't last, and that's all it was, the secret of Aurelie Morea: luck, genes, not a thing she could call her own and as for the voice, truth was she never matched that first night for style.

"It's about more than a father. What about Grandma? And I must have had a grandfather, I mean, mustn't I?"

"You tell me," Mom said, "you spoke to him last." I blushed. I shall tell you a story, 'cause my life is full of them, all curled up like spiders down the plughole: A couple of years before that night, I'd thought I'd found my grandfather. Helena had told me about some website; the library had just got internet. I typed in *Agatha Easy* and *Georgetown* and forty-seven names came up. Most of them seemed to live in Chickasaw Nation, I.T. I was not sure what this signified, but I made a note of it all the same. Anyway, after a half-hour of searching, a Jack Easy (also known as John, as Joe and Johnnie and plain old J) came up. He was sixty-nine years old and a retired car mechanic. He lived in Georgetown but had travelled some 'cause he'd also been in New York, New Jersey, Nevada, Idaho and Austin. Best of all, he had posted his number on the net. I called him from the lobby payphone in the library foyer. A girl without a past to be sure of will grab hold of anything and call it a father. A woman answered.

"Who?" she said. "He's having his medicine. Call back later."

"It's his granddaughter," I said.

"Uh-huh," she didn't sound surprised, "Call back later." She hung up.

I called Mom in excitement. "I've found him."

"Who?" she said.

"Granddad."

Mom laughed. At first I supposed she was happy, but then I noticed her laugh was kind of slurred, like coloured clothes running into each other in the wash.

"Have you been drinking?" I said.

"Where you find him?"

"On the internet. I'm calling him back after he's had his medicine."

"Send him my love," Mom said. She hung up too.

When I called Jack back, he picked up straight away. "Granddad?" I said, my voice shaking. There was a pause. "I mean, are you Jack Easy?"

"Yes?" he said, though he didn't sound sure. The line was bad, but I could make out the accent alright and it felt like home.

"It's Agatha's daughter," I said.

"Yes," he said.

"Georgetown," I said.

"Yes."

There was a pause.

"I'm researching the family tree," I said.

"Yes," he said, and then, "Can you lend me fifty dollars?"

"Listen," I said, "it's important. Before my money runs out, understand? I need to know something. Mom's boyfriend, before I was born, I mean."

"Yes."

"He was a white guy, right?"

"Yes."

"Do you know his name?"

"Give me the fifty dollars, first," he said.

I heard a woman's voice in back say, "Mr Easy, have you been posting on the internet again?"

"Yes."

"Have you been tricking folks out of money again?"

She comes on the line, "Look," she said, "I don't know who you are, but you ain't who you think you are, if you think you are who I think you think you are."

"Excuse me ma'am," I say, "I'm calling long-distance."

"I'll say you is."

"I'm calling from England. I'm Georgetown Easy. Ma'am, I'm researching my Afro-American ancestors." I ain't got no shame, no sense, no nothing at all and I fit to bust as I sing, "I'm Mr Easy's long-lost grand-daughter." In my mind we are embracing on Oprah, I am wiping a tear from his cheek and my mother has straightened her hair for the occasion.

"Is you now. Is you just. Ain't you just. Mr Easy has

twenty long-lost grand-daughters. Mr Easy got a nephew been to the moon and a bullet lodged in his temporal lobe."

"I don't understand."

"Some folks ought to know not to believe everything they see on the internet."

"But you don't understand – he said he was, he said he knew my father."

The woman let out a sigh smelled bad to me from across the Atlantic. "Mr Easy, is you the son of President Jefferson?"

"Yes."

"And do you have a sister call herself Marilyn Monroe?"

"Yes."

"And, Mr Easy, do you have a little nigger girl granddaughter living in England?"

I hung up.

"Look, George," Mom said, "this obsession with history –"

"My father ain't history. Even if he's dead, he ain't."

"We's a family, ain't we? You and me, so what we need nobody else for?"

"Everybody needs something to look back on."

Mom kicked at the stepladder; it left a bare stripe where it scraped down the height of the wall. Mom swore. "You want to look back on something? Look back on Henry number eight and his sixteen wives."

"Six wives, Mom."

"You look back on that and on rationing and Queen Her Majesty Victoria. Why not?"

"Because it's not mine."

"It yours just as much as anyone else's." Some families do not have discussions about the meaning of history. Some families play trivial pursuits and watch TV. "You born here, near as, it's yours. You want it? Take it, it's as good as you'll get. Or what's the matter? You want your own private history stretching all the way back to Moses? You want to draw a line in the sand, say this black history, this white? There is only one kind of history and it's dirty and grey. We're all descended from each other, all screwing each other, it's all everyone's and nobody's, and there ain't no such thing as us and ours. The English all German anyway, the Australians English, the Americans, Lord knows."

"You're so —"

Mom looked at me.

"So —"

She raised an eyebrow. "What? What am I, Georgie? Tell me."

"Inconsistent," I said.

I went to the bathroom. After all Mom's paintwork, I couldn't even pee and feel at home. I splashed cold water on my face, vowing that I would not sleep until I had the truth of the matter (and as a back-up I would ask Helena what she knew about the European Court of Human Rights).

I swaggered back into the lounge ready for Round Two.

"Jimmy didn't do such a bad job," Mom said.

I shrugged, "Didn't see what was wrong with the way it was."

"It's a change." Mom said "And you know what they say about a change."

"It sucks," I said.

Mom said something to the effect of everyone making mistakes, blah, the virtues of forgiveness, blah, blah, how she hadn't forfeited her right to be spoken to correctly in her own home on account of a weakness for filing. Mom headed for the kitchen.

"I'll ask Tantie," I said, "I'll ask her what really went down."

"Sure," Mom said, "sure. You ask her."

"You can't expect her to keep your secrets forever."

Mom described two half-circles with her hands, as if to indicate the vastness of her indifference.

"Just answer me one question," I said.

Mom laughed.

"One."

"I answer one question, you think I don't know there'll be a dozen more chasing its tail?"

"If you loved me, in the least, you'd give me a question," I said, but not with anger, with a chill in my voice at the realisation that what I said to hurt my mother might be true, and turn out to cut me deeper than the hurt I intended her.

"Oh, is that how it works?" Mom said, sleek, pushing a cuticle back with a thumbnail.

"That's how it is."

"You think love has rules?" She batted eyelids at me.

"I think it has conditions."

"I didn't bring you up to think that way."

"I think my own way. I'm all grown up, Mom." And I didn't know why my mother couldn't see that. She could see that a ceiling needed painting or a wall needed papering, but she thought that me and her could make do and go on the way we had been since I was five years old.

"Not that I noticed. You want to stop looking at me and take a look at yourself. The world is moving on and Georgetown Easy's still at the bus-stop looking for her purse."

I was making an effort not to cry. If I cried, Mom would have folded me up in those dough-pounding arms and we would have settled ourselves back into stalemate, and I was sick of a stalemate in which I'd always be the loser. "I'm going to Tantie's," I said. "I'm moving in."

This did not affect my mother in the cataclysmic way you might expect. Its impact had been somewhat undermined by overuse. I must have threatened it (as a teenager, not for years before that day) thirty, forty times and got so far as packing a bag five or six. I once spent a weekend in Tantie's box room, so my mother ought to have known it was not entirely an idle threat.

"Fine," Mom said, casual as spilt milk. "Maybe it's better that way."

"I mean it, Mom, because we're through here."

"You hear me arguing?"

"Fine then. Then that's fine. That's — I'll pack up tonight then."

"Cool-o," Mom said, eyes drier than mine, breathing softer. "Cool-i-o."

I strike a chord, sound each one of 'em out:

Jimmy's untroubled bassline,

Be-dum-be-dum,

Mary's staccato,

Ka-ka-ka-ka,

Agie's bluesy bassoon,

Oop-doop-be-boop.

I hype the lot of them

Gas them, fracture

call Jimmy fly daddy-o

Agie baby

Mary a monster with more soul than the Lord's own wishbone.

I tighten the peg and change the key.

I bring them in and send them out

in my own sweet time

and it's breakneck.

I start with Mary, singing in the pocket

then I slide-slip and syncopate

the hell out

of whatever time we're meant to be in.

We go on for weeks,

trading 8s in a smooth chase,

and once I got her running she cannot stop, she's blowing hysterical

till Jimmy's scared she'll be all blown out.

And another thing:

she hits notes with me that he can't get.

Jimmy jams with me, the swing of my hips suggests a new ground beat,

the curve of my lips puts a new change to mind.

When I'm around, he can't stop picking.

He strums till his fingers bleed, he thumbs till his wrist aches.

It crosses his mind.

As for Agatha, she's my front-row doll, my standing ovation

and I got myself what I need:

a place to call home, a way

to flush myself clean of those beauty queen genes,

undo that Promethean paternal feat,

stop being breathing proof of the impossible,

the Archimedean bath water,

the earth-bound apple,

the philosopher's daughter.

Some kind of week

Jimmy was sick in bed the night I called round, shouting down "That woman is working me into the ground, let there be no confusion over that point at the inquest." It was their sixteenth wedding anniversary, and Tantie was getting misty-eyed over a photo of the two of them, Tantie in a brown silk sleeveless had to be seen to credit it, Jimmy in a borrowed suit and a bowtie he'd stolen from the Oxfam shop, mistaking the old dear who told him the clothes had been donated for the sake of the African poor. "You remember?" Tantie said.

"Course I do. I was the best man, wasn't I?"

Tantie laughed. After screaming a tantrum at the orange organza Tantie had intended for me as bridesmaid, I'd been relegated to chief dresser of the groom. Given Jimmy's recent arrival to the country, and the love shading into fear he had for his bride, this was perhaps a larger task than my aunt intended for my eight-year-old self. Still, we achieved our goal with five minutes to spare and had allowed ourselves a moment of congratulation. "How do I look?" Jimmy had asked.

"Fantastic," I said.

He beamed (Jimmy had always had a smile you could get yourself lost in). "I have everything I need – my suit, my flower," we had stolen one of Mrs Wilkinson's peach roses, less because it almost matched my aunt's chocolate orange colour scheme and more because I knew they were Mrs Wilkinson's favourites, "a ring," we had chosen the wedding band from Ratners, a bargain at £3.99 and, we had agreed, indistinguishable from its £200 twin in the shop next door, "and a speech."

"Uncle Jimmy!" I said, "But you haven't got a best man!"

Jimmy put his head in his hands. "Shit!" he said. "I knew there was something I had not remembered to remember. Shit!"

I let him appreciate the seriousness of the situation.

"What is a best man? Precisely, I mean."

"God, man," I rolled my eyes and pulled at my dress in exasperation, "he holds the rings at the wedding and gives a speech afterwards. And he makes the groom feel not nervous when the bride is late."

"Mary will not be late."

"They're always late," I said. "Don't you know anything?"

Jimmy looked nothing less than alarmed. "This best man. Do you think it is very important?"

I nodded. "Everyone has a best man. You can't get married without one. It's practically the law."

"I see." Jimmy was pacing the room, stroking his chin like it was good luck. "Where can I get one of the best men?"

"You just pick someone. Someone you like."

"It can be anyone?"

"Well not anyone. You need someone knows a lot about rings, see, and then someone sure to get on with the bride."

Outside the taxi was beeping its horn. Jimmy looked at the clock. It was four minutes to two and a five-minute ride to the church.

"Georgetown," he said, "would you do me the very great honour — that is to say, would you be my best man?"

"No problem, Jimmy," I said.

Placing the photo back on the shelf, Tantie settled herself down to business. "So," she said, "Empire Tobacco. I drafted a letter."

The University's new Empire Tobacco Chair of Post-Colonial English was my aunt's most recent campaign and I'd promised to help her with her fundraising drive. Tantie did not know what Post-Colonial English was, but that didn't mean she wasn't prepared to set herself dead against it until somebody gave her a reason not to. As for the tobacco trade, it was the big blue-black booger man to her Br'er Rabbit act. Her only trouble was in choosing what made her maddest about it, "They like big John Kong with his great donkey dong, they just about screw everything in sight, you know what I'm saying? Everyone flat on their back while Mr Puff Puff do his business."

I was surprised my aunt had time to worry about a lecturing job. In the old days, when I was growing up, Tantie had been prepared to let some things pass. She had kept in her head an account book more complicated than the devil's, with gains and losses of the moral variety all scored out and so it was possible that something like this could once have been balanced by a donation to a children's home or scholarships for poor black kids. But it seemed Tantie's standards were subject to inflation and her days of deal-brokering were over. She told me, "'Vengeance is mine,' says the Lord, quite true, but don't say nothing wrong with giving the Almighty a helping hand." I sometimes worried it would all get too much for my aunt. She may only have been in her forties, but, as she loved to tell me, she had done living enough for two lifetimes, and there were days when she took to her bed with the strain of it all. Underneath her huff and puff, Tantie was like a peeled banana: she bruised easily. The little spites and bites of this life that the rest of us learn to shut up and put up with still dug deep into Tantie's flesh. If milk boils for long enough it grows a skin, but blood ain't like that and Tantie bubbled over with the righteous indignation of the well-fed and well-clothed who remembered when life wasn't always like that.

"Fetch my files, honey, and move that bag. What you got in there anyhow? Louisiana?"

"I moved out of Mom's."

"Oh, Georgie, what for?"

I shrugged. "We ain't been getting ourselves on too good."

"Since Georgetown?"

I nodded.

"You know, Georgie, seems to me like you got a choice and you need to make a call. You can keep punishing your mom for what happened before you was even born, or you can start considering some kind of a future."

"Uh-huh."

"So what you think?"

"This goes deep Tantie, deeper than who my daddy is."

"What the matter? You think she don't love you?"

I shrugged.

"You crazy girl. Course she loves you."

"I guess."

"There you are. And what's more important than love?"

"How about truth," I said.

"Ha! You say that 'cause you've had too much of one and not enough of the other to know how lucky you are."

"She got me a fake passport. Her and Sanderson. That's the lengths she's going to – she'd break the law to keep me from knowing myself."

Tantie doodled a sunflower on the files I'd carried

over to her. "I knew about that."

"You knew?"

"Course I knew."

"What else you know?"

"Enough not to get myself messed up in this. So you're moving out, where you gonna live? What you gonna live on? Or ain't you worried about the practicalities, hmmm? Maybe you're gonna feed yourself on truth."

"I thought maybe I could move in here."

"Tsch!"

"I could pay you rent. Just as soon as I can get some work."

"You got work."

I shaded in the sunflower Tantie had drawn and felt the blood in my cheeks confess.

"You lost your job? Lord, girl, this is some week you're having."

I mumbled an apology. It was Tantie who had scored me that job in the first instance, a PA at Price and Hart, typing minutes, taking phonecalls, booking hotels, dinners and flights and helping them reach their ethnic minority recruitment target of 0.3 percent. My aunt's grudge against Price and Hart dated back to 1870, around ninety years before she was born. This was the year Mr Price and Mr Hart opened their first shop just round the corner and sold spices my aunt claims were not theirs to ask money for in the first place. It so happened there was certain information floating round Price and Hart that was very useful to someone like Tantie: where they sourced products, how much they paid for them, that kind of thing. I guess I had been a double agent and now was unemployed twice over.

"What you lose it for?"

"Surfing the internet on company time."

"The internet." Tantie stopped dead. "You looking at porn?"

"Tantie!"

"Were you?"

"Of course not." I had been searching for Easy, Georgetown, Texas on every genealogy site I could find.

"Then what business they got what you do?"

"'Cause they don't pay me to surf the internet, do they?"

"When you gonna start sticking up for yourself George Easy? Hmm?"

"You know me, Tantie," I said, "easy come, easy go."

"I know. Trouble easy come, Georgetown easy go. A person can be too easy come, easy go, you know what

I'm saying? Nothing ever change in the world that way, except for the worse."

Tantie boiled the kettle up and, in a mug, mixed fresh ginger, lemon juice, demerara sugar and clove to clear Jimmy's cold. "You're not the only one doing this internet thing, though. Right?" she said.

"I suppose."

"But you're the only one get sacked?"

I shrugged.

"What the union say?"

"I'm not in the union."

"Lord, child, didn't I tell you to get in the union?"

"I don't do everything you tell me," I said.

"This is discrimination. You can take them to an industrial tribunal." I could see Tantie making battleplans, walking down the high street with a banner held high, chaining herself to the Chief Executive's desk.

"Tantie. It ain't discrimination, it ain't prejudice, it ain't racism, sexism or anything else. You can't pin this on anyone except me. You want to shout at someone, shout at me."

"I'm on your side. Don't forget."

"No you're not," I said, "you're on whichever side gets to fire the first shot."

Tantie pulled her chair into the table. She took an orange from the bowl and peeled it, real careful, with her worn old fingers, Jimmy's tonic getting cold on the worktop. When she got the peel off she picked out all the white threads till that orange was bare naked, then she bit into it like other folks eat an apple. After she'd finished, a pool of juice on the tabletop, she said, "Why you do it?"

I shrugged.

"Quit shrugging me," she said, "I ain't your mom."

"It's not like it matters," I said.

"You were fired, Georgie, yeah? You lost your job. What you talking about it don't matter?"

"Helena says she'll look out for me at the council, they always need admin people. Or I can work here."

"Nuh-uh. No way, lady. Think again."

"I'm only following in the family line of things."

Tantie took a swing at me, stopping just short of my nose. "Smell these fingers. Well, smell 'em lady. Onion, hmm? Now it don't matter how much I scrub them up or soak them out, when I die St Peter ain't gonna need no ID from me, he'll just be able to smell me coming. Look at these feet." Her feet were bunioned and callused and raw. "You think I'm going to let my family do that to themselves? I didn't set up here to give you a job to fall into; I worked here so you wouldn't have to. You get yourself down the job shop tomorrow and you find something else. Respectable."

"Yeah, but I could help out weekends maybe, just to earn my keep."

"You can't cook good enough."

"I can chop."

"You're too slow." Tantie scooped up peel and trundled through to the kitchen. She swore when she saw Jimmy's drink still standing by the kettle, and boiled up fresh water. "Anyway, there ain't no room, even if I wanted to have you."

"There's the box room."

"Aurelie's in the box room."

"Aurelie?"

"Leave your mouth hanging open like that and you might catch your dinner. Aurelie. Yes, Aurelie. What's wrong with that? Girl needs a roof over her head."

"Didn't know you took lodgers is all."

"There's more than that you don't know."

"Bet Jimmy is mighty pleased having Aurelie walking round the place." It didn't take nothing from Jimmy's love for Mary to tell you he took on a volcanic glow when

Aurelie passed by. After all, every man in town was the same and most of the women too.

"Jimmy's got other on his mind than that girl."

"Sure," I said.

"You're just sore. Anyway she ain't a lodger. Aurelie a guest."

"You mean she's not paying you?"

"Well she ain't got the money."

"What about Arii Cook's money?"

"She don't like spending it. Says it bad luck money."

"Well it's bad luck for you her purse ain't as loose as she is. There must be royalties or something."

"I don't know."

"Well of course there is, on both sides."

"It ain't polite to talk about things like that."

"Polite!" I had not known this was a word in my aunt's vocabulary. I looked at her, rattling a teaspoon in the mug, pulling her cardigan round her and looking old. "Fine," I said, "Fine, if that's how it is."

"That's how it is. I'm telling you how it is."

"If you want to let your own niece go roofless."

"What I want," Tantie said, "is for my niece to swallow her pride down, go back home and not bring me into a fight with her mother that's so past its best-before it makes me sick. You're twenty-three, George, and you're a little old to be asking for a father."

The Tahitian Pearl

"He's got gut bug," George said, and Mary took it out on a chicken wing.

"Gut bug? Too much rum," said Mary, "fourteen years and he gets worse with every one of them."

"Happy anniversary," George said and kissed her. She broke the lids of two Cobras on the worktop and we went through to the café. "You know what's really got Jimmy," she said.

"No." I couldn't think of a reason for a man to miss his own anniversary party or anything worth making George's Aunt Mary mad at you for.

"After band practice last night, three o'clock they finished, and on his way back, the man hadn't eaten since lunch, not a hundred yards from his door, Jimmy gave way to a kebab."

"Rest his soul," Bob said, flying past with a dish of queso and chips, a bottle of No.10 filling out his jacket. Everybody knew Mary would rather Jimmy strayed with a woman than fast food.

It was a party on the verge: everyone was still three-quarters sober and the music kept to a decent level, but it was coming, you could feel it in the air. Gag and Troy, there for my sake, were sat down already in the far corner, next to Diddy's wife Talitha, and their kids. On the long table that ran along the window sat the friends Mary had picked up along with her criminal record, professional protesters who found a meaning in everything. Blooz Hot stacked up by the snacks, and sat in the centre of the room was Bo, the finest man in the whole town, but so far gone on George he was coming back on himself, and his uncle Son Son, whose hands were shaking as bad as his voice, with his hair all turned white and his whiskers too, his eyebrows, his eyelashes even, sinking back further into his chair every time Mary threw a pan in the sink or a chilli in hot oil. Son Son's nerves wouldn't hold together, and he couldn't keep from staring at Aurelie, standing in the corner, reading the newspaper cuttings

Mary collaged on the wall.

The whole place was lit with a hundred, hundred tea-lights, nestled among pebbles on the tabletops, trailed along shelving and windowsills, tied in knotted string ropes that hung down the walls, brave ones exploring the rafters above us. Mary ran around, frying pan in one hand, fish slice in another. She wouldn't take an evening off for any family occasion, not even for her own wedding; she refused to pay good money to eat something out she could have fixed better herself. "Cooking ain't work," she'd say, "no more than eating, Lord, no, no more than breathing, you hear me?"

The menu at Zambezi was made up from whatever Mary felt like making, which was decided by the shape of the moon and the stage of her cycle and which Ethel James track she had on the stereo. That night she brought out an egg pie, then a hamsteak with jezebel sauce and a fried catfish Bob declared indecently good, pork ribs ("You don't spare the flavour on these, no and not the dry rub," Mary said when Bo asked how she made them so good), New Orleans barbecue shrimp and, just like always, always, always in that place, a macaroni cheese that tasted in such a way it made you realise how wrong the rest of the world had been making it all these years.

I sat with George and Agatha and Bob, and we talked about the last sixteen years of Mary bossing Jimmy and Jimmy teasing her back and we drank beer and then vodka cocktails and we ate like we hadn't been fed in weeks.

Gag and Troy kept in their corner. Every now and then you'd hear Gag laugh at one of her own jokes or a snatch of her Edith Piaf story or a blue joke she was telling, and as time went on, Talitha and some of the protesters stopped their own conversations and listened into Gag's, and bit by little the room fell quiet, voices dropping away to nothing until I heard, clear, Gag say "I don't think I've ever really gotten over Bohemia, if I'm frank, my dear."

All eyes were on her and she shammed oblivion, loving each second, wearing every piece of jewellery ever given to her and three shades of fuschia. Troy topped up her glass. "Café de Flore. That was the place. On the corner of St-Germain and rue St Benoit. The patisseries!" Troy pinched a rib off her plate. "There I was, April, taking Betrand's Mitzi for a shitzi, and I wouldn't have gone near the place if I hadn't seen Simone go in, but I knew her from the magazines. Oh, she had a style about her, that one, hair she could sit on, longer than mine is, and she'd wear it all twisted up on her head, just so. That's the French for you though, very chic, very – anyway, I order *chocolat*: came in a glass like this, flakes like that – and who was in the corner but Jean-Paul, Sartre, I mean, and *well* I had to come back after that, didn't I? And there he was every day, from nine in the morning until lunch, then right through lunch with nothing more than an omelette, and from just after lunch until dinner, just the whole day long of it, the same table, the best table always, in the back, but with a view to the street. You'd see him picking dog-ends off the floor (huge fingers he had, never seen fingers like that on a man of his size) stuffing his pipe with tobacco, he'd just sit there and smoke, and don't ask me how he got to know half the things he knew for I never saw him with a paper, never mind a book, just his smoke, his coffee cup rattling away in its saucer, glasses of red wine on the table, real marble, I'm sure it was, and mirrors just everywhere and – why not – because everyone there, we were all of us young and beautiful, of course." Gag ran her finger round the rim of her wine glass, her old hands shaking, and the room held its breath, but all I could think was what a stranger this woman was to me really, with memories crawling out like woodworm.

"He once bought me champagne, just so I could taste it, he said, because he said….well, never mind what he said, but I was quite, quite drunk by the end of it all, just like an English girl, they all said. Ah, what do they say, *Je suis née sur une banquette du Café de Flore*. Indeed, ooh la la," Gag caught Troy's eye then gave a giggle and people laughed, a couple of them clapping their hands against their knees in appreciation. I sat with my arms folded tight around me, my fingernails digging into my arm. For all her talk of shell shock and syphilis, how many of Gag's war stories were true? As a child I'd loved to hear them, I'd got drunk on second-hand absinthe swallowed from teaspoons, my head aching from black coffee, red wine and cigar smoke strong enough to turn your stomach. But as I listened over the years, over the rustle of nylon petticoats against fishnets I heard something that gave me hiccoughs: silence. For there was never so much as a gunshot to spoil the romance of it all, never the sound of a child screaming or a young widow crying. There was never so much as an air raid in Gag's Paris by moonlight; no Velodrome, no ghettoes, no trains or boots in the night. Gag's exploits in the name of international relations resembled every wartime in Paris movie you ever saw, so that by the time I was nineteen myself, I wasn't sure that she hadn't just fallen asleep watching *Casablanca* and woken up calling herself Ingrid Bergman. I wanted to believe in it all, the dreams and the magic, but then there was Mum's discomfort when the stories started, Gelda's own contradictions, the stories whose loose ends refused to tie up. Most of all, I thought, if things were as great as Gelda made out, then why wasn't she in Paris now? That night as I watched her performing for the crowds I felt certain: this life she spoke about was one she'd invented. And where, growing up, Gag had been for me proof of the possibility of escape, now she was a warning: one day I'd end up the same, spinning stories for strangers in bars, imagining how my life could have been, trying to forget how it really was.

We were clearing back the tables, Bob scooping up the last of the rice with his fingers, Troy picking bones off other people's plates, and Bo was setting up the sound system when down came Jimmy to a holler and a round of backslapping and feet stamping. He looked a little rough, but then Jimmy had an awkward look about him permanently. His shirt collar was forever too loose and his trousers hung low around his hip bones yet rode too high on the ankle. The gap between his two top teeth gave him a goofy look that rubbed up strangely against his serious demeanour, the chip on the bottom one made it pointed as a dog's tooth. When he started with the blues (Jenny Finch stamped him out a book called itself *Teach Yourself Blues in Thirty Days*. That's a joke, everyone said, until he did. But, as Jimmy said, "Either you're born knowing the blues, or else life makes it its business to teach you, or else you'll never learn.") Anyway, when Jimmy took up with the blues he decided that would be his name – Dogtooth Tebiah. Mary laughed harder than a rainstorm. But Jimmy dug in, refusing to answer to anything but. "Jimmy T," she said, "when you going to learn, a name got to be earned, it got to be given, you know, can't be demanded. And what's happening to the good name you got already? It wounds a mother like no other thing I know to see its child throw that gift away."

Jimmy never talked of his mother; he never spoke of anything that had happened in Africa. Not of what it was like in jail or what it had been like out of it. He sang no songs from home and he always spoke in, swore in, dreamed in (he told us), English. When he danced, Mary and Agatha teased, for he moved like a European they said – his hips stiff and knees straight at right angles to one another and his weight held high in his body. But sometimes he'd sit in the same place for hours, days of it, just staring at something you couldn't see and sometimes you'd say the slightest thing and Jimmy would jump like you'd slapped him, but then, no matter how deep the funk he got in, he caught Mary's eye and gave her a smile like sunlight on dappled water.

Jimmy headed over to George and me and poured himself a long glass of water (but even the water at Zambezi came like it wouldn't elsewhere, in a great glass jug with mint leaves, citrus fruits and ice like diamonds) and Mary took herself off to their part of the house as her protesters did the washing up. Then Mary came back in a plum dress with ruffles cut to her breast and the soft part of her back, and with make-up on, and the whole place went quiet and Jimmy said something to himself and stood up and held out his arms and then they danced to *My Baby Just Cares* which had been their first song, and everyone got the wet-eye, as Mary called it, and husbands started nuzzling wives and Bob ran his hands up and down Agatha while Bo looked over in George's direction and she pretended not to care, and altogether everything seemed part of every other thing and the world seemed rounder than it had ever been.

After Troy and Gag had left at ten for last orders at

The Coach and Eight, the two of them drunk as each other and singing all the way down the stairs, I picked at peanuts and watched the couples move across the floor. There was one other person not paired up: Aurelie danced on her own, her limbs waving, like seaweed in a warm ocean.

Talitha and Diddy almost went into her and, losing their stride, stepped out to join me. Talitha frowned, "What's wrong with that girl?"

Diddy, out of breath after a James Brown track, allowed his weight to fall into the chair next to me. "Now she's only a little stoned or so, never did anyone any harm that I could see."

"She look all right to you, Bo?" Talitha said, calling him over from his turntables.

"As right as that girl ever does." He couldn't take his eyes off her.

"What you thinking?" I said, though I might have made a pretty guess.

"I don't know. What's she got – a mother half-crazy, a father half-crazy? What does that make her, you tell me?"

We pulled some chairs round to join with the table behind us where Mary and Agatha sat arguing over whether Mary would have been better charbroiling the catfish (and maybe a little collard greens on the side) than frying it, and whether Agatha would have been better keeping her tongue and her lazy be-hind at home if all she can do is eat and criticise and so on. The men still had their eyes swivelled on Aurelie. Diddy said, "You know her mother and father fought like fire and water. I reckon the two of them still fighting it out, what is she now, not black, not white, half genius, half beauty queen, and the poor girl don't stand a chance, pulled one way and then another, it's a wonder she don't fall apart."

"You know," Bob said, "I read that when she was born, Arii didn't want nothing to do with her, just got up out of the bed and called herself a cab to JFK. She was on a plane to London before they knew; she'd ditched that little girl there like left luggage."

Diddy poured himself a glass of water, sweat dancing on his brow, "Well I read the moon was made of green cheese, but that don't make it true. Who knows what happened? Not you, not me, not Aurelie, none of us, 'cause the woman didn't leave that child as much as a note. Not a word."

"A cool million though, I heard," George said, crossing over from the kitchen, standing a bottle of Cointreau on the table.

Right then the music stopped and Bo sprang up and put a long player on, shaking his head at George, who giggled. Bo was always wanting to play with the tempo or try a little scratching, or mix in some Motown with some two-to-the-floor beat and he could only just stand to be putting on these old tracks one after another.

"What do you say about it, Unc?" he asked Son Son.

We all looked at Son Son. In the days before Paradise, George had told me, Son Son ran some place off Oxford Street and when Arii was in town she'd come down sometimes, sit at a table they kept for her right at the back. Son Son didn't say anything, but peeled the label off the JD.

Agatha gave a laugh to cover the silence and said, "Well, there's rumours to spare about that one," meaning Arii.

Son Son shook his head. "I've listened to everyone these twenty years talk about where it went wrong, was it this film, that deal, this man, that one. There never was one big thing, life ain't like that, it's lots of little things, lots one after another till you can't take it no more, broken hearts and babies you wanted and you didn't want, too much champagne, not enough love and time going by faster than you can catch a hold of it."

"But the drugs, Son Son," said Bob, "it was the drugs that killed the girl."

"I don't think so. No more than you can blame the rope for the hanged man."

"You don't think it was on purpose though, sure now, you don't think it was suicide?"

A shiver ran through me then, for the room where they found her wasn't a half mile from where we sat.

"Now," said Jimmy, "how Son Son going to know a thing like that?"

Son Son said, "I know half as much would have killed her, and she wasn't some kid needed her dealer to find a vein. She knew what she wanted that one. Tsch, it's a bad story. One of the worst."

There was a hole in the conversation then, for we all wanted to hear this bad story, but didn't want to ask. No matter how many times you read it, no matter how many pictures of Arii Cook you saw, you always wanted more.

Someone poured Son Son another brandy. And another someone crushed him some ice. And he said, "She did it because she enjoyed it, then she did it because it was there, and then, well, it wasn't a case of her doing it so much as it doing her. And she got that way before she was twenty-one, not three years after she got off that plane and long before Jack Morea."

There was people blamed Jack Morea, you see, for what happened to Arii. Her fans blamed him for the suicide (for no matter what Bob liked to believe, there wasn't many thought it could be anything but) and his fans said his breakdown was her fault. Jack Morea wouldn't say a word about it, hadn't even told Aurelie, by what Mary said, what went on, and you'd still see headlines in the back of the Sundays, every month or so, claiming new proof of what really happened between the two of them: Arii's voodoo or love letters from Morea to other girls.

"And all this business, this was all when she was –?" Agatha looked over at Aurelie. "This wasn't when she was –?" her hand was on her belly pulling at her dress.

Son Son looked over at Aurelie then dropped his eyes.

"Lord, Lord, Lord," Agatha said and sank back in her chair and squeezed a hold of George's arm, "things never got that bad, did they. How do you get over something like that, it's in the blood, it's in the mother's milk – it's inside of you."

People were passing a joint around the circle, a joint

that went over my head or behind my back because everybody knew that sensible Helena Jones didn't smoke, not even cigarettes.

Bo took a deep, a deep, deep, drag, "It's a terrible thing."

Son Son said, "Aurelie doesn't know a thing about it. I'm sure she don't. That's why her father's kept her on that island all this time. But she feels it, she was born feeling it, I seen them, crack-babies, like nothing human, just a bundle of needing, wanting something will kill 'em to have. And this one, she got the hunger real bad, just doesn't know what she's hungry for, but she'll hit on it soon enough and then – tsch, na," Son Son snorted. "Arii Cook was a good-looking girl and in another world, a softer one, she might have lived her life a different way, but what she did she did, and what she did to that baby of hers, is nothing less than murder. Her father so worried about the girl finding a needle he's kept her locked up these twenty years. He thinks what she don't know can't hurt her, but there's things you don't have to be told, and here she is now, and mixing with Sanderson too, and Paradise never was the place that I'd want it to be, I mean jazz and smoke go together like – well." We waited while Son Son hacked, "It's time, that's all there is between that girl and –"

Agatha let out a moan, "Lord, Son Son, don't talk about it so."

"I seen it, that girl's future laid out in front of her like – like a shroud," the preacher's note creeping back into his voice though it was thirty years since he'd been in a pulpit. "Her momma never loved her poppa and maybe he never loved her – when that's the place you come from course the world seems something to fight against. But she's like a fish been hooked. More she wriggles, more she's stuck and you know why? All this little-miss-two-fingers-up-at-the-world, all this running away and falling in love and all, all, all of this, where does she think it comes from if not Arii? It's all decided long ago. She's a re-run, that girl. A straight re-run. We'll find her one morning like they found her mother."

Mary was angry, "You speak some nonsense, Son Son, sure you do. A crack-baby's a baby same as any other. Ain't nothing that a bit of love can't overcome. Ain't none of us sat here got off to the start we'd have liked, but you rise above it, is what you do and now Aurelie's here, I'll see she's fine, and you know when I say something, well then, it's fixing to get itself done." She bounced the heel of her hand off the table, making the drinks chatter together in their glasses then snatched the joint from Jimmy's lips and passed it on to Bob.

A couple of stragglers who'd been making out half-heartedly in the corner came over to say goodbye; he kissed Mary on the cheek and she took Jimmy in her arms and rocked with him a moment. Everyone was fuddled with booze and growing a second hunger even after all that food and this was the time for Mary to brew coffee or pour tea, and offer sausage sandwiches, but she didn't. She stared at the table and when Jimmy poured her Southern Comfort she didn't raise her hand for enough till he was two-thirds up the glass. Bo took his sweater off and hung it round George's shoulders, who pulled it close without looking at him. The empty room was grown cold; most of the tealights had burned themselves out. The group of us sat in the middle of the room shivering, lit by what light escaped from the kitchen and the moon bright outside.

Son Son said then, "The strangest thing I heard – and if it came from anywhere but where it did I wouldn't have believed it – the story was Arii did leave that baby of hers, left hospital so quick after birthing it they didn't get a chance to tell her it was sick. But it was, and really sick. I don't know, it was the heart perhaps, or the lungs

– something to do with what Arii'd been taking. But Arii snuck off before they'd found a way to break it to her, before she'd held it in her arms even, and by the time Jack Morea got there, it was dead."

Talitha's eyes were big, "Do you think it's true?"

"What?" said Bob, "How can it be true when you looking at the girl?"

"If she's who she says she is," George said dead, standing up then, her chair catching at the floor.

We all watched Aurelie then. All still, except Mary who was twisting and twisting a napkin round in her hands and Jimmy watching her. He put his hand out on hers, she raised her eyes to him, and something passed between them.

I left them to their smoke and jazz, and on my way home, just as it was closing, stopped at Hollywood Video. There wasn't a single Arii Cook film in the battered classics section, not a one of those arthouse flicks she'd done when she first came to Europe, not even one of her bit-part blaxploitation roles she'd sunk to by the seventies, but I found, stuck between *Gone with the Wind* and *The Maltese Falcon,* an old Arii Cook biopic they showed on late night TV sometimes, *The Tahitian Pearl.*

I sat home alone with the lights off, a bottle of beer in my hand, the next day's hangover already making itself at home, and I watched the thing through. I watched her dancing hula-hula for the French tourists, not more than six or seven; then, a little older, even prettier, selling shell necklaces to fat Americans.

The Paris years were a hurried montage – there was Arii on the Dior catwalk, on the cover of Vogue, there were hand-held shots of the Eiffel Tower, her sitting on the balustrade at the Sacre Coeur, walking arm in arm with Alain Delain on the banks of the Seine, sitting in a boulevard café smoking cigarettes. The whole thing was set to *Je t'aime* and if Gag had seen what they'd made of her city (sly little shots of Pigalle, Arab youths loitering) she'd have cursed in every language she knew.

Most of the film was set in America. There was scene after scene of Arii rowing with Hollywood directors when she turned up high or wouldn't take her clothes off, and the lead actress just loved all the high drama of it, you could see. And somewhere in the middle of this, she met Jack Morea. And I wanted to know, is this how it happened, is this when she met him, when she was already past helping? Because it seemed to matter, how far down she was, and whether he tried to save her and failed, or whether he pushed her further over. And what was it held them together and pushed them apart, the philosopher and the beauty queen? And could it have ended any other way? But none of this was really gone into because one half of the film of Arii Cook's life was all about her death.

The day she died there'd been a custody hearing over Aurelie, only Arii was too stoned, in the film at least, to show up and after spending the afternoon with someone's husband she'd taken a phone call from an old friend, an Earl Skinner, who was short of an act for his club that night, and Arii owed a favour and never could say no, and would always do anything to save her from being alone. She was like a seashell, she said, and when all other sounds died away she resounded to the rhythm of the tides on the shore of a place that she couldn't get back to anymore and anything was better than that.

The film set of Paradise was nothing near: it was a rooftop bar, five times the size of the real thing. The actress playing Arii couldn't sing. After the gig was through, Arii Cook, the actress with latex wrinkles that the real Arii never had, cleared out a hotel mini bar, scooping the bottles up in her skirt and spreading them on the bed. There's a knock on the door, room service, the whisky

she ordered, a bottle of it, and a cut glass tumbler, no ice.
The waiter knows her. Everybody knows her, but there
is something particular about the glaze of his eyes and
he's pretty, with long thick eyelashes and milky skin.

"Come sit with me," she says, patting the space on the
bed next to her. The actress does a bad job of pretending
to be drunk.

The waiter smiles, but doesn't move, holding the
whisky still on the tray.

"Come, here, on the bed," she said, "do not be
frightened. I am not so old am I?"

"No, miss."

"I was beautiful once. You don't remember?"

He looks straight ahead of him.

"Beautiful like an island sunset, like the darkest part
of night."

He still doesn't move.

"Won't you come and sit with me?" She looks at
him. He is shaking, shaking from head to toe. What is
making him shake – desire? Fear? He can't be more
than seventeen. It is laughter.

"Fuck you," she says, she hurls an ashtray at him,
"Fuck you!"

He puts the whisky on the side and comes over to

her. Close to, he is not so pretty, nor so young; there is something hard in his eyes and his face is mean. She curls her knees into her chest and hugs a pillow to herself.

"You want pills?"

She stares out at him. And you can see it, she won't beg from this kid, this prick in a bowtie.

"Do you want it?"

He twists his lip and makes to go but she grabs hold of his shirt sleeve, pulling herself up. There's a moment, then she nods.

Arii left no suicide note, the papers said. All the autopsy could do was list what she'd taken, not why. And Jack Morea, if he knew anything at all, never told, and so the biopic version, written by one old lover, produced by another, went down in history as the truth: Arii passes out, wakes again, pukes and checks the TV for news. She takes a couple of pills, washing them down with the whisky, then, at three-thirty a.m., depressed drunk, desperate drunk, but with the optimism of the little white pill still ringing in her ears, still tickling her funny bone, still jangling her nerves, she makes a phone-call. Her hands shake as she dials the number. He answers. "Well?" she says.

"You lost," he tells her.

She downs whisky. She doesn't use a glass and her face is past emotion. "Can I see her?"

He says nothing.

"Can I speak to her, then?"

He says nothing.

"They said I could see her? Jack? They said I could?"

There's a pause. Then Jack Morea hangs up on his wife for the last time.

Eve and Adam had a garden
Everything was great till one day a boy says
Pardon, miss, my name is snake

Sanderson Miller and the love worm

Sanderson Miller bought Paradise after Son Son had a breakdown. People said it was a funk overdose, what with hearing Aurelie sing every night; after all, everybody knows too much funk can be deadly. It's just possible that girl sent him edge over. Bo tried to scratch some money together to get the place in his own name, but Son Son's bookkeeping was improvised free-style like his jazz, and no one would lend Bo the money on the strength of it. Though it broke his heart to see it, he couldn't stop Paradise becoming another of Sanderson's deals.

But the reason that Sanderson bought Paradise was nothing to do with business, not even anything to do with the ready supply of half-dressed, three-quarters-undressed girls who strolled in and rolled out every night. Sanderson bought Paradise to be close to Aurelie. Trust Sanderson Miller to fall in love with a ghost. After twenty years of screwing around, he finally decided he was a decent man after all. Love found a place in his heart not completely grown over, a soft spot under the calluses, and it ate him up from the inside. When I called in to see him, his skin was hollowed out and his lips were parched. Sanderson got a love-worm and from that time on it wouldn't matter how much he got, it wouldn't ever be enough.

The trouble was, Sanderson Miller wasn't meant to fall in love. When God made Sanderson, it wasn't for love's sake; it was as part of the old contract, part of the deal God made with the devil to guarantee Satan a number of souls incapable of redemption. You see, Sanderson was born to damn himself, destined to land sticky-side down. He didn't have a choice in the matter, and if he had, he'd always have chosen hell anyway. Now all of a sudden Sanderson started thinking of salvation, angel harps and all that, and when he kissed his girl he felt a prayer on his lips.

It happened all at once, in the mid-point of a crescendo on E flat. Not Shakespeare or Gershwin or any other genius of loving could tell you how. My personal feeling is it was something to do with subatomic particle theory. You see, when Aurelie hit that E flat, she sent waves through the air could interfere with a body, those waves hit Sanderson full on, a nuclear tsunami, and Sanderson started to tremble until the shaking knocked his heart out of time with itself. You couldn't have foreseen it, and I do believe there ain't no replicating a falling in love like that. It was a one-off. Even Sanderson had thought he was immune. When Sanderson fell in love, he fell bad – he landed black and blue, twisted as he fell and he didn't think he could ever get himself up again. He just lay there, staring at the sky, enjoying life from a horizontal locale. From down there his highs seemed as insubstantial as cirrus cumulus, his lows as comfy as a feather bed.

"So. Here you are," I said, when I called in at Paradise mid-afternoon in the middle of a sound-check (Aurelie bust mics regular as; got through pianists like other girls got through lip-gloss). "Getting old and looking for something to ease you on your way."

He was a broken man. He let out a sigh been bottling itself up these past thirty years, and it came out smelling bad. "Now, Georgetown, I'm too old to go chasing every stick that comes my way." More like Sanderson was a wise old goat who knew you couldn't keep chasing desire when you'd gotten so old you couldn't keep up with it. Sanderson could run himself breathless with a new girl every night or he could settle down.

"Too old to bother with me no more, it seems," I said. "You ain't stopped by since you got back."

He reached in his pocket, pulled something out and held it out to me. "Look what I got for you."

"I'm too old for chocolate."

"It's not chocolate. See. Take it. Here." It was a friendship band I'd made must be fifteen years back and it meant something he'd kept it all these years. "You've grown a hard heart there, girl. Don't you never make no mistakes?" He stroked his whiskers, running his fingertips against the grain of the growth. There were as many white hairs as black. "You still make them daisy chains?"

"I'm not your little girl no more, Sanderson."

"Well give a man some credit to change himself over too. Look at that there," and he smiled over at Aurelie who was setting up on stage and he said, to me, or to himself, I don't know, "The purest thing I ever laid my hand on, why I want to spoil all that?" Sanderson was the kind of rootless man would cling onto anything upright that came his way.

"She don't love you," I said.

Sanderson blew smoke rings into the air.

"I know," I said. "I seen the way she look at you. Remind me of somebody else I know." Time was, Sanderson would be happy enough with the company, if you know what I mean. Time was, Sanderson cared more about making love than holding on to it. All that changed the day he saw Aurelie. She wrapped him round himself till he didn't know which way he was pointing. "You know what this is, Sanderson," I said. "Karma." Up to this point, life for Sanderson had been soft as skin, simple as making love, straightforward like a road out of town in a fast car. After knowing Aurelie, Sanderson could see what women had been telling him all his life, that life was complicated. Aurelie was a whowherewhywhenwhat of a girl and it made his head spin. As he'd said to Bo, "All I been doing, these years long, Lord, I thought I was living. I was just breathing in."

"All them broken hearts, all them lies you told, Sanderson. What goes around comes around."

Sanderson shifted himself round to get a good look at

me. "What's this about? You want to know what regret looks like? Well open your eyes girl; you're looking straight at him. I tell you, this is different; with Aurelie I seen the light."

"You ain't seen the light," I said, "You just old and scared of dying."

"What you want, Georgie? Spit it."

"I'm looking for work."

"I ain't hiring."

"Bo says he could do with help."

"And I know why he says it, but he ain't thinking with my wallet."

"What about in the kitchens?"

"I gave you an answer."

I looked at Sanderson, rough as a long night, smooth as an early one, and it made me mad to think how easy he threw off Mom and me now that he had Aurelie. I'd spent years just trying to catch his eye, in love with him before I knew what love was and never quite giving up on the idea, but you don't need to be a big man to have an eight-year-old girl look up to you. I could see that now.

"As a matter of fact," I said, "you can tell me a thing. We'll call it old times' sake."

Sanderson put his cigarette out. His face barely

flickered. He made a signal to Bo, who'd been drying glasses at the bar, and pushed a seat out away from the table with his foot.

"I wanna know who my father is."

"Shouldn't you be directing that question in somebody else's direction? If you catch my drift."

I stayed where I stood. "Mom won't talk about it."

"And why you suppose that is, Georgetown Easy? Where's all this come from on sudden?"

"A plane ticket. And I'm running out of time."

"We all running out of time since the day we born, ain't no need to do anything hasty."

"You know who he is, don't you, Sanderson?"

"You're like the monkey who wanted to live in the desert, don't know what's good for itself. What you be doing with a father these days anyhow? You too old for a father is what. I practically is your father. Who gave you pick-a-back up two streets? Who bought you shoes?"

"A daddy is more than shoes and pick-a-back," I said, "and what am I going to do when my kids come along asking after their grandfather, do like Mom and tell 'em mind their business?"

Sanderson took his eyes off Aurelie then, letting them land on me. "You got a baby on the way?"

"What if, Sanderson. I'm saying what if."

"A man got enough to do dealing with the life he's living without what-ifs."

"Don't tell me you're scared of Mom and Tantie. You got a mind of your own."

"I made a promise, Georgie, or don't that mean nothing to you?"

"And you never broke a promise?"

"Some things – I don't know. They go back. Seems like, the years over, I've let too much slip past me and secrets are about the only thing I managed to keep a hold of. There's been bad times, and I'm sure you're gonna tell me whose fault they are, but if I've learnt anything, it's when an old secret gets broke, there's no telling the consequence. I don't know. But there ain't no fixing a broken confidence."

It made me mad as hell to see Sanderson sitting there mighty as. I shook my head and headed for the door.

"Hey," he called after me, "Maybe I don't know, you thought about that? Maybe your momma even don't."

I kept my voice low and steady, "She knows. Why make all this business over it else?"

Sanderson shrugged, "It seem to me you'd do a whole lot better stop chasing the parent that don't want you and spend a bit more loving on the one that do."

That did for me. I walked back up to Sanderson, stood between him and the stage to guarantee his attention. "I know something," I said. I had a piece of the truth and I wasn't giving up on it.

"What you know, Georgetown?"

"I went to Texas."

He opened his eyes till they were as round as a baby's, but Sanderson never could look innocent. "And?"

"Nobody knew me, Sanderson. Nobody knew no Georgetown Easy."

"Hell, you got to understand, folks in Georgetown don't always answer a question straight as you ask it. Folks in Georgetown —"

"What you know about Georgetown?" I said.

"Nothing," but Sanderson's denial snagged in his throat as if the lie had barbs that caught at him.

"You never even been there."

"I been there," Sanderson said, like everyone had been there. Like being there wasn't proof of anything.

"When?"

Sanderson started jumping like a needle in a groove. I could see the sweat squeezing out of him. Now, there was only one reason I could think of why Mom would tell me she didn't know Sanderson back in Texas, and why Sanderson would say he didn't know nothing 'bout Georgetown. The two lies fitted together like the two halves of a broken heart. Sanderson Miller was my father. Before I could fit the words together, I felt something rise up from my gut to my heart and stick in my throat. I stumbled to the door. And old Sanderson? He flicked his lighter and called after me, "Your Aunt Mary ask? We never had this conversation."

Love is not poetry and it does not rhyme.

It does not fall in stanzas, nor fit

neatly in covered pocket books.

It is soundless, wordless, awesome and aweful.

All the old love songs lie.

Sanderson silenced poets with a love unutterable,

even rendered me mute.

We converse in something more fluent:

our fingers lace and my anger unravels,

my fears untwisting as our arms entwine.

He enfolds me and releases me, holds me tight and

lets me go.

Sanderson takes off my clothes and gives me innocence,

cradles me in the roots of a fig tree and I

let myself be tamed by this witch-whisperer

who insists

it's he who's grateful: I remind him

of when love was a feeling and not an act,

and the Lord's name meant more than a cuss.

And if love could compensate (if his 24 carat heart could pay

                    off the devil on my back)

or the gold leaf of his caress could gild my rage,

I'd drink the ambrosiac amnesia he offered,

love him back and forget revenge.

For there are eyes like whirlpools

that draw other eyes to them, souls like whirlwinds

that draw other souls in.

I was born with a beat but I got me a tune

Never sang till the day I saw you, Sanderson

And since I saw you I couldn't stop.

But I know it will end.

Our parting will be like our coming together

Swift and breathless

Blink and you'll miss it.

He's too late, and that's the truth of it:

Kamikaze pilots fly alone.

When I say 'I' or 'me', I refer of course to the self that has been created for 'me.' There's no escaping those inverted commas: 'I' is product, the result of complex and unconscious social mechanisms.

Jack Morea, *The Theory of Soul*

Maybe this maybe that

A strand of limp tinsel hung about the cabinets as I put the Christmas display together. I'd suggested something on Christmas pudding, but Merg maintained that desserts were of less historic significance than savouries and we'd compromised on *Stuffings Through the Ages*. Merg had been in a bad mood all morning. After a week of festive spirit, humming Dean Martin as he shuffled round the archive, even throwing a quid in the bucket when the Rotary Club Santa stopped by and generally giving all signs of having been taste-testing the sherry at Tesco again, Merg had spent Christmas Eve morning moping till I just couldn't stand it any more and put it to him straight to tell me what was wrong.

"There's been a complaint," he said, face long as a donkey.

"What kind of complaint?"

Merg put down a mug of greying tea, the cheesy smell of day-past-best-before milk curling towards me, "Mary."

The last month we'd put on a coffee house exhibit. It was about the best display we'd had, with all the chocolate pots and whisks, the sugar bowls and dredgers brought together with a sense of purpose. Merg had even sweet-talked the V & A into lending us some biscuit moulds, but before he'd pasted the last of the notices onto coloured card, Mary had got up a petition against it. Merg had fidgeted with his cardigan buttons as Mary stood there, her anger raising cobwebs from the cabinet tops. She had all the rhetoric of a TV evangelist. "You know what coffee smells of? Sweat. You know what sugar tastes of? Blood. You know what chocolate remind me of? The brown skins got whipped so you could drink yourself fat."

According to Mary, the coffee house, with its cocoa beans, coffee and sugar and spice wasn't just the product of slavery, it was the cause of it. The silver and china bits we'd assembled were symbols of oppression, and Merg and I were collaborators. Mary never had approved of our take on the past, the two of us having negotiated a path through history devoid of bloodshed, war and politics, populated by questions of aesthetics and etiquette. (My MA was on the impact of the French Revolution on desserts. Merg had written a thesis on consequences for the development of cooking utensils of the British experience in India.)

Merg showed me the letter Mary had written. "I mean, we have to be pragmatic," he said.

"Mary doesn't," I said.

Merg was a good man, but there were things about the world these days he couldn't keep up with. I knew he was homesick for the days when there wasn't a council policy on diversity, when you didn't have to translate thirty-seven parts of a full-service tea-set into Gujarati, when there was only one side to every story. After all, he was almost as old as Gag, if only a third as senile. He was a refugee from another era and refused to be dragged into a political arena, but according to Mary you couldn't blow your nose without making some sort of statement. "There's stories get told and there's stories that don't and it's people like you what's responsible," she'd said.

"So what are we going to do?" I asked Merg.

"I'll draft an apology." He frowned at the title I'd pasted above the cabinets, and I saw I'd missed an 'f' in 'Stuffing'. "Pass it by cultural liaison."

I patted his hand. "It'll be something else next week," I said, "knowing Mary."

Merg muttered, unconvinced. "She's smelled blood," he said. "All they need is a letter in *The Gazette*, all they need is one more excuse and that's it for us. Then we'll see if she's happy when this place is a Starbucks or Café Cadabra."

Mary's world was populated by two kinds of people: them and us. I was always 'them,' and the way she went on about things sometimes you'd think I'd personally stood over her with a whip. Even Agatha saw the crazy in that. "Guilt ain't inherited, right to feel aggrieved ain't inherited," I'd heard her say. But then Mary twitched her behind and said, "You think so?" in a way that there was no arguing against.

Jenny came at twelve with a gluten-free Yule Log. Merg made a big show of delight and the two of them disappeared into the boiler cupboard that Merg had spent half the morning decking out with mistletoe.

George called for lunch with leftovers. We sat under

the sieve display, cross-legged on the floor and bit into sweet potato pasties, transporting ourselves into carbohydrate overdrive and trying to ignore the banging from the cupboard. I told her, "I'm going to see him."

"Who?"

"Jack Morea, of course. Aurelie gave me his address."

"Just like that?"

I shrugged.

"What you going to do, turn up on the doorstep? Why don't you write the guy?"

"I wrote to him already."

"And?"

"Maybe he didn't get the letter."

"Maybe this, maybe that. You got enough maybes to set up shop with the things." She took another bite of jam cake.

"I just wish there was someone to see the world like I do," I said.

"So do I. And I wish it was me for you and you for me, but I'd do as well to wish my brown eyes blue, your blue eyes brown. We see things different."

"What's to see different? Either you see things the way they are or you —" I let this piece of rhetoric hang limply. "I bought you a ticket, George. A freaking ticket and you know what I think about that, but you wanted to go and I got you a ticket."

"A father's blood, Helena, a father's a point of fact."

"Whatever."

"Jack Morea ain't got no magic wand turn you into Aurelie."

"I don't want to be Aurelie."

"You want to be anyone but who you is, want to believe anything but what's in front of you."

"Since when are you Open University professor of mindreading? Since never."

We were shouting now louder than Jenny was moaning, saying it the way it was, the way we usually didn't. George fought with her mum and the two of us laughed about it later; the same with me and Troy. That was how things worked until we'd both woken up one morning not quite knowing who we were or how we got there and needing somebody to blame.

"Look at it, H, look at it." George grabbed the book from me, tipped it by one corner, shaking its pages loose, "You don't even know what it means." George flicked her wrist out over the equation, "Garbage."

"But that's why I am going to see him. Everybody

knows there's a sequel –"

"It's a confidence trick, the emperor's new clothes, that's all it is. He's sat on that island, I bet, and he's laughing. And what next, Helena? You'll be going through that shelf one book after another until you don't know what you think. The answer ain't in there." George sent the book scudding across the floor, sending up dust, "and it ain't out there." When George's hand moved up it moved with purpose, pointing out of the door, into the world. "It's in here," she tapped her temple, looked so much like Agatha I could have laughed.

"Is there any salsa?" I said.

George spooned sauce from her lunchbox to mine, "What you going to ask him anyway; why your mom died? Why you and Troy can't get on?" She ate, angrily, shovelling it in, hardly chewing, spilling half of it down her front.

George and me might have been best friends, but we were nothing much alike. George's attitude to life was summed up in a simple up-down of the shoulders that got her by just fine but was never enough for me. When you come from a family of lumps and bumps and things that die in the night, you do tend to think more than most about what exactly it is – life I mean – what you get and what you're going to do with it. "You know what my cancer risk is?" I said.

George put her fork down, answered me nervous, mouth still half-full, "Helena —"

"Well, there you go. You think there's all the time in the world and there isn't. Before you know it there I'll be, up on that shelf next to the rest of them. Why shouldn't I read a book? What's the harm? I get more sense from it than any of you lot and that's the truth."

George mumbled her answer, her fork teasing rice grains in her lunchbox, "No harm in reading, but you act like —"

I clicked down the lid on the Tupperware box and shoved it back at her, crossed one ankle over the other out in front of me and folded my arms.

"Who you so angry at?"

"No one."

"What then?"

I picked at a blob of sauce drying on my trousers.

"Who you so mad at?"

I let out a breath I'd been holding too long. I lifted my arm, waving it limply at the ceiling, gesturing at something bigger than the room; it fell back heavy to earth.

"You need a holiday, that's all. I mean you could have come to Texas with me, we could have, I don't know, we could have – or even still we could go, you got money, we could...why not?" George swung round on the floor, crossed her legs in front of her and grabbed hold of my hands with both hers. She squeezed my fingers between hers. I didn't squeeze back. George put her head to the side. "I thought you liked it here."

"I did."

Until Aurelie. She walked in here, and it was as if I'd been watching the world until then through the cracks between my fingers, not daring to see it full on, catching glimpses of it now and then, pieces of bits of shapes, shadows that never really made sense. Aurelie peeled back my hands and showed me a world that was bigger and bolder, more colourful and closer than I'd have known it for and ever since I couldn't stand anything of my old world, this old town, that itched against me with its clammy hand-me-down feel, that clung, that oozed, when you pressed it, with decay. This town thought it knew everything, had seen it all, but I knew now there was something beyond my life here, there was more to it.

"You know what I think?" George said.

But before she could finish, Jenny breezed out of the cupboard, trailing Merg behind her. "Who's for tea?" she said, all brightness and dimples. "Helena, go in my bag, and you'll find a chocolate swiss roll I won't be needing. Poor lamb, now tell me, how will you be at Christmas?"

"Fine," I said. Christmas dinner at Gelda's was a horrendous prospect; she'd been defrosting a gelatinous bird in the crusty avocado bath for the last forty-eight hours.

"And Troy?"

"You know Troy."

There was a lumpen silence clumped between us. I saw Jenny and George exchange a look, which never happened. I checked my teeth for corn. "What?"

"Merg saw your Troy yesterday," Jenny whispered.

"Now Jennifer –"

"She'll find out soon enough," Jenny said firmly. "Better from a friend than a stranger."

"What?"

"I saw Troy yesterday," Merg said, glumly.

"And?" I said.

"Fell down drunk in the street."

"One o'clock in the afternoon," said Jenny.

"Is that all?" I said. "He does that regularly."

"Exactly, Helena." George folded her arms.

Jenny laced her fingers together.

"It's not like he's an alcoholic. He's a student." I said again, more slowly, since they hadn't understood, "He's not an alcoholic." That didn't seem to make it better. I looked at Merg. I looked at Jenny. I looked at George. I looked at the floor. "Fine," I said. "I'll talk to him."

Troy was watching *Star Wars Special Edition* on a loop. His digs in the Clays skulked among a mass of broken paving, big dogs on tight leashes and wet washing strung up in small yards, hid back from the street behind a heap of rusting caravans. Your feet curled up inside your shoes when you walked down the Clays. I tucked my hand up inside my sweater sleeve before ringing the doorbell.

"We need to talk about something," I said. Troy's lips were moving with the dialogue. "Are you listening?"

"I'm trying not to."

"It's important."

"More important than the destruction of civilisation as we know it?"

"Troy!"

"OK, OK." He hit pause. "Shoot."

"Merg thinks you're drinking too much."

Troy stared at me, "Is that why you came round?"

I stared back.

"Only I thought you said it was important."

"Give yourself the night off, why don't you." There was a bad smell in that room, a smell of biological origin that lingered, stronger some days than others, which I'd never been able to identify, though I suspected it was linked to Boz, Troy's six-foot, pink-haired med-student housemate (it was hard to think of anyone less suitable to be in charge of a prescription pad than Boz). I took shallow breaths. "Are you?"

"Am I what?"

"Drinking too much. God, Troy, have you been smoking?"

"Do you think you could keep this lecture to one thing at a time?" Troy paused. "Yes, I am drinking too much," he said, and he looked at me, one eyebrow raised, the other resting. The look said *what're you going to do about it?*

"Don't you think you should stop?" I said.

Troy switched eyebrows. "Is that it?"

Well, what was I supposed to say? Do the whole Mum pull-your-socks-up-sonny-jim, the whole hands on hip, foot tapping, your father and I speech? Of course not. Troy's idea of himself and his place in the scheme of things was monumental – it eclipsed all smaller belief systems (major world religions, political ideologies). It would take more, much more, than a lecture from me to shake Troy's complacency, and as I stood there, still catching my breath from the smart walk over, my heart pumping, and watched Troy pick dirt from under his toenail, for the first time I didn't feel exasperation at him, or impatience. What I felt was pure and uncompromised envy.

I'd long had the notion that Troy and I were each an imperfect half of a whole person, our strengths and lacks compensating on a cosmic scale for each other. If Troy and I were balanced on an emotional see-saw, my self-doubt balanced out by his self-confidence, then he had the best end of the deal. Even when Mum and Dad died he'd gone on regardless – an emotional hovercraft riding out the roughs and taking death like he took life, taking it easy.

As he sucked Ambrosia custard off a Micro-Chip, I could feel the simple evolutionary response that governed our relationship kick in: fight or flight – at it full belt till the other begged for mercy or storm out in a reckless search for the moral high ground. "Look at yourself, you're a mess," I said, but it was half-hearted. Why couldn't he be civil? Why couldn't he be more like me?

Troy threw himself out of the sofa and at the TV. He switched it off, spun round to face me, his arms folded and a new kind of anger coming from him. That was the thing with Troy. All my efforts to puncture his cumbersome self-regard, cutting remarks and mortal put-me-downs glanced off. Then I make a perfectly sensible point and he got upset. I gave up. "I'm going to see Gelda."

"Good luck."

"What do you mean?"

"She's gone."

"Gone where?"

Troy shrugged. "Tahiti."

"Tahiti the place or –" I realised there was no other Tahiti. "What the hell is she doing in Tahiti?" Package deals, reader offers, holidays planned and agreed on in advance – these were tolerated; last-minute flights to under-developed island nations were not, especially now. Gelda and I had had a little chat at her eightieth birthday party the week before – surf and turf for sixteen geriatrics and six bright pitchers of green cocktail at Oz

Bar – and Gag had been most reasonable. I explained that, what with her age and blood pressure, higher than Troy on a Saturday night, she was uninsurable. We'd agreed: no more foreign holidays. "Troy, you know she shouldn't travel without insurance."

"What are you – a public information broadcast?"

"What's she doing in Tahiti?"

"She's gone to find Jack Morea."

"What?"

"She thought you'd be pleased."

"But Jack is in the Hebrides. Do you mean she's gone to the Hebrides?" Troy was clueless at geography and Gag had a thing for whisky and men in kilts; it could all still make sense, and Harris wasn't even abroad, which meant that if her heart should give way, or her liver, more likely, she might have more to rely on than witch doctors.

"No, I mean she went to Tahiti. Shut the door on your way out, H."

I punched up Gag on my mobile. "Gag? Where are you?"

"I'm in the piano lounge, dear."

"I mean, where *are* you?"

"Tahiti. Didn't Troy tell you?"

"But why?"

"On holiday, of course."

"From what? You only just got back from Mexico."

"Darling! That was weeks ago."

"Come home," I said. There was a hiss on the line, and my own voice coming back to me was broken up in a way had nothing to do with satellite links. "Gag. This is silly. What about Christmas? We need you, Gelda. Come home."

And then – and whether it was a dud battery, a rogue cloud, or Gag hanging up on me to give her full attention to the waiters – the line went dead.

I've got a right to sing the blues

Billie Holiday

It comes in many flavours

New Year's Eve, Mom told me she was moving in at Bob's place and that she and Tantie were putting the house up for sale. Mom said she was still a young woman with her own life to lead. "You think I'm too old for a fresh start? Think again. You like Bob, don't you?"

"I like him."

"Well then," Mom concluded, like I didn't like the postman, milkman and corner shop man too without wanting my mom to move in with him.

"There is too much talking 'bout the past," Mom said, "Time somebody started talking 'bout the future."

The future was coming up like mushrooms overnight. I was renting a room from Helena, who'd found me a job at the council. As for Sanderson, I left him to one side, like mustard. What was there to say? What worth celebrating or recriminating over? After the words in all directions, between Mom and me there was now only silence.

Mom had left the kitchen until last, and it wasn't until the night before she was due to move out that we sat down together, surrounded by a regiment of pulses, which we divided into battalions of black-eyes, lima, kidney, butter, cannellini and haricot. We crated up the plump green cardamom pods, nestling them next to the bitter cumin seeds, wrapping each jar in newspaper to keep the hot from the bitter, the floral from the citrus, and keeping the oils separate from all. Last of all, Mom packed up a box of fresh lemons and oranges, loading the top with bananas and mangoes, papaya, yam and beetroot in a bright embrace. When our precious cargo was boxed safely, we started on the utensils, Mom packing these most careful of all, handling them like a surgeon does his instruments. Mom always said she didn't believe in nostalgia, that she grew out of romance the day she turned thirteen, but Mom had a story for every spoon ("This the one Jimmy bought me over from Africa") and every gadget ("This grater grate even potato ever so fine").

Something that had been going, like Helena would say, twenty to the dozen, had wound itself down at last, and I don't know if the stopping wasn't after all more dizzy-making than the going. Of course, a woman doesn't stop being your mom just 'cause you don't live with her, but Mom's complicated system of punishments and rewards could not be administered at a distance; she couldn't cook me mash potato with chilli butter when I did something to please her, or lock me in my room when I didn't. We could not spend a Friday night together as if by accident, as if it was just a coincidence we were in the same-place-same-time space, both complaining about the television. We would have to make confessions to the fact that we wanted to spend time together. We would have to say things like *I miss you*, things like *It's good to see you*, and I didn't know if we were up to that yet. I was about to broach this (and it surely fell under the heading of things we don't talk about) when Mom said, as she straightened the tin cans so their labels faced all the same way, "I meant to tell you. Mary is having a baby."

"What?" I said, 'cause Mom said it simple as saying Mary was having roast pork for dinner.

"She's having a baby."

"Well, how did that happen?"

"How you think?"

Mary and Jimmy had been together fifteen years and I hadn't ever heard either of them mention a baby. "Did they try for it?"

"I don't know."

"Didn't you ask?"

"What do I care?"

"You the baby's aunt ain't you?"

"Aunt," Mom said. "Right." Now though Mom's reaction might not make sense to a strictly logical individual, to anyone who was familiar with the last twenty years of Easy relations, the reason for my mother's agitation was obvious: Mom and Tantie probably saw this event as competition. Mom would see this conception as an elaborate attempt by Tantie to:

1. Upstage her own impending domestic bliss with Bob

2. Cast doubt on Mom's own

    i)   womanhood

    ii)   desirability, and

    iii) fertility

I guessed that I wouldn't stay an only child for much longer. Mom and Bob would undoubtedly practise for one of their own, which would of course weigh more than Tantie's, have more hair, and, if male, much bigger balls.

Mom taped up the last box and sat back against the cupboard doors, her legs lain out in front of her, her head back, eyes closed, all her energy gone from her. "Maybe she keep a hold of this one," she said. "Who knows."

"Plenty people give their baby away, Mom," I said.

"Plenty people give them away." Mom repeated the words but twisted the tone.

"Everyone deserves a second chance, now, don't they?"

Mom muttered something and started picking at the embroidery on her apron. She looked so young sat there right then, and she was, not even forty. Outside, the light was falling. Everyone's mother is beautiful; the beauty of mine lay in her cheekbones, stronger than any person's I knew, her lips, her eyes, the fold of the skin of her neck. My mother was magnificent and all at once as strange to me as a penny found in the street: precious and not believably my own.

"You've got me," I said, reaching a sweaty hand out to rest on hers. "Don't forget."

Mom let out a sigh that didn't do a whole lot for my self-esteem. "Yes. I got you."

"What then?"

"Nothing." Mom looked round the room, lost in her empty kitchen. "It just don't seem fair is all. Mary and her happy family, a mom and a dad and a baby. A fresh start."

"Well, you've got yourself a fresh start, haven't you? With Bob, and as for you and me, well –"

"You and me never stood a chance, Georgetown. There was always too many secrets."

"Maybe secrets ain't such a bad thing," I said. This was my first attempt at an apology, for if I had known that Sanderson was the thing I'd been searching for, I might not have spent so long looking.

"Course they is," she said. "Look at you and me. All lies and promises, that's what we about. Lies and promises and nothing real to get a hold of."

"Maybe it doesn't matter," I said, "I mean, maybe there are more important things than the truth." Even as I said it, it sounded unlikely.

Mom laughed, an evil sound with no joy in it, like the devil breaking wind.

"And maybe you and Bob – you know, in a few months, maybe." I could not look my mother in the eye. "You know."

"You think I wanted things to be like this? Since you old enough to talk, you and me been wrestling like strays with a bone. I'm sick of it. If the truth don't matter then what's the point in anything?" Mom flattened her hair against her head, pushed her chin into her chest, "You keep a secret long enough and you begin to hope it'll start keeping itself. You forget what the truth ever was."

I said this story began with a bowlful of doughnuts and it seemed to me to be true at the time. The story I set out to tell, the truth I set out to uncover began with a bowlful of sugar doughnuts, and ended as my father and I embraced atop the Empire State, surrounded by a loving crowd of chastised family members. But somewhere along the way, around the time Sanderson blew back into town perhaps, or maybe the day I decided to board that plane that I don't believe ever brought me back down to earth, someone seemed to have decided that not only was the happy ending nowhere in sight, but I was on some other mission altogether. I lost track of what the story was, of what I was looking for (a name? An address? A photo?) Now Mom was talking about babies and secrets and sounding like she had more than my father on her mind.

"I talked to Sanderson," I said.

There was a silence so long I felt like my lungs would burst.

"What did he tell you?"

The blood was in my cheeks. "That my real name is Georgetown Miller."

Mom banged her fist down on the floor. "Sanderson Miller is not your father." She looked right at me to make sure I understood.

I was just considering how best to smooth the furrows of my mother's wrath when she said, "Sanderson is Mary's babyfather."

I felt all the blood drop to my feet, not in a rush, but as slow as treacle falling off a spoon. "I have to pack my things," I said.

"Sit down. Well sit down!" Mom said. "You want the truth? Well peel back your ears some 'cause it comes in many flavours. Twenty years I've kept that woman's secret, twenty years and then some and even now she's got Sanderson spreading lies to cover her own tracks. She'll not rest till you as far away from me as her baby is from her. I'll tell you how it was." Mom looked into the middle-distance, like she was entranced by the story she was about to tell. She caught a breath deep enough to last her the whole sorry tale through, and began:

"Mary comes in to our room late one night, must have been three in the morning or so, and starts throwing things all in a suitcase. Clothes, make-up, her Bible – Lord, as if that was any use, the journey she was on – everything she could get to hand she just flung it all in. Mary came home late often enough. Now I was used to Mary coming home late and used to her bringing men back with her." Mom looked over at me. "What's the matter – you surprised? Well ain't no need to be surprised: Mary didn't fix her high and mighty act until we landed east of Atlantic. Back then she used to say sexing came so easy to her she must have been born to it. Used to act like the sun came up just to hear her crow." Mom threw a rice grain over the room. "Anyhow, I had seen plenty, sharing a room like we did, but I had never seen no suitcase, 'specially not one so shiny new and with a smell of leather something wonderful. So I lay there, pretending to be asleep, wondering what Mary was doing with a suitcase, when neither of us ever went nowhere and wasn't likely to be invited anywhere worth going, until I couldn't keep the thought in any longer and I said, *Where did you get that from, Marygirl?*

– *Get dressed*, she says, *and hush your mouth.* Her breath came fast like a waterfall and her eyes was dancing. I had seen Mary drunk plenty of times. Plenty. And she wasn't drunk.

– *Where we going?* I said.

– *Get dressed*, she said, *Sanderson's waiting downstairs.*

– *Sanderson Miller?* I said. I had been in love with Sanderson my whole life long. The whole sorry lot of it. Loving Sanderson is the first thing I remember, and despite everything that happened in between, my love for him was the one good thing I carried from that town," then she laid her head back against the melamine and looked across at me, "Except you baby, except you. Maybe one day there was a chance for me and Sanderson –" Mom stopped. She traced the curve of the lino pattern with her little finger, so slow she seemed barely to be moving at all, as if she was in no hurry to finish the sentence, as if now we had begun on the great story, we would never come out the other end. "Momma used to say regrets are free, so help yourself. Well I helped myself plenty to the thought of Sanderson Miller and what could have been. Anyway, I looked down to the street, and there is his sand-coloured Mustang waiting, the engine running and I can just make out the shape of his butternut head. I pull on my clothes so fast I forget my underwear." Mom tried a laugh, but her mouth just cracked open dry, no sound came out.

"Mary said goodbye to Momma. She left her with the cartoons running, fresh milk in the fridge and a note saying she loved her. That's one thing I remember. Maybe the rest I could have forgiven, but she wrote *I* not *we* on that note, *I love you Momma*, it read, and I didn't think to correct her because far as I knew we would be back the next day or the day after that, just as soon as the three of us had had whatever fun she had planned. But Mary knew right then we was never going back.

"We got up to Dallas before I asked where we was headed. Sanderson says two words. The only two words he says to me for a thousand miles, *New York*. He says plenty to Mary though, plenty like, *baby*, plenty like *sugar*, plenty like *I got it all to plan, all laid out in my mind, just how it going to be*. And I saw him stroke her belly, and that's when I knew. Mary told me we going on holiday, like you and me were babies both and I didn't know her and Sanderson was in the worse kind of trouble there is. But maybe she was right, 'cause there I was, sucking my teeth, my little girl next to me, my big sister nine months gone and me acting like the belly she had on her was too much corn candy, like it was my first rodeo. Anyhow, that's how it is for miles of night, Mary in the front with

Sanderson on the leather seats, you and me on the back on the plastic seats. And the heat, Georgie, the heat!" Mom lost herself for a moment in the heat of a southern night, somewhere 'round Delaware.

It was dark now outside, and I strained to see Mom, the linoleum cold against the backs of my legs. Then, all on sudden, something hit me full force like a linebacker. I remembered. I remembered the smell of that back seat, the cooking plastic and its inch-thick dirt and Motown playing on the radio. The truth reverberated round the empty kitchen, clanged like biting down on the prongs of your fork.

"So we got to New York," Mom said, "and even then I was expecting Mary would just have the baby and then we'd go back home. Most girls getting caught out travelled interstate for the birth; if you had the money you could always find someone to take it in, and Sanderson had the money. Course I hadn't heard of anyone going as far as New York, but Tantie was always one for taking it outfield. And I was so mad with her. Mad like you wouldn't believe, so much that it hurt me. She looked down on me since the day you was born, you see, and I never knew why, and that night I saw that it wasn't because I did it, or got caught out, it was because I kept a hold of you. That was what Mary couldn't stand to see.

"Sanderson had a list of addresses he was following through. Each one we got to Mary would tell me to wait with you, wait in the car, then Sanderson would march Mary up the street and then half an hour later they'd be back, cussing each other. I guessed they couldn't find no one to take it in. After a couple few days, whether it the heat or all the driving I don't know, but Mary says the baby is coming. Sanderson paid for a hospital, a real smart place, and Mary got a room on her own and good food and TV, not like me and you on the bathroom floor, and he even slipped a gold band on her finger so the nurses treat Mary real nice, like she was doing it on purpose, not on accident. Like that's where the shame lies, in it not being on purpose.

"Sanderson and I waited outside her room, drinking coffee. You only know the beat Sanderson, the down and out Sanderson. You don't believe it but Sanderson was a man to grab hold of and hold on to, time upon. He must have been twenty-five, twenty-six, and this wasn't the first child laid to his name, but there was a simpleness to him, a pride and a joy in the manner of his being uncommon to see. Wasn't easy being a black man those times, those places, but Sanderson wore his skin like the finest leather coat and he'd call the white folks nigger and they'd smile and take it as a compliment. For all his dealings, days before and days afterwards, he pitched straight at life and never flinched when life hit right back at him, and as we stood there I knew him for a fine looking man. Too fine for a brother-in-law anyhow. *What we waiting for*, I said, *You and me got nothing to stick round for, you got a car. I got, well, I got me. And Georgie.* He always had a place for you see, baby, 'cause you brought out something tender he thought his daddy had beat out of him. *We could set off*, I said, *go west. Or Canada, always like the sound of Canada.*

"Sanderson thought about it. Don't care what he says now, he thought about it, but before he could say one way or another, the doctors called me in. The baby was coming. I held Mary's hand. It was an ugly birth. Birthing you was like seeding a pomegranate, but Mary and her baby was fighting each other, not knowing if they wanted to be separate or whole. Mary asked for Sanderson and I went back to the waiting room to call him in. He wasn't alone; while Mary was pushing and heaving away, Sanderson was selling it from under her."

"Selling it?"

Mom nodded.

"To who?"

"A man in the waiting room."

"You mean an agency?"

"No, not an agency. Why an agency be at the hospital; got enough people looking for them without going to the hospital. And then there was no form to sign that I saw, just the cash, blocks of it, and really why would an agency come out to the hospital when you'd have thought unloved black babies fell from the sky, there was so many of them."

"So what man? What did he look like?"

"A white man, that's all I know. In a suit. I saw him and I saw the money. Ten thousand dollars of it, he said." Mom turned for the first time to look at me, the movement stiff, "Now you tell me since when a little baby was worth ever so much as ten thousand dollars to anyone but his own mother? Hmmm? He could have picked one up for free from so many a place, so why was he paying so much for this one? He didn't even know if it was a boy or a girl. Didn't ask."

"But Tantie didn't take the money. Mom, Tantie didn't take the money off of Sanderson, though. Right?"

"She took it and gave Sanderson his cut like the old pimp he was. She gave that three-hour-old thing away, checked herself on her way, and her heels didn't touch the ground. She took me and you and bought a plane ticket over here." Mom rocked herself side to side, her back sliding against the cupboard doors. "And I wonder, even if she don't, I wonder where that baby is now. A man don't pay out ten thousand dollars on a baby unless he's sure he'll get every cent of it back in his pocket."

"So what did Sanderson say when you asked him?"

"I never asked him. Not a one of those two has ever said her name to me or anything about the thing these twenty years. And it wouldn't surprise me if they carrying on all this time, even after Jimmy, nothing would surprise me."

"I always thought —"

"Why you think Sanderson stop by all those times? Always just happening on a bit of gold tack he could throw my way, or something for you?"

"We can find her, though. Track her down and bring her back and —"

"And then what Georgie? And then what? It's too late. Even if we could get anything out of Sanderson, we're twenty years too late, don't you see? I pray it's dead. I pray it died the next morning with the sunrise. I watched her hand that baby over and I should have grabbed the thing with my own hand and brought its skull down hard on the hospital floor. Should have painted the ceiling with its brains before I let him have it."

Mom's face in the twilight was old, and I wished she would cry if expressing tears would stop the free-flow of whatever was leaking inside of her. "So there you go, Georgie, you got the truth. Now what you gonna do with it, that's your problem now."

I threw my fists and feet at Tantie's door. I called her name into the heavens. She looked down from the bedroom, in her dressing gown and haircap, "Georgie!"

"Get down here."

"Oh my Lord, where's Agatha? What's the matter?"

"I said get down here." I launched another assault.

Tantie hurried down the stairs and unbolted the door.

"Nina Ella," I said.

"Yes?"

"Nina Ella."

"Georgie, let me fix you a brandy, you're frighting me."

I grabbed my aunt's hair, "Don't turn your back to me," I said. "Mom told me."

"What?"

"Nina Ella!"

Tantie shrank into herself, like the wicked witch of the west she surely was.

"What would you do, Georgie?"

My answer came back like gunfire. "I wouldn't sell my baby," I said.

"Well plenty girls did," she said. "Plenty."

"Who the hell to?"

"Rich folks. Rich folks who couldn't have them of their own. Good folks. Northerners mostly."

"White folks?" I said.

"Some of them. Get in here, Georgie. I won't talk like this in the street."

I followed her in. Over the floor and the sofa were placards, all face down, with the splint glue drying on them, ready for whatever battle Tantie was fighting next.

"All this time I felt sorry for you."

"And now? Say George, you really think the money made it any easier?"

"I guess it must have done."

"Georgie, I don't understand, you knew I gave that baby away, so tell me what difference does the money make?"

"You sold your own baby for an airplane ticket."

"Not for an airplane ticket, for another chance. Another chance for me and for her. What kind of life would she have had back in Georgetown?

"I turned out all right."

"Because you got away. And what let you get away? My babymoney, so don't come here laying it down lady." So that was how it was, I thought. Tantie had bound the three of us up with her money. This lie was tied so tight around us, it could not be unpicked.

Aurelie came through to fetch a glass of water. She gave Tantie a smile, taking care to leave me out in the cold, and I felt somehow (must have been the hour, must have been the adrenaline) that all the troubles of this family didn't start in Texas, they started the day she got up to sing in Paradise.

"Looking back changes things," Tantie said. "When you got your neck twisted backward, everything is simple, causes and consequences all lain out. Back in the days –"

"Don't feed me shit," I said. "Ain't any time on the planet what you did was half-way right."

"The thing about Georgetown –"

"Don't bother," I said, "I've been there, remember.

I've seen it. I know it. It's a place with right and wrong like any other town."

"So," she said, "you think I should have done what your mom done, hmm? Brazen it out in that town with half the decent folks not giving her the time of day and all the rounders thinking she's easy picking? Once plucked, easy fucked and the whole damn town talking about crazy momma, her two whores and their two bastards?"

"If that was the consequences. I mean," the room was pivoting round us, "consequences. Thought you believed in them."

"I live with the consequences every day."

"And so does Mom. In a way means something. You let me think it was her. You let me think this was her fault, all the secrets, why we came over here."

"And what are you saying? That it's mine?"

"Whose else is it?" I saw how it was. Tantie always coming between us, picking at Mom with one hand, spoiling me with the other, all 'cause she was so jealous of what she'd thrown away. "You wasn't a child," I said, "you was nineteen. That wasn't your baby, Mary. It wasn't yours, it was all of ours, mine and Mom's and –

"George, your momma and me, we dealt with this.

Dealt and done with it while you still playing with dolls. Ain't a family alive without its problems but least —"

"Problems? A baby ain't a problem."

"What you know about anything? We did our best. Only problem now and that's you — causing trouble, leaving nothing be. Butcher can't blame pig if he gets blood on his hands. You've got no one to blame for the way you're feeling right now but yourself."

"A hypocrite, that's what you are. Poking around in everyone else's business, petitions on this, boycotts on that, and the whole time —"

"You know girl you want to watch you don't dig up more snakes than you can kill."

"I ain't listening to you Mary. I'm through with listening. You know I seen you cry for strangers plenty of times. Plenty. I ain't never seen you cry for your own."

Tantie pushed her lips out at me. "What do I care what you think?"

"You probably told Mom to get rid of me at the same time. Or could you not get enough to make it worth your while? Four-year-olds don't fetch so much cash as little baby girls."

"Agatha had no business stirring all this up. All that has nothing to do with this."

"This – what this?"

"Your father. That's what began this, well ain't it just. She told you my secret; did she tell you hers?"

That made me madder than anything, Tantie trying to shift the blame off herself.

"I don't care who my father is," I said, "any more."

I used to like being Georgetown Easy. The sassiest kid in town, I stepped off the airplane and onto that school yard and I was brand new. I ran the fastest, I laughed the loudest and they couldn't get enough, the other kids, of the way I talked and rhymed, my funky little butt-rolling strides, cute as a button, and I knew it and they did too. Never crossed my mind to be like them local girls, eating turkey roll sandwiches and bitching; wasn't a girl but Helena worth bothering with, and as for boys, they got bothered all right, but I minded my own.

When I was eight I told my mom I was done with pigtails, grew myself my own little Afro, strutted round the yard like Miss Thing. Older I got, sorrier I was for those local girls, with their mousy hair and blotting paper skin. I couldn't tell one from the other, the all of them trying so hard to be the same, like beans cooked too long, they all mushed into one soupy thing. But it was a struggle, I tell you that now. I never was an easy fit in that place, always riding up and twisting round. I never felt the shame of having less money; too poor to paint, too proud to whitewash, that was us, and I laughed for years when Mom said it to Mary and Mary smiled back, before I knew what it meant: that we were stuck someplace ten thousand miles from the last place any one of us might have called home and not one thing nor another. Now I was wishing – what had she brought me to with her lying ways – wishing I was plain English scone, margarine and fish fingers. I didn't want to be different any more, or special. I wasn't brand new Georgie Easy; I was the same dirty old story negroes been telling each other these two hundred years, and I was shamed and tired of it. Didn't care the place, just wanted somewhere to set myself down and catch my breath, 'stead of always running from something, some thing, I didn't even know what.

I looked at Tantie. *Don't mess with Texas*, she used to say when I was growing and used to sass her, and a word from her would do more than ten from my mother to hush me. *Don't need nobody teach me to ride my own horse*, she'd say, and I looked at her then and seemed she was thinking the same thing; never had a moment's doubt in her life, that woman, but that she was right as the sun was shining and the wind blowing, and thought she could sit on the fence and the birds would feed her. "Does Jimmy know?" I said.

"Leave Jimmy be." Tantie's voice had a sharp edge of panic.

I pushed past her towards the stairs, caught her with my shoulder so she had to steady herself on the wall.

"Leave it Georgetown," Tantie threw my name at me like it was a curse.

I climbed the stairs two at a time, pawing with my hands to help pull me away from my aunt's sharp nails.

"Georgie, Georgie," she was screaming at me now, reaching hysteria as I came to the top of the stairs, "Jimmy already knows."

I didn't hear her. Or else did not believe it. Or maybe even, by that point in the evening, I did not care. I flung open the bedroom door, I hit the lights. I saw straight away why our fight had not brought down my Uncle Jimmy. He was not asleep. He was sick. Real sick. Coughing blood and crying, his eyes two hollows of incomprehension. I turned to my aunt, frightened.

"Get out," she said, "Go on. And tell your mom, tell her from now on we are two families. You and your momma can stick together in the sacred convent of the righteous and me and Jimmy and the baby, we'll stick together, don't worry about it. And Aurelie."

I left. I did not see how I could ever go back.

Perhaps he'd thought to keep me out of sunlight,

imprisoned in his bone

white marble library, until my black skin faded

to the paper-pale pallor of his own.

He might as well have hoped to conduct the ocean with a twig.

I read until my eyeballs bled, found my mother

pressed between dead weight of cowhide,

read until my brain turned cannibal,

devoured itself.

So now I'll have revenge in place of answers: become her ghost and haunt him.

Play with him like a kitten with wool, twisting, unravelling as I go.

Sometimes it's worse to win a fight than lose
Billie Holiday

For what it's worth

There were folks on the tables, folks on the floor, folks outside, their ears up against the door; there was a kind of hysteria that night, I mean more so than usual. The whole place was in a state of agitation shading to paranoia with people keening for their fix, the conversations leaning on misgiving: what if the girl didn't show (*she hadn't let them down before*), what if she wouldn't sing (*that's what she did, easy as bleeding*). They fought amongst themselves for the seats closest to the stage or in the trajectory of her vocal, but one path was kept clear, the gangway between Aurelie's spot at the mic and Sanderson's place at the bar, and though Aurelie sent her most honeyed notes along that very direction, no one got in the way, they didn't dare. It wasn't Sanderson they were afraid of, his shooters or his heavies; it was Aurelie. You see, by this time the papers were fetching up stories about her, and then again some people are plain too big for a small town – their heads swell up in a way means nobody else can get by, and their bellies, always after too much feeding. Time was, Paradise was a place for a beer and a whisky and good music you could shake to. Now it was all about Aurelie and all we were good for was applause. Everybody likes a little crazy, but even champagne, I heard, is a thing you can get too much of and what Aurelie did to you, she asked no permission for. The bluer the blues, the better you feel, but not with her singing: all vinegar, no oil; that was Aurelie. She hated us and so we hated us and then we got wise and turned on her. Aurelie hadn't sold her soul to the devil, more like it was the other way round; sure there wasn't many standing there that night, the men especial, she didn't have something on.

Jimmy, Bob and Diddy were her fallen angels, playing for her each night at Paradise until it closed at two, then at an after hours club until six, then jamming till the sun was high. They had the scars to prove it: Bob's callused lips, Jimmy's bandaged fingers, Diddy's crooked back were the only wages she paid and the only reward they cared for. Their gigs were all that kept our family playing from the same sheet, Tantie at Paradise for Jimmy's sake, Mom for Bob's, though neither of them happy to see their men used so. Not even Tantie's miscarriage two weeks before had softened the clot between her and Mom.

Course in my heart I had forgiven Tantie. I never did find a way of holding onto a feeling that strong, and fiercer it was, happier I was to let it go, and maybe that's a good thing and maybe not but I can no more be another way than a cat can play guitar. Anyway, I had forgiven my aunt; I just hadn't found a way of telling her so. Losing the baby pulled her and Jimmy so close there was no squeezing between then. I watched them then, Tantie leaning into him, his arms wrapped round her, and though there was nothing I knew to stop them trying for another, they were grieving like there was no starting over. Mom was angry in a way put all her former rages in the shade. I think I comprehended Tantie in a way Mom never could. For Mom love was simple, an old blues riff, a twelve bar with progressions logical; for Tantie love was only ever jazz – improvised, unpredictable, precious and precarious. Loving a thing and losing it was not a possibility for Mom the way it was for Tantie.

By eleven Aurelie was singing so fast, shooting staccato

accidentals like gun-fire, that Jimmy was sweating just trying to keep up. The crowd was in a stupor, they never could pace themselves, those every-timers, just on the verge of insanity (don't doubt but that sound could persuade a mind to leave a body behind for good, or a soul for that matter: there'd already been one casualty, even before that night). Jimmy and Diddy were fading by midnight, but Bob kept blowing, his eyes on Aurelie, and the two of them fell into a call-and-answer must have lasted two hours until Aurelie flicked the switch and Bob carried on solo, his harp wailing and calling for her to come back to him. I'd never heard Bob play like that before, and it seemed to make Mom sweat some, she was flapping like a lobster in the pot even before Aurelie came up close to Bob, him keeping it steady, growling under the five hole draw. She held her ground and then, right when you thought two people couldn't get closer to one another, took another step into him, past touching, their bodies hungry into one another, ripped the harp from his hands and, eyes all on him, put that whole thing to her mouth and, no hands, played *Baby Don't Touch Me*. The crowd were in raptures, spasming left-right, husbands and wives showing no shame before each other and brothers and sisters thrashing their limbs at once. She held the harp out towards him; he cupped it with tender palms and pressed it to his lips. Mom cried softly next to me. Aurelie climbed octaves, reaching after something so sweet it wouldn't be decent to describe it. Mom sobbed as Bob moaned in return then coaxed, tongue blocking, lip puckering, a broken anti-climax from the girl.

"Aurelie doesn't belong here," Mom said, her voice distant as the crowd surged to the bar, thirsty now the show was over.

"No," I said, "I know."

"It's time she went back," Mom said, "to wherever she came from. You'll have to tell Mary to let the girl go."

I shook my head. Me and Tantie were past the stage of asking favours, and Tantie could no more give Aurelie up than her own liver. If we wanted to cut this boll-weevil out of our cotton patch, I was going to have to sharpen a knife. I downed an Angel Hair and crossed to Aurelie at the side of the stage. Sanderson had fitted out the old store-cupboard as her personal dressing room, with red velvet cushions and a glitzy mirror, the kind with lights running around it, the kind Sanderson liked to think had class. Aurelie's dress that night was sequin red, a Shirley Bassey number too big in the bust and twenty years ahead of her. As I watched her, Bo came past with a tumbler on a silver tray.

"George," he said, the smile falling off him, "didn't see you there, girl."

"What's that?" I said, nodding at the glass.

"Oh," he said, "well –"

"It's a Black Bullet, isn't it Bo?" Aurelie said. She came up, took the glass, and looking at me the while, downed it straight. "Aniseed, cola, Kahlua and – what was it you said, Bo?"

"Treacle," Bo said, his voice sticking to the sides of his throat. He limped back to his place at the bar. What did I care if he was mixing the girl exclusives?

"What do you mean by Bob?" I said.

Aurelie turned to look at me, gave me the up-and-down and went back to glossing her pout.

"You come here all angry with the world, well what's it ever done to you it ain't done to the all of us, and what we done to you, you got to come here rip Jimmy apart, rip Bob from Mom, us all at each other, ain't none of us had a day's peace since you got here. Seems like the biggest favour you could do this town is get yourself a dose of laryngitis."

"If it'd stop me from singing, I'd sew these lips together

tonight. You've seen what it does to them; what do you think it does to me?" Aurelie looked over to Sanderson, giving orders to the doormen. "Trying to stop me singing, sister, it is like trying to plug a volcano."

"I ain't your sister," I said. Aurelie had this mid-Atlantic shit going on, fake as her eyelashes. That was Aurelie though, playing dress-up in her mother's clothes,

"And what your mom and Bob got, I'd give anything for it."

"Anything to break it up, you mean," for Aurelie was like that, like a cuckoo laying its stinking egg in the happiest nest, and other people's happiness. It was like tinfoil to a magpie with her; she never could resist the lure of it.

"Sometimes I forget is all. Life's more than a song that you can get lost in."

"It's time to move on, Aurelie," I said, "leave while you still got the chance to come back."

She stopped the pretty-making then. She smiled at me. "Singing in Paradise, it's all I got, it's all I'm good for, Georgie."

"There are hundreds of bars, thousands; you could get a job in any one of them."

"My mother sang here."

"Well she ain't singing no more and if you want to start following those footsteps, well," I said, "you know where they lead."

"Just singing the blues, sister, you know about the blues."

"I know you ain't nothing but a ghost and some us quick to see through you. Right now you got people fooled, they looking at you and seeing Arii, but you ain't nothing to her and when people see that, well, like I say, you want to leave while it's still a choice."

"It'll break Sanderson's heart."

"You think there's a girl in here hasn't been a woman some time with Sanderson Miller? Only difference is you believe the same lies he told us all."

Her face cracked, a little. "You're jealous."

"What I got to be jealous of? Sure you got a pretty face, smooth voice and you got money to play with, but what's any of that? I got me. I got me, Aurelie, and after you paid your last bill and the last of your band's gone home, when there's no one to see you and no one to hear you, what you got, Aurelie? When the lights go off at night, who you got? Nothing."

Next door the Blooz Hot boys were going through

achromatics, the crowd growing restless for their next fix; Aurelie checked her face in the glass and I followed her through to the main room, shaking as she climbed to the stage. The midnight set was when Aurelie let things shake out a little bit funky, heavy on the bass and drums, with scratchy riffs and choppy keys mixed in, and sometimes Bob would let the horn go, and no one was above a little Wonderland. The music seemed to pull your forehead up and down and make your lip curl. It was an argument against mortality, hands clapping and the every-timers each letting out a screech the Godfather would be proud of, one by one their hips working their way loose of their seats, feet side-shuffling, hot-stepping to the beat.

Forget all that. That night Aurelie waved the band away; she looked at me for a beat or two, just so I'd know that this song wasn't meant for Sanderson, and it wasn't meant to get the every-timers high; this song she was singing was meant for me. And she sang:

Southern trees bear a strange fruit
Blood on the leaves and blood at the root
Black body swinging in the southern breeze
Strange fruit hanging from the poplar trees

There was a gravel in her throat had not been there before, and a hopelessness you couldn't fake. The voice echoed round the room, bounced off tables, and came at you from every side, but still it was empty. The way she sang leeched marrow from bone, blood from vein, it reached its fist around my heart and pulled at it. She sang with memory, which is what blues is, with sorrow and around me life was going on, people ordering drinks at the bar, trying their chances with the drunken girls, but I was back in Texas, back home, and I heard the screaming. For the first time, I smelled flesh burning.

I pushed through the crowds, shrugged off the hands that reached after me, turned from the faces that smiled at me. In the ladies I splashed cold water on my face. My skin was grey. The toilets were not one of Paradise's features. You learned to take your own paper, and hold your breath. In the cubicle I perched there, skin away from the sticky seat, my stomach cramping, when the door through to the bar swung open and hit against the dryer.

Over the sound of water running I could make out a voice. "Why d'you do it? Tell me. Go on." There was a beat pause and the voice went on, "Well I know why anyhow. You did it for him," there was the sound of the hand dryer came on, "didn't you. Always," feet on the tiles, "him. All these years later and you've never changed no more than a leopard does and not sorry for it either." There was the sound of the door swinging open. "Bringing the police round. The police, for Lord's sake, and you wonder what for Momma never got out of that chair." It was Tantie's voice, thrashing like a wet fish in a tight space.

"Better she knows about that than finds out about the other," Mom said, in a voice so deep I hardly knew it for her own.

I came out of the cubicle quick to catch them. Mom and Tantie started then froze. "Oh my Lord, Georgie. Oh my Lord." Tantie was coming at me with her arms trying to catch me to her, and Mom was shaking her head.

I ran past the both of them, ran into the thick and the heave of bodies on the dance floor. Someone grabbed me from behind. It was Sanderson. "You got to help me Georgie, I's in trouble, quick before –"

Too late. A hush dropped on the place and Sanderson, me, everybody there, watched as a crinkle-headed blonde crossed the floor, deliberate as murder, stepped to Aurelie, shaking her rings and jangling her bangles, and slapped Aurelie hard against the face. Her jewellery rattled. As for Aurelie, she didn't even blink.

"Who is that?"

"That," said Sanderson, wretched as a comedown, "that's my wife."

Ain't nothing more precious than a secret or a person too poor to have one. Everyone wants everyone else's and everyone's after keeping their own. We all pick the same dirt over, trying to bury our own mess deep, scratching it over till they all, all the shameful stuff, mixed up one with the other. Seemed Sanderson had more secrets than even he could keep track of. He tried to hide behind me, "Keep her away from me, Georgie, don't let her near me, you hear?"

"Never mind the wife. Lord, Sanderson, it's Aurelie you got to watch for."

Sure enough, Aurelie cut a path over to her man. "Sanderson Miller," she said, so soft was only the two of us could have heard her. "Almost taught me the meaning of love, didn't you? Now I want to teach you something." She raised her voice so the place could hear her, "You know a man got one use only, and even then he's second best."

There was applause from the every-timers at this.

Then Aurelie parted those lips like cocking a gun, and we got ready to witness a jazz murder (the bloodiest kind) when a scream flew over from the far side. Mom had punched Tantie fat in the lip; deep blood spattered on her blouse.

The crowd couldn't pick between one fight and the other and while they was distracted, Aurelie stepped in to Sanderson. She pressed her lips onto his, he tried to lose himself in the kiss, but Aurelie pulled away. "Goodbye, Sanderson," she said and then she lassoed every person in that room with a gold hoop of a note that purred in her throat, and she moved to the door, her hips jigging and the crowd behind her. Next day paper said she'd kept them skiffling down the street till sunrise, pied piper she'd dance them to hell and back, and once that voice opened up, even Mrs Miller had no choice but to fall in.

When the last of the crowd had gone, Sanderson shut the door and peeled the sisters one from the other, took four shot glasses together and poured out whisky, sat himself down. I started to cry. Mom knew, Mary knew, Sanderson knew. So who else was this all about but me? All this troubling on account of me and for why? I didn't think my daddy was a movie star. You know I never thought he was president neither, but child that

I was that night, I thought there wasn't a truth so bad I wouldn't be happier knowing it. "What's the matter, baby?" Sanderson said, his voice empty.

"Whatever we did, whatever happened in Georgetown," I said, "it's got to be time to get over it. We can't live our whole lives like this, ashamed."

"Ashamed?" Mom and Tantie spoke together, the word burning in their throats.

"I ain't ashamed," Mom said.

"You're ashamed?" Tantie asked.

Sanderson downed his shot, "See now but you've got this girl all mixed up."

"What you think happened?" Tantie said.

"Something that makes our name a cuss in that town twenty-five years after the fact. Something that got you at each other this time after. Something bad."

Mom and Tantie looked at each other, daring each other to break their vow of silence.

"What happened," Sanderson said, "was your grandfather." He picked up the bottle, screwed off the top, "His name was Loyal; he was a good man. You ought never to be ashamed on account of him." Sanderson drank from the bottle in a way I'd seen him despise other men for, for Sanderson indulged his vices in style.

"Sure, you would have loved him, given a chance. He was a historian like you. Took him five years to track it all down but he did, and he published it too: family history all the way back to Africa. That caused a storm, I can tell you, a man like Loyal Easy saying his people had been free negroes early as 1860 and with the proof of it to hand, and descended from royalty too."

Tantie lifted her eyes, "A storm, that what you call it, Sanderson?"

"Ain't my business to call it anything more."

"A storm, you say?" Mom shook her head, "Hell, I hate to see your hurricane."

The three of them sat all in a row, their bodies sloppy, their eyes wide-open, facing right into me, not seeing me at all.

"Mom?" I said. "Tantie?"

"The day JFK was shot," Mom began, her voice harder, brighter than I'd heard it before.

Tantie followed up, "November 22nd, 1963."

"The day he was shot," Mom's voice tightening like a pegged string.

"Only up the road, not two hundred miles from the door, Dealey Plaza, Dallas, Texas, USA."

"The day he was shot, they killed your granddad,"

Mom's voice breaking on the final word.

I looked to Sanderson, all the lifeblood drawn out of him.

"They took him from outside the schoolhouse."

"Daddy was a schoolteacher."

"A principal."

"They took him straight from there."

"They said it was robbery but we found his wallet still in his pants pocket."

"And the dollar bills he'd just got from the bank still folded inside."

"They said it could have been any nigger got caught out like that."

"Daddy was never no one's nigger and it was only ever him would do, after he published those things. Some people were saying the school teacher needed teaching lessons."

Mom and Tantie fell silent, so still they were, I could not see if they were breathing. Sanderson cast his glass at the far wall side. "You want to know the greatest lie, Georgetown, in that whole damn nation? Not everyone cried the day JFK got shot. Some folks, was all they could do to keep from singing."

Mom reached out a hand to Sanderson's, and he

grabbed a hold of it. More quietly he said, "A black man with pride is a fearsome thing to some folks. And I never saw a man with more self-same pride than Loyal, or a man who better deserved it."

Mom started up again, "They tied his feet and his arms together, tied him to the back of a car, pants down to his ankles, and pulled him along High Street."

Tantie slipped her hand into Mom's. "When they got to the end of High Street, they turned round and dragged him back again. They did fifteen runs."

Outside I could hear Aurelie circling round this direction again with two hundred feet dancing behind her. I hoped that Sanderson had his gun to hand. I waited for Mom to say something. I waited for Tantie to start up. Even Sanderson was still. It came to me that maybe I was the only one could break that silence. That I would have to do it, but I did not have the strength. I could not open my mouth. I could not move my tongue. I thought the four of us would stay frozen in quiet that way forever and this thought filled me with a happiness such that I thought maybe I had died already for I had never known anything like it, a blissful hush, a peace.

Sometime before the sun rose, could have been twenty minutes later, and it could have been hours, Mom's bottom lip started to tremble. Slowly, slowly, it pulled itself loose. Tantie and Sanderson and me watched Mom's mouth open. She said, "I made a world for you, Georgie, I made you a world," she looked at me, and I saw that she would not cry, "where bad things didn't happen, where there was no past to hurt you. I hid you in that house, you and me and Mary and Momma all on top of one another, and I wouldn't let so much as the sun see you." I wanted to go to her. I wanted to fall on the floor before her and put my head on her lap. "I was fifteen, Georgie, what else I know how to do but keep a secret?"

My mouth, my throat was dry.

"I wanted to save you all that, the past, Georgie. It was the past killed Daddy; the past was killing that whole town, the all of us, 'cause it's without end. Things happened there's no putting right and no forgetting. How you tell a thing like that a baby? How you tell that thing at all I don't know."

My eyes owned tears that I wouldn't let fall as long as Mom held up. "Why you call me for a place like that, Mom? Why you call me for Georgetown when that was the place it was?"

"Wasn't the place did that murder, Georgie."

"Still —"

"Let me tell you something; ten years I was mute. Ten years I wouldn't give that town so much as the breath from my body. But you can't hate the place you come from; you can't hate what made you without hating yourself. After I'd birthed you, I held you, the both of us was shaking, both so exhausted, and downstairs Momma was watching the cartoons not knowing you was even thought of, and Mary was over in Dallas singing, not knowing you was brought into the world. I sat with you in my arms and I was so full of love for you, just wasn't room for no more hate. You washed it clean out of me, Georgie. You waved your hand, you uncurled your tiny fingers like this, and I didn't know whether it was you or me was moving, I didn't know where you began and I ended. Then you screamed and I felt a shaking in my chest, felt my voice coming back to me, moving in me. I was fifteen and a southern girl, Georgie, my universe stopped at the city border. Georgetown was all I knew of the world. And I looked at you, and you was my everything, the future and all I had and all I wanted. And I pressed my lips on you, and I told you that, I called you Georgetown."

Mom and Tantie sat with their arms wrapped around each other, deep in a grief I could only touch the surface of. There was a banging on the door of Paradise. Sanderson strolled over to it. I tried to call out to him to take out his shooter, stood between Mom and the door. Sanderson had barely twitched the bolt when Diddy fell into the place, wheezing and clutching at his chest.

"You all right, Diddy?" I said.

"Georgetown, fetch him a brandy," Sanderson said.

Diddy shook his head, "Not me, not me." He walked over to my aunt, he coughed something terrible and eventually Tantie gave him her eyes and Diddy found the air to speak, "Mary, it's Jimmy, he's fallen right over. You'd better come quick."

Not the notes you play

They'd taken him to the general on the far side of town, the ambulance siren mixing with the echo of slide guitar. The cancer had started in his liver, the doctors said, and spread quicker than the British Empire. Now they had him where Helena's dad had been, in a ward where, like Mom said, "Ain't nothing for the nurses to do but arrange flowers and wait."

Jimmy's brown face stood out in the whiteness. I sat by his bedside while he slept, Mom and Bob having kidnapped Tantie. Mom was gonna fix her hair and rub olive oil into her feet and Bob was gonna fix some macaroni cheese that Tantie would eat whether she wanted it or not. The man in the next bed to Jimmy wept without drawing breath, water falling out of him like someone was squeezing on his insides. Eventually Jimmy stirred.

"How you doing?"

He smiled. "How am I doing?" He tasted each word, as if testing one of Tantie's new sauces. "Well, I got an answer next time some smart alexander asks what I'm doing for the Millennium."

"Jimmy," I said, "don't – there's, we'll get you out of here."

Jimmy raised both eyebrows, very slowly, and then I heard a gassing sound and then his throat kicked it and I realised he was laughing. "Hee hee hee. You always were an optimist," he said. "Georgetown, you are a lovely young woman. Now do me a favour and stop pretending you don't know what is going on here."

"You could have done something," I said, angry at the calmness of the man, "told someone. They have treatments, you know. You hear about it all the time. All the time."

Jimmy let out a long breath. "Your aunt and me, we have spent our whole life fighting. Our whole life. In the end, a man needs a bit of dignity, you know." A woman wheeled round with a trolley of Kit-Kats, an urn of tea and I took a little polystyrene cup of watery squash. "What can we hope for in our old age – and I am old, Georgie – if not a little wisdom? I know enough not to fight the inevitable. And besides, medication interferes with your sound. I couldn't let Aurelie down. Now who else could she get to play axe like me?"

I reached into my bag. "I brought you flying saucers."

Jimmy's eyes narrowed. "What else?"

"Liquorice shoelaces."

"Put them in the drawer," he whispered, his eyes on the nurse station. "At the back, behind the underpants."

"They treating you good?"

"Best poker of my life."

"Poker?" I said. "And there's me believing all these years you weren't a gambling man."

"Well," he said, "crazy stakes you can get in here. Quite seriously."

I didn't laugh and Jimmy looked at me thoughtful, like I amused him but he was too obliging to laugh.

"You know, I always thought it a terrible thing, dying. Turns out it's easier than falling over your own shoelaces."

"Don't," I said.

"I feel like I been putting something off and putting something off, and, now I'm finally getting round to it, I'm wondering why I spent so long avoiding it. God is good, Georgetown. God is good and he knows what he's about."

"Don't put a face on," I said, "I don't want it. I've no time for that or for messing and I'd rather you cried on me than lied about it."

"I've shed my last tear, Georgetown. I am sixty and I have lived more life than twenty other men might do. Besides, it's the shock of it you're feeling, and then, with your blood, getting angry always was a way of passing the time. I've had months to play with. I've been on an aeroplane; do you know what that means? I've seen two continents and fallen in love and sometimes I've done things with my guitar that were worth doing, so why would I waste time now getting angry?" His eyes drifted to the TV set hanging in the corner, his face mellowed into the easy breeze of the chat-show conversation.

The hospital was old and tall, and its rooms, this ward at least, were circular, great towers with a staircase running up the centre. I watched the visitors coming in and looking lost, defeated by the identical beds, and walking uncertainly, in Sunday best, searching out loved ones from under sheets and drips. I felt cold; my toes, my fingers, my bones, all cold.

"I saw a man on TV this morning," Jimmy started up as the ad breaks came on, "said the world ending December 31st. Called it the Millennium Bug and said all those missiles going to go off like popcorn. So I'll be keeping your sun loungers ready for the rest of you." Jimmy laughed as if he was determined to do it. "Your aunt is keeping well?"

I lied silently. I did not tell him that I found rotting meat in her fridge, that she hadn't bathed since he came in here. "She's OK," I said. I had already decided that now Aurelie had gone I would move out of Helena's and into Tantie's.

"She's a practical woman. I admire that."

"Well," I said, pinching the edge of the bed, "you know, she ain't as practical as all that."

"She's a doer, not a thinker. She'll be OK."

"Hmmmm," I said, "yes."

"And she don't need anybody fussing over her."

"Yeah, well," I said, "she's got it anyway."

"God knows who she is going to sue this time," Jimmy said.

I smiled.

"You are allowed to laugh," he said, but I couldn't.

A nurse stuck down a plate of food before Jimmy, who smiled his thanks. Jimmy still had a killer smile.

"God, what is that?" The food on Jimmy's plate showed the inadequacy of the word 'grey'.

"Mince?" Jimmy said.

"Minced what?"

Jimmy shook his head, "Mince and cabbage."

"You're sure?"

"It's what I asked for."

"Can't believe you asked for that, man," I said.

Jimmy looked as if he couldn't believe it either. He beheld his plate with fascination. "Tell Mary, if she's looking for a new campaign."

I didn't suppose that Tantie would be in a crusading frame of mind for a while. Her and Mom were still shaken after that night in Paradise. "Hell, Georgetown," Mom'd said when we talked about it later, but more in grief than anger, "what did you think you gonna find out, you know? You think there was some wonderful news we keeping from you on purpose?"

Sometimes it as much as you can do to shrug. Mom showed me the article my grandfather had written for the newspaper. It was a story with not a lot of joy in it.

Not that it was a story should go untold, but it hadn't got a lot of comfort in it and I guess comfort was what I was looking for. I'd been searching for a past I could never have found. I guess most folks like me are the same: you have to go back a long way to find a happy ending, and that's if you don't get lost on the way, get stuck back in the cotton fields, burning with an injustice you only ever read about in books, trying to right a centuries-old wrong.

"You ain't born to put this world right," Mom said.

"Tantie thinks so."

"Mary's wrong, and, anyhow, seems to me she made enough mistakes of her own. You put on this earth to do your own thing." Then she said, "Oh girl, it's all pigswill. All the jumbled up leftovers of someone else's mess. You want to go swimming in them custardy slops, you want to dive down in the old cabbage leaves and mash potato? What you think you gonna find down there? And how far back you want to go? What if you go back, all the way back to Africa; what difference it going to make?"

I tried to explain some of this to Jimmy. He was unsympathetic, "They told you, Georgie; you got what you want."

It didn't feel like it. "It doesn't make sense to me."

"Things make sense to those two won't make sense to other people, 'cause their world's not like ours. What do you suppose life was like for those two after that day? Your grandma's ghost left so quickly it forgot to take the body with it. As for the rest of that town, well everybody knows that spilt blood doesn't achieve anything but give people a taste for more. All you can do is the one thing you never have, and still won't. All you can do is trust they did the best for you."

I sucked my teeth and drew my shoe against the linoleum.

Jimmy grinned and reached out a hand at my knee that didn't quite make it before falling back on the bed. "You will have one of your own one day, then you'll know. Then you'll know, asking you why the sun shines and who put it there. No parent can ever tell a child all it wants to know, but all these things, these are things you'll work out yourself someday."

"I can't guess at my father like a math problem."

"Perhaps so, perhaps not. Maybe you got the whole thing on back-to-front. Remember when Helena's mother went to see Nina Simone, do you remember, in London some time, remember? *How was it,* we said. Nina Simone at the Albert Hall, full band, all the old classics and all that anger, all that passion. *How was it,* we said? *Oh,* she said, *she got the words wrong some places.*" Jimmy laughed.

The nurse came and took Jimmy's plate away. I watched him slyly from my eye-corner. I tried to memorise the way his features lay, the curl of his hair, the colour of his skin. I shut my eyes to test how easy I could reassemble him. "Do you remember," Jimmy said, "that time you thought you found your grandfather?"

I smiled. "God, man. Don't remind me."

"What was the name of that website?"

"Familytree.com," I said sheepishly.

Jimmy said, "You put us through some times, Georgie."

"I'm not the only one," I said. "Do you remember when Alice Manning came to tea?"

Alice Manning was the other black kid in my class at school, a real light-skinned girl – honey coloured, with hair like molasses, enough good looks to make you sick – who'd been adopted by a white couple with three kids of their own. Mom was sure that Alice would be better off in the orphanage than living with Mr and Mrs Manning and was forever trying to rescue Alice and welcome her back to the bosom of the black community (round our way Mom was the bosom of the black community. And it was some bosom). Mom would not let up until we invited poor orphan Alice Manning round for tea. When she came, all pigtails and party frock, Mom practically gave her an examination in black culture. As Mom ladled out fish soup, she said, trying to sound it out as casual as she could, which is about as casual as a B52 bomber, "Who your favourite black martyr, Alice sweetheart?"

I was brought up reciting and revering the black martyrs – Martin, Marcus, Malcolm, this in place of times tables and the Green Cross Code, but poor Alice Manning didn't know what to say and she just about pissed herself when she saw that old fish head float up and wink at her so she sat there for the whole meal and didn't open her mouth to speak a word nor eat a bite. Mom whispered to Tantie, "That girl don't know nothing 'bout her own culture. She ain't even ate peas and rice before, can you imagine?" Like there was just one black culture, like all us Africans, Jamaicans, Afro-Americans and Aborigines are linked in a world of jerk chicken, ganja and Bob Marley records.

Tantie shook her head and said, "It nothing less than brainwashing, is what it is."

Jimmy and I had giggled conspiratorially and did so again at the memory.

The bell rang for the end of visitors' time. Jimmy, who was still chuckling over the memory of poor Alice Manning, said, "And do you remember when you got married?"

I pushed back into my chair. I had thought Jimmy was riding right by me, but I guess the medication must have confused him some. I swallowed, moved my tongue soundless against the roof of my mouth.

"You were twenty-eight or so," Jimmy said, "beautiful day. Your mom gave you away, Blooz Hot played the reception, though of course everyone agreed the new guitarist wasn't fit to hold the pick of the old."

I squeezed Jimmy's hand. "And then," he said, "there was that time Mary sang up at the town hall. Some protest thing or other, and everyone said, *why this girl hasn't sung all these years*, and Mary said, *that would have been my foolish husband, and he mightn't have known much about singing, but he had a heart like a continent, you know. He had soul,* she said." Then Jimmy said, "I will offer you a piece of advice, and since I am on my sick-bed perhaps you will listen to me for once. Here it is: don't worry so much."

"Don't worry so much?"

Jimmy elaborated, "You know, watch more TV."

"OK."

"Since the first time we met, you are always worrying

about some problem or other."

"That's what we do," I said, "we all do that."

"Take a walk on the wild side, as our friend Sanderson would say. After all, the blues is not the notes you play, it's the way you feel. There ain't no such thing as poetry for beginners. You can't learn that kind of thing. Soul is soul, you've just got to –" His eyes were faraway, focusing on something that mystified him and that I could not see, would not even know where to look for. A cough ravaged him, and I sat there, helpless as he shook. The nurse looked over, met my eye for the briefest time and dropped her gaze, tweaked some chrysanthemums. "Georgetown, I am glad you're here," Jimmy said.

Tears tracked down my face. There was no hope; Mom had told me that, his face did and his bony hands, but I still believed, in the face of test results and expert opinions, despite white blood cell counts and BP readings, in something greater.

"There is something I have been meaning to ask you," Jimmy said. Meaning to ask you, for ages."

I squeezed his hand, unable to speak for if I had opened my mouth who could have doubted but that it would all have come flooding out.

"Georgetown, will you do me the honour –" he

coughed again, "the very great honour," his voice was a croak, "of being my daughter?"

And then he was holding me in his arms and we were crying together and laughing. "No problem," I said, and let the water lap over me, the pain wash out.

The Chilhuacle negro

We peeled tomatoes for Tantie's salsa, boiling up panfuls of water, crossing the tight skins with a sharp knife and plunging them in. Steam clung to the white tiles, droplets hanging from the louvred doors. "– Growing concern this week about the safety of genetically-modified crops and the possible impact on human health –" the radio said. "– And abroad, Serbs seek refuge from NATO bombing campaign –" The news blared out and Tantie peeled tomatoes without a murmur, her fingers easing the fruit out of its jacket like her whole attention was taken up on a job I'd seen her do with one arm broken and her eyes on a book. Things were coming loose in that household. There was grime in the grouting, and where

Tantie's two ovens neighboured up was an inch gap had been colonised by peas and onion skin nestling in with rice and spaghetti halves. Mornings I'd come down to the evidence of Tantie's midnight snacking – eight pork chops gone from the freezer, the bones piled on the sofa arm, half-cooked rice with mushroom ketchup stuck to the frying pan or whole bowlfuls of greens floating in the sink, leftovers Tantie had eaten straight from the pan.

It had been that way since the funeral. Tantie, chalk-skinned, straw-haired, was practically desiccated with grief. Her eyes, that were always wet with joy or pity, were dry as Sahara. Tantie was flat out of juice and wasn't none of us knew how to get it flowing again. Even her cooking was flat (though none of her customers would dare to complain), her chicken coating didn't wrestle your tongue like it used to, her black olive couscous didn't tie it in knots and though the salsa we were making had exactly the same number of home grown tomatoes, the same pinch of chilli Tantie had been pinching for seventeen years, and the onion was cut in the exact same size cubes (just between a dice and a slice), it was like ketchup to its former incarnations.

But Mom was getting sleeker and glossier by the day. Her hair had an oil all its own, and the way she moved these days was petroleum jelly. Mom and Bob were a month away from marriage and Mom was so giddy with it she had no means of steadying her sister. She was even on a diet, trying to reverse forty years of indulgence with four weeks of good behaviour. "What you starving yourself for?" I said, "Bob surely loves you how you is," and Lord knows if Bob liked his women treat-size rather than feast-size, he wouldn't have gone near Mom.

"I want to look good, don't I?" Mom said. "I picked me out a dress and all."

Mom showed me a picture she'd torn out of *Bride*. It was all lace and sequins, moulded in a fishtail and plunge neck, in brilliant white.

"Mom –" I said.

"I know. It's beautiful. Not cheap, but, you know, a woman only does this sort of thing once in a while. I got yours picked out too."

"So it's definitely a church wedding then?"

"And why not? I'm a true believer." Mom hadn't been to church in years, but Mom said God is like your kidneys – you know he's there, doing his business, without you have to be all the time telling him how grateful you are on account of it. "God and I have an understanding," Mom said, "I don't ask nothing of him and he don't ask nothing of me."

I wasn't sure what the vicar would make of this, or Mom in sequins, lace and a plunge-neck. Her diet meant sprinkling one tablespoon of bran on her regular food. For breakfast she had blueberry muffins with bran, mid-morning she might have a cream cake with bran, and for lunch she had pork chops, fries and baked beans, all with a sprinkling of bran. Tantie, a disciple of the no pain, no gain school of weight loss, wasn't impressed, but Mom pointed out it cleansed the system something worth believing.

After we'd done with the tomatoes, and to keep Tantie from crawling back under the covers, I persuaded her we had the time to get to the cash and carry and back before the evening crowd came in. Driving the van had been Jimmy's job, and Tantie didn't even have a licence when he got sick, but, self-made woman she was, (and her latest call was "busy hands, busy mind," like holding a potato peeler, or gearstick, or learning to crochet, could take the place of a husband in a broken heart), she took a week's crash course with Pass Masters and, I was convinced, bribed the examiner with a sausage roll and pickled onion combination to get her licence. As we hit the dual carriageway, it was evident that Tantie thought fifth gear was a luxury option, like using your headlights

("What's worth seeing?") and indicating ("If I'm going left the whole world can see me going left, if they can't see this great van, is they going to notice a blinking little light?"). She used the rev indicator as a prompt, only moving up a gear when the needle hit red. I tried to offer advice, but Tantie reminded me she's the one with the licence and she wasn't carrying no back-seat drivers. Tantie demanded absolute silence when she was at the wheel, though this didn't stop her monologuing on about how if the government provided better public transport she wouldn't need to drive at all. Tantie crunched into third, almost hitting the central reservation. She was overtaking a police car at the time. For a Texas lady, she sure was a speed demon. "I been thinking," she said. "About time I found this daughter of mine."

I saw the policeman go for his car radio. "OK," I said, without really hearing her.

"Is that it? OK? OK? I'm talking 'bout a daughter here," Tantie had her foot flat on the pedal, a sure sign of stress, and the van was screaming like a child with a nightmare, "not old shoes."

"Sure," I said, "but it's like finding a pearl in an ocean, is all."

"You think I can't find her? Hmmm?" Tantie turned

to look at me, letting the speed drop and weaving like a bumblebee. "I didn't say I'm gonna look for her, I said I'm gonna find her. I said it." The foot jammed back down on the pedal. I was thrown back into my seat and the rear van doors fell open. The police car hit the lights and siren.

"OK, OK," Tantie said, "I'm pulling over. Get you past."

It took Tantie a minute to realise it was her he was stopping. When she did, I braced myself for Tantie's outburst – she had a fistful of statistics on the number of innocent black folks get stopped, a whole speech all committed to memory – but she took the breath test, showed her papers and drove the rest of the way at a steady thirty. Something was definitely wrong with Tantie.

We got to the cash and carry and Tantie went back on pilot light. She made her way past morning goods, took a shortcut through the seasonal aisle and made for greengrocery. There, she scooped up armfuls of chillies, shading from green to sweet red, like a rainbow of heat. She selected anchos, wrinkled and thick-fleshed, taking in a lungful of their sweet earthy smell. Next she picked out a couple of devilish arbols for flavouring oils, then some red habaneras that go great with fruit, if you can stand the heat of them. Tantie used to grow her own chillies in pots on the windowsill, but the sun this side of the Atlantic was tamer than his Texan cousin, and aside from the Bangalore Torpedoes, she'd let the idea go. These days, Tantie was dependent on Mr Dhir for her supplies. We checked the remainder off the shopping list: tan, mild green anaheims for roasting and stuffing, bullet shaped serranos for pickling, dark raisin brown pasillas and choricero, sweet and mild and big as your hand, the secret ingredient of Tantie's famous chocolate cake.

Mr Dhir shuffled over from the novelty items rack where he'd been hanging up whoopie cushions. He had something to show Tantie, "Look, please, look what I have for you." He beamed with pride as he uncovered, in the palm of his hand, an owl pellet.

Tantie caught her breath. "Don't tell me!" she said.

"Yes," he said.

They whispered together, "Chilhuacle Negro."

A tear glistened in Tantie's eye, and Mr Dhir, who was one of Tantie's oldest friends, and as committed to the causes as anyone, swallowed and ran his hand across his face. Tantie had been after a Chilhuacle Negro for at least fifteen years.

We heaved up four five-kilo bags of onions, Tantie insisting on opening up every one and checking for bruises, softness and bolted bulbs, six kilos of potatoes, passed for eyes, shoots, and awkward nobbles, peppers, oil, corn, flour, salt, sugar, garlic, and a jungle of fresh herbs. It was good to see Tantie in control; outside the cool dustiness of the warehouse and the hot damp of the kitchen, Tantie couldn't make her mind up on anything these days, didn't know whether she wanted her eggs boiled or easy over, as if, without Jimmy to argue against, her own mind was a strange thing to herself. Mr Dhir boxed everything up for us and his son carried our shopping out to the van.

This whole thing with Nina Ella had hit out of nowhere, blind-side. For so long my absent baby cousin had been a part of our emotional furniture, like the chip in the dining room table, missing for so long we didn't notice it was gone and for which we had long since stopped imagining ways of improvising a solution. "What if you don't find her?" I said.

Tantie shrugged.

"And what if you do?" I said.

"I hear what you're thinking Georgie. I hear it so loud my eardrum is bleeding."

"All that soul-ache over my father —"

But, like Mom, Tantie would never believe I was old enough to stop taking advice and start giving it. "You ask me, someone that lose himself ain't worth looking for. Nina Ella's not like that. She's not hiding herself away. Hell, she don't even know how lost she is. So things didn't work out with you and your dad," she said. "You don't have to help me."

"I'll help," I said, knowing that this was the beginning of the great Nina Ella Project, but that it might not be a bad thing if it took her mind off Jimmy, and what happened back in Texas. "The past, you know, Tantie, it kind of weighs you down, you know?"

"I'm not looking for the past, now am I? I'm searching for the future." Tantie started up the engine, pulled on her seatbelt, cranked the gear-stick into first, and stalled.

In the space of a month, Tantie had gone from worrying about a million things to caring about two: finding Nina Ella and closing the museum. I couldn't help but think that somehow the two had gotten mixed up together. "That's how it works," she said, "one thing gets mixed up with every other thing, and you think you can separate them? Like cutting an arm from a hand, like sieving the sea for salt, or," she said, "like taking a baby from its mother." Her lasso sure could bind tighter when it wasn't at full stretch. With the museum it was as if the passion that used to be spread out wide was focused on one spot. Tantie had timed her indignation to the beat: even Helena knew that place's days were numbered. I guess history comes in and out of fashion like that sometimes, and Helena's kind was going down fast enough to give you nosebleed. The letters pages of *The Gazette* were filled with suggestions on what the place could be but Tantie was one step ahead of the competition. She had it all planned, "Something big, something gonna put this town on the map." She raised her eyebrows, dropped her chin, all meaningful at Merg last time she went to picket the place.

We watched his Adam apple do the work. It was no sweat for old Merg, really; Jimmy's death had given him a bad fright. After fighting retirement for years, he'd on a sudden let the line go slack. Mom had seen him with an H. Samuel catalogue. Helena had heard him and Jenny discussing cottages in Cornwall.

Tantie enjoyed her moment. She moved round the museum like she'd inherited the place, shoulders circling, hands held just so, half-dancing with the pleasure it brought her to see Merg and Jenny shaking at the prospect. Jimmy hadn't been gone six weeks but Tantie was back on her horse and kicked her spurs so hard she drew blood, went for it like a buzzard and guts. It scared me. The worst I had to cope with was history, belching itself up, making its presence known. As for my aunt: how many times do you pick yourself up? And didn't matter what happened now, wasn't no happy ending could compensate for what had gone before, but fighting was what she knew how to do, and she fought.

"What exactly were you thinking of?" Jenny asked.

"Leicester got the National Museum of Space, you get me?"

"Right," said Jenny.

"Sheffield got some National Museum of Pop Music, see? Pop music. And – Georgie, where's that tram place?"

"I don't know," I said. "Don't bring me into this."

"So," said Tantie, as if all this was building to a logical point, "what we gonna get ourselves in this here place, it's the National Museum of Black History." Tantie sealed her sentence with a stout nod, glided back on the floor.

"Here?" said Jenny.

"This very room, sister, what's the matter? Not keen on the idea?"

"It's just," Jenny looked a little pinker than usual, "I mean, here?"

There was more shoe shops than black people in our town.

"You got a better idea?" Tantie said. She smiled at Merg. A long time back, and I mean before Jimmy, when we'd not been here a year, Jenny had angled for jewellery. Jenny had fluttered and muttered and Merg had stood his ground, and for a while the two of them had split one from the other. Mary, I don't know why, but Mary, probably out of spite to Jenny, asked Merg if he liked Steven Spielberg, and when Merg said yes, took him to *The Color Purple*. Merg paid for the tickets, Tantie followed the story in her paperback, hissing at every departure from the version in her lap. Anyway, wasn't but the next morning, just as Merg was fixing to get his first taste of grits (as a paying customer, don't make no mistake) when Jenny turned up for the first time at Zambezi all humble pie and cleavage. Merg had trotted back, dazed but no damage done, from Tantie. And that's all there was to it, one date, one half-night together, but I knew what it counted for. Tantie might have acted like she thought Merg was a lost cause, but I knew, welcome as Jenny was to him, she hadn't given up on making him see right.

Jenny pulled at a row of pearls she'd got in plastic. She was secretary treasurer of the local Historical Society. They organised battle re-enactments on midsummer's eve, playing at a history with winners and losers and a voucher for a meal at Castle Tandoori for the best death scene. Jenny fixed Tantie with her eye. "Leave it with me," she said.

That same night, Tantie came into my room, disturbing a real sweet dream. "I think I found her." She jabbed at my behind with a surprisingly bony finger.

"Found who?" I said. "And where you find her? Under your pillow? It's the middle of the night. I was having a sweet dream. Leave me alone."

"Nina Ella Aurelie."

The three words ran after one another so, they didn't make any sense to me. "Go to bed."

But Tantie had sat on the end of my bed with her feet tucked up under her, shining like I don't remember the last time I saw her so happy. "I been thinking," she said. "She the exact same right age."

"Who is?"

"She got the look about her, she got my funk and then she got my voice."

"Tantie," I said. I didn't mean any disrespect to my aunt, who's got the second best voice I ever heard, but comparing those voices was like comparing silk and nylon. "You're not saying Aurelie is Nina Ella?"

Tantie saw my doubt. "A woman surely knows her own daughter."

Just like a girl with no past will grab hold of anything and call it a father, so I learned that a woman with no future will grab hold of anything and call it a daughter. Maybe this was how madness started. Maybe it ain't always a violent thing. Maybe it just lets itself in quietly by the back door, and one day you come home and find it sitting in your chair, wearing your pyjamas and drinking your cocoa.

"Where's this coming from all on sudden?" I said.

"You think this is sudden? I been looking for years. I been looking since the day I lost her, near as. Every penny I had I spent on lawyers, detectives, I registered with every agency there is. Nothing. Well, blood surely knows blood."

"You can't believe Aurelie is Nina Ella. That's crazy. We know who her parents are. Everybody knows." But as I said it I thought, I never had seen a photo of Arii Cook where her stomach wasn't flat as shore after the tide gone out, and the two of them stuck away on that island those years, who's to say what went on? And then there was that same thing been troubling me since I first laid eyes on Aurelie. She was black, real honest black and her mother no darker than a week in Ibiza. "Well, what does Sanderson say?"

"You know Sanderson. Won't remember anything he doesn't want to."

Sanderson's memory was shot to pieces. After that night in Paradise, after he realised Aurelie wasn't coming back, every bone in body seemed to turn to butter. His wife scooped him up and rode him to Paris. He's there now, I bet, under the Eiffel tower, sitting in a café, stirring his coffee, his mind twisting itself round the idea of Aurelie and the thought of him, big man grown small, will be enough to cure me of any broken heart I might catch my life long.

"I think it's crazy."

"When a thing is so crazy you can't hardly believe it but still you do," Tantie said, "then it's the truth. It all fits together, I see it, all the pieces like scrambled egg settling back to plain white and yolk as I think about it. Simple as an unshelled egg."

"It would be one big coincidence," I said, seeing my

aunt getting upset and not wanting to push her edge over.

"Not a coincidence," Tantie shook her head. "It's fate, it's destiny. It's logical as that."

"I don't think you should tell Aurelie."

"She got a right to know."

"Yeah, but maybe she ain't ready for the shock of it."

Tantie thought this over. "I gonna prove it. Not for myself, 'cause I know, but for you. For Nina Ella. I gonna find me some evidence, some fact." There was an electric rustle of wrapper. Tantie sank her jaws into a Nestlé Lion Bar.

"Since when you eat that?"

"You know what?" Tantie said "I'm getting too old to be fighting other people's wars. From now on, I'm fighting my own."

"Except for the National Museum of Black History," I said.

"Except for that," Tantie agreed.

If only silence.

If only there could be an unknitting of words

and the songs in my head could dissolve

like footprints under a resolute tide.

Back home, the sea was black, the sky was grey

the only trees too busy clinging

to rock with bony roots

to grow too many leaves.

The sun rose pale and clouded and set

fraying round the edges like an addled egg.

On rainy afternoons spittles lashed the shoreline and I imagined this, tonight: the heat of the stage lights, smoke curling up at me

and a silence waiting for me to fill it up tight

sweet and brimful.

I fancied hitting a note and holding it,

but I ain't got the gas for that these days

now I sing myself hoarse and dream of the sea

black and the grey sky and the only trees too busy clinging.

Nothing changes.

I'm still an island

lonely as an urchin in a rockpool

waiting for the tide to come back in and screaming.

The air is thick, I only hold my head above water

and hope this time someone will hear me.

Every note carries with it

into the sharp wind a small piece of me,

Is it better to stay silent?

I'm dying in slow motion and still they encore.

And where's my bounce? Where's my beat, my hook?

Why can't someone write me a clear chord progression?

All this jazz!

Every living being is a social fossil. We carry in our behaviours, our attitudes, our very beliefs, traces of the people and systems that shaped us.

Jack Morea, *The Theory of Soul*

Times and places unknown

Agie straightened her hair, tissue paper wrapped around the ends and the irons pulled down with a sputter. She heard me through and then she said, "You can't come here asking me what I think and think you're consulting the black community."

"I don't," I said. Of course I did.

"Mary got every right to be angry. Every right. She gave you her lecture on cultural oppression?"

"Yes."

"And a dozen more, I'll bet. Well, you had it coming, that's a long time been coming. Pass me that oil." She shook her hand, bangles jangling at a jar. I handed it to her.

"It's stupid," I said, "they're just things."

"That all it is to you? You making a whole lot of noise for just things."

"It's my job she's losing me here."

Mary thought she was clever but she couldn't hold more than two ideas in her head at one time: right and wrong, black and white. Confidence of a continent she had, and as immovable, but instead of doing some good in the world she was always out to cause some trouble. Agatha tipped her head to the side, looked at me in the mirror. She'd heard me mouth off about the museum one time too many to have much sympathy.

"Well what does she want – that we just throw them away? What's that going to change?"

"Well now, maybe you're right, but what you got to understand is, a thing ain't just a thing; the past, it ain't just something that happened, you know? And Mary been through all sorts lately."

Mary would sooner change the planet than look at herself, I thought. We'd all been through all sorts, but you didn't see me trying to bring the world to heel like it was my own personal lap dog. I folded my arms. "Racist, that's what she said. Racist. Because of coffee cups."

I caught Agatha smiling before she could help it.

"Mary wants to think of a new insult," I said, "she's been handing out the same old shit for too long now."

Agatha gave me a look that made my shoes seem interesting. She could cuss like a professional, but she wasn't about to put up with it from me. I said, "It's not our fault, it's not like we invented history. We do our best. It's a good museum."

"Don't let Mary catch you saying that."

"I said it to her face."

Agatha gave me a look full of new respect. "And?"

"She looked at me like I'd slapped her. So what, she practices that look in the mirror, I bet; she wasn't any more surprised than if I'd said I liked my toast with margarine. *It's a public disgrace, is what it is*, she says. Well, the world's a disgrace to her."

"Well now that ain't quite how I'd put it, which ain't to say it's not true, but," Agatha blotted her lipstick, pressing down on a sheet of Kleenex, "she entitled to her opinion."

"All the problems in the world and she's picking on this. What happened to the blue whale? What happened to free elections in Burma? She's not been right since Jimmy."

Agatha burned her little finger on the tongs and

cursed. There was a minute of blowing at fingers and looking for germoline. Then she opened a pot of blush. "Come here girl. You any good with this stuff?"

I stood behind her, brush in my hand.

"Mary's alone now." Agatha said.

"She's got you and Georgie. And –"

"You think that's the same? Listen, Helena, it don't matter how full it is at Zambezi and how many arms she got wrapped round her; in her heart, now Jimmy's gone, she's alone."

I drew thick stripes on Agatha's cheek.

"And I tell you something else, which I ain't even said to her, no, and not to George neither, but I don't think when Jimmy was alive she ever give up on the idea of moving out to Kenya. Course, Jimmy wasn't having any but still I don't think she'd given all up on the idea of it. You know she wrote to his sister?"

I shook my head.

"Course you don't. 'Cause wasn't even Jimmy knew about it. But there you go." Agatha nodded as if things all made sense now. She turned back to the mirror.

"What's that got to do with –?"

"Damn, girl, what you done to me?" Agie snatched the brush back off me and set about toning down the blush. "Mary's not going back to Texas, is she now, and she ain't got no other place to go on to, so if this here town is going to be her home, then it's going to have to pay her some attention. Not for Zambezi, not for the cooking, but for herself. Mary just wants her feelings to be taken some account of, and it would have been nice when you and Merg Merton putting your little display together if you'd thought past the end of your noses and remembered we not all looking at things from the same angle and what's no kind of deal to you is a very big deal to some." Agatha admired her cheekbones. "Mary just wants a little smoothing over. You know, half the time I don't think she mean to pick a fight, but people getting all so defensive, well it brings it out of her sometimes is all."

"It was just a display, really, if you'd seen it, the coffee house thing, it was just –"

"Listen. You open you eyes and what do you see?"

I gave a half-shrug, not daring a full one, "I see what's in front of me."

"Exactly. You see what's there, you see what's in front of you," Agatha spritzed perfume on her bosom, "But Mary see more than that, she see what's behind what's in front of her, and what's behind that, it's all joined up, see, for Mary."

"You have to let it go sometimes."

"But see she's not angry because of what your great-great-great-to-the-power-of-ten-grandfather did two hundred years back. She's angry with what you doing now."

"Which is what?"

"Acting like the world began the day you got yourself born. Acting like history is something that's been and gone and is dates and places but not people, like feelings don't count for nothing if you can't stick them behind glass and charge people to look at them." She came over to where I sat on the bed. One eye made up four glitzy shades of plum, fat lick of kohl and armoured lashes stating her intention, the other bare and beautiful. She held my hand. "Things happened Helena," she said, "and the consequences of that happening ripple through times and places unknown to them what's responsible. Ripple through my whole life, if only you knew it, right through to today and right through this conversation. You asking me what you have to do to put an end to it? Well I don't know. You want me to pinch you, wake you up? You think I haven't tried that before now? There won't ever be an end to it. There's folks still bleeding. Meanwhile we got Helena Jones telling us it's not her job to give out Band-Aid." We sat there for a moment, a half-moment, and then she stood and got busy with the eyeliner. Agatha looked at me straight. "You came here today so I'd tell you not to feel bad," she said. She didn't tell me not to feel bad.

I walked back home, dodging the drunks out of Market Tavern, and thought about what Agatha had said. I didn't even know why I was fighting Mary, not really. Merg was practically as old as Gag and needed putting out to pasture, and though I never could leave as long as his retirement plans relied on him being able to hand over to me, I needed something more than that place. I felt it now, the smallness of it. Sometimes I'd see people round the town, people I grew up with, pushing prams or arm in arm, and there's me, still playing in the doll's house. At the same time, the museum was the one thing I had that went back past the last two years. I could go to work each morning and shut the door on the world, forget about whatever operation Mum was having that day, or anything in the real world and disappear into a place where everything was arranged just the way I saw fit, catalogued and cross-referenced and certain. It's something I am good at, the past. I'm sure my parents told me stories, but the tales I remember are the ones I told them. Both of them, in the end, my mum and dad, right at the end, they didn't ask any more for the future; they wanted to be tucked up in the past and I could do it and I used to think it mattered, keeping the past and passing it on, remembering – but it's someone else's past. Someone else's treasures I'm guarding.

***

When I got home Troy was asleep on the sofa, muddy footprints on the rug and his caterpillars on the armrest. I shut the door with a bang and, when that didn't work, poked him with the *Radio Times*.

"Helena!"

I knew right away he'd been drinking. "What are you doing here?"

Troy approximated the vertical, "We're twins," he said, all solemnity.

"Apparently," I said.

"And do you know how many twins there are in the world?"

"Tell me," I said.

Troy let fly a belch that told the whole sorry story of his evening, beers, liquor, weed and vomit. "What I mean is

— we're unique, I mean —" he stood up flamboyantly, arms outstretched as if about to conduct the Philharmonic. Then a pained expression took hold of his face and he stumbled back into the sofa. "We're twins," he said lamely. "They chucked me off the course."

"Oh," I said. "Why? I mean, exactly?"

"I missed a few —" Troy belched again.

"Essay deadlines? Lectures? Fees?"

"Yeah," he said.

"Are you OK?"

"Not really."

"Yeah. Well. You'll get over it." Troy always got over stuff; there was vaseline between him and the rest of the world.

"What would you know?"

"I'm just saying you'll find something else."

"What if I don't want to find something else?"

"Then you'll hang out here until I kick you out and then I suppose you'll hang around Gag's until she boots you and then one day, who knows, you might even grow up."

"I think I'm going to spew."

I was going to tell him not to be so melodramatic, but he was limping already towards the en-suite, and

I put the radio on to cover the sound of him heaving. Troy got like this, sometimes, after too much to drink: sentimental about the shared DNA. There was a deep vein of schmaltz in that boy. He'd been a sweet kid, I could admit that much, I supposed, and he wasn't a bad brother, just a bloody annoying one, whose feet smelled and who got life caught round his head sometimes but who really shouldn't have got to me the way he did. It wasn't Troy's fault, this space between us, the fact of our difference. I shouldn't blame him if, where I expected a looking-glass image, he was a funfair mirror, showing me flaws I didn't know I had, proving, just by being himself, that I couldn't blame my shortcomings on genetics or on Mum and Dad. Troy, so completely, so determinedly, so obviously different, proved there was no alibi for any of it, which left me with the possibility that I was like this because I somehow chose to be. I could just as easily be Troy.

I boiled a kettle and tipped the crumbs of a coffee jar into a mug. Troy came into the kitchen, the whites of his eyes darker than his skin. "Are you OK?" I said.

"Fine," said Troy.

"Did you hear from Gag?"

"A postcard."

"The naked fireman?"

"No. A volcano. She sent you porn?"

I gave Troy the postcard I'd stuck to the fridge. Troy looked at it a moment, turned it over then said, "I didn't even know she was allergic to avocado."

I gave him his coffee black.

"All this stuff about Paris." I said. "Do you think any of it is, you know, actually true?"

Troy shrugged, "Have you got any biscuits?"

"Crackers."

"Cheese?"

"Out of luck."

We went to sit in the lounge. Troy put a CD on, one of mine. We sat for a while. In between tracks I could hear a tap he'd left dripping in the bathroom. "What if we rented it?" I said.

"What?"

"The house. What if we rented it out?"

"It's Mum and Dad's house."

"Yes, but –"

"What are you saying, H?" Troy took any reference to their actual death as a personal affront.

"I'm saying, maybe you should care a little bit more about how I feel than how Mum and Dad would've, could've, should've felt, you know?"

Troy slumped back in the sofa. The problem was we'd been living in the conditional for so long now, we were having trouble adjusting to straightforward present.

"Have we still got Hungry Hippo?"

"I dunno. Somewhere."

Troy sprang up, all arms and legs, and ran up the stairs three at a time. I heard him in the loft and then he came back, Hungry Hippo held triumphantly. We lay on our fronts on the rug, the game between us, like we used to and played best of three. He thrashed me so we made it best of five. He still won.

"You know I don't think kids appreciate just how totally cool it is being a kid."

I was about to say that I hadn't noticed Troy had ever stopped being a kid. But I didn't. I looked at the shadow of our heads on the far wall, the two of us alone in that big house and I said, "Yeah."

"Maybe I should move back in here, it would be –" Troy was all legs and elbows on the floor; he put his hand on my shoulder, awkward, "We're twins, Helena, we can –"

"Things can't go back though, can they? I mean – we've got to get on with life." I didn't sound enthusiastic.

What did normal people do? I could hardly remember a time when there weren't hospital trips at all hours, chemo come-downs, and what was I getting on with? I never even bought those shoes, the red patent ones; never got so far as pressing my nose up against the shop window. "Anyway, how things were, that was never that great, was it?"

"I suppose."

"Overall, you and me, Troy, we've got more to look forward to than back on, don't you think?" I paused. I wanted to squeeze his hand but he'd wiped his nose on the back of it.

"H?"

"What?"

"I'm sick of fighting."

I didn't know what to say. I'd always thought Troy had rather enjoyed it. "Me too," I said.

"Why do you always do it then, hey?" Troy reached out and put his pukey hand on my head and ruffled my hair.

I pulled away.

"What've I done now?"

"You're the one who picks fights."

"Am not."

"Are too. You enjoy it."

"Why do you have to be like this?"

"Why do you?"

And so we went on. Variations in B minor of the same fucking row we'd been having our whole life. That's twins for you; that's brothers and sisters. Each wanting to be their own person, needing to stick together. We went on, going for soft spots, showing no mercy, until Troy stormed out, tripping over his own feet on the way.

It ain't what you do it's the way that you do it
That's what get results

The truth ain't a number

Tantie's blouse was pressed with blade-sharp creases. Her hair was Tefal straight and her make-up showed she was a woman who didn't believe in compromise. She'd pinned on every ribbon she could find: World Aids Day, Drop the Debt and Colon Cancer. She was a maypole of resistance. "How do I look?" she said.

We waited in the lobby of the town hall till they called us in to the meeting, Tantie scrutinising the portraits of DWEMs that hung about the place. She had a list of signatures to back her up (that chilli chocolate cake of hers could get results) and an acronym – my aunt was always happiest when she was representing something bigger than herself, and now she was self-declared Chair of the Black British Memorial Society (BBMS).

Tantie gave her attention to the three worthies that had sprouted like mushrooms over night in the square when the council changed, back in '87. After four vandal attacks (not a one of them traced back to the kitchens of Zambezi) the statues had been moved inside. Tantie circled them, snorting in an exaggerated fashion; there was Maximus Eyre, slightly lopsided, Gulliver Sykes, astride a mare, and Heribert Hubermaier, his chiselled trousers billowing in an imaginary breeze. Gulliver Sykes had invented a mechanised loom that created employment for thousands of previously idle children. Heribert Hubermaier had fought and won in the African colonies, quelling rebellion, outlawing barbaric practices and spreading the word of God behind him like a fart. And Sykes, well, he was just rich and white and dead. Tantie couldn't keep a lid on her disrespect. I eyeballed the ceiling as Tantie let a bit of drool spill on Heribert's foot just as Jenny Finch (roots and perm both needing doing) and Merg (carrying her handbag) came in the door. Tantie shook her head as they passed, Merg half-shrugging as Jenny swung past, her neck stretched, her chest inflated, as if to show her deep, irreversible, damn it, her pathological disapproval of people like us.

"Did you see that? Twenty years I been here and it still don't feel like home," Tantie said. I knew what she meant, and I wondered sometimes what it was, why we never could sit snug with everybody the way we wanted. Tantie took a deep breath and screwed her fists together, "Well it's time this place got to roll over Beethoven, make a little space for me." She looked at me, I smiled back. She wasn't fighting for a principle, or for Jimmy's memory, she was fighting for a space and a place that she could call home. And I'd come along not caring a piece for museums of any persuasion but just wanting to make things right for her after all she'd been through.

The all of us sat in the Great Hall, lined up along one side of wooden table: Merg and Jenny, Helena, Tantie and me and, opposite us, sat the council chairman, a thin red-haired man called Colin Sowter, whose plum trees Helena and I used to use as goal when we played down the street about a million years ago. "You've all got a copy of the agenda," Colin Sowter said. "There's a lot to cover so –Yes, Mrs Tebiah?"

My aunt was waving her bangled arm in the air, "I have an objection."

"As you'll see from the agenda," Colin said, "everyone

will have the opportunity to discuss their various objections in due course —"

"No, no," Tantie said. "I have an objection to the agenda."

Merg poured himself a cup of tea.

Jenny Finch snapped a custard cream in two.

Colin Sowter raised one ginger eyebrow.

"Says here I get five minutes."

"Both proposals will get an equal —"

"Both?"

Jenny let a custard cream dissolve on her tongue and spun a new solitaire round her finger.

"Lord, there's wars been fought, there's people bled and died ain't nobody got to the bottom of, and all it's worth to you is five minutes?" Tantie waited for a reaction that didn't come. "Well," she said quieter, so only we could hear, "it's a one in two, anyhow, fought longer odds than that and won."

"Or," said Helena, under her breath and giving her flattest smile, not forgiving Tantie yet for losing her her job, for the museum was being shut down, that much was agreed, "they'll turn you both down and give the lease to Starbucks." She gave Tantie a look as if the global onslaught of coffee outlets was her responsibility entirely.

Helena and Tantie was a problem. I'd tried to think of a solution that, like separating yolk from white and turning the one to meringue, the other to custard, would leave both my aunt and my friend sweet. The truth was, like a piece of shell in your favourite pudding, some things are without remedy. I let them fight it out in catty looks and sharp remarks.

Eventually Tantie allowed herself to be reassured that there was no conspiracy in the order of speakers, and allowed Jenny to load up her slides.

"Here we go," Jenny gave us all a thick smile. "Here's the idea," she said. "A museum of famous local personages." She widened her eyes at Merg in a pre-arranged signal and the slide changed. "Sykes and," another look, another grainy black and white, "Eyre. Hubermaier, of course." She flicked through her slide show, doled out handouts of pie charts and spreadsheets, and next to me I felt Tantie relax. I could even hear her humming, her fingers waggling on the table, thinking this was no kind of competition at all.

"The idea has the full backing of the Historical Society," Jenny said, and I almost felt sorry for her. Tantie could have her – never mind for breakfast – Tantie could have her like swallowing a fly.

I watched Merg going at his glasses with his cardigan sleeve, squinting at Jenny in the sunlight. He'd got a life sentence with that one. I mean, Tantie could have found enough chillies needed seeding and enough peas needed shelling to keep twenty Jimmys running round after her for an eternity, but see, at the bottom of it was love, and what was at the bottom of Merg and Jenny? A fondness gone sour like milk, and you could see it in his pinched expression, his permanent bad-smell look, this was something way out-of-date.

"With the millennium," Jenny was still full flow, "I think everyone realises it's time to think about our cultural heritage in a new —"

"What's with this our cultural heritage?" Tantie had been quiet for far too long, "ain't no cultural heritage of mine. And don't get me going on the millennium," she said.

"Yeah," I said, "believe me. Don't get her going on that."

Tantie had a lungful, "Everybody looking for the millennium. All looking for that day that's gonna set everything back to zero, fresh start, nothing on the clock, all born again with sins forgiven. A day's a day like any other but if you ain't got God, and you incapable of saying sorry, what you got? You got the millennium."

Helena gave a hysterical cough.

"Mary," Jenny said, all huff, "Our museum," You'd think she passed the thing in her stool she sounded proud enough, "will be open to all people, black, white, yellow, green."

"Well," said Tantie, "I will leave the yellow and green people, whoever they are, to argue for themselves, but I would like to know how many famous local black personages is going to be in this thing of yours. Me and Agatha, let me tell you, we invented being black in this town." Tantie had a point. "Sounds like you just painting lemons and calling them oranges. This museum no more representative than the last."

"Jenny doesn't have a quota," Merg explained. "Decisions will be made according to merit, black, white, as you say —" Merg caught Tantie's eye and cut himself short.

"So what black people you got?"

"Well that would be for Colin to —" Merg was looking like he wished he didn't open his mouth. Jenny was looking like she felt just the same about it.

"Who you got?" Tantie was rocking on the back two legs of her chair.

"Statistically speaking it's –"

"The truth ain't a number, boy, so let's talk about names and places."

Merg made like a goldfish.

Tantie turned on Jenny then, "Is you proposing this or ain't you? Don't go passing your own farts off on others. You putting these people in or ain't you?"

"It depends –"

"Everything depends with you, don't it? On what, I'd like to know? On what. Who you think you are, deciding who worth remembering and who forgotten?" I wondered if my aunt was going to run through the entire canon of Black Martyrs.

Merg stepped away from the projector and took refuge behind the table, more at ease with a quarter ton of oak between him and Tantie. "I don't want this to become political," he said.

"Well that's a shame, 'cause guess what? You start talking about hierarchies and history and who's in and who's out and it gets political faster than milk boiling. I don't want no library of famous personages, full of has-beens and never was-es. I can't stand to hear another word 'bout any of those fools never did a thing but make money for theyselves. You hear me? You should do. I'm paying your wages. I want something for the all of us. Black history ain't just for black people no more than a art gallery only for them what paint. How's things ever going to change when we passing on the same old shit that stinks? What you think of that, Merg Merton? Tell me. What do you think of that?"

Merg and Tantie looked at each other. Looked so long that people began marking the look, if you know what I mean. He was green like spring tomatoes and Tantie was mango – ripe and ready for chutneying, sweet as she was and fine as cream gravy. I'd been seeing Merg as long as I could remember but I never really gave him my attention. Seemed to me then that Merg was a man could have done something in the world, with a smart head on him and a sharp tongue. But he'd hid himself away, held his breath and swallowed his own farts, never having a passion lasted longer than a B-side. Merg was a good egg but when he was gone, wasn't a person would bother telling his tale. A story needs a point to make, a middle after the beginning and after the middle an end and Merg must have been touching seventy and no further on in life than once-upon-a.

Life's a mudpool but it's no good trying to stay out of it. I was covered in top to toe dirt, so filthy with life by five years old it didn't matter what I did after, I'd never get clean as Merg kept himself. Tantie smiled at Merg, and it wasn't pity exactly but she was glad to be she; glad, no matter the hardness of the thing, to be made that way. First time since Jimmy I'd say she looked pleased to be alive: pure flesh, fat and sassy like a hog in slops and her laugh broke out then, like a baby on bourbon and Merg coloured up like a schoolgirl.

Jenny saw the look, like we all did, that went between Merg and Tantie. She moved her head from side to side slowly, "The irony of it. I mean, an American, coming over here, lecturing us about cultural imperialism." She chuckled, her laugh like a teaspoon rattling in an empty coffee cup.

Tantie's nose twitched.

Colin seemed suddenly to get the joke, "Yes, that is rather the pot calling the kettle black!"

Merg whispered something from the side of his mouth.

"What? Oh. I see," Colin caught Tantie's eye and busied himself with his papers. "Not black in the racial sense, obviously."

"Obviously," Tantie said.

Jenny smiled, "What I mean to say is, it isn't Merg and I who are racist."

Tantie threw her eyes at Jenny, "All of this just a way to pass the afternoon for you, ain't it? All of this a change from scones for you, and strawberry jam. People have died trying to fight for the right to black history. People been imprisoned, you calling Martin Luther King a racist, you calling my Jimmy —"

"Of course she's not," said Merg, but his voice had a wobble to it and it wouldn't have taken more than a breath to unseat him.

No one looked at us. Jenny said, her face screwed up as if the light shining from Tantie's self-made halo was getting in her eyes, "I think we're getting a little hysterical, now Mary."

"I wish you were, Jennifer Finch, I wish you were." But it wasn't Tantie back-chatted her, it was Merg, looking at her like he'd never really seen her before. Jenny buttoned her mouth and felt for her diamond.

Colin started putting his papers back in his bag. "I feel a touch of migraine." He looked at Tantie like she was a rat in his runner beans. "Leave your details with me, Mrs Tebiah. All proposals will be considered, according to the criteria."

Tantie lay her forehead down on the table. I saw her shoulders rise and fall. I'd always thought, seeing Jimmy roll his eyes behind her back, or tease her, that Tantie was carried forward on her own momentum, but she needed a straight man, Tantie did, she needed someone standing in back. As for me, for the first time I felt a little of that fire in my own belly, felt like there was more than a line on a family tree held me and Tantie together. "And who's going to consider the criteria?" I said.

"The criteria are agreed," Colin said.

"Yes," said Jenny, "the criteria were agreed some time ago. They're approved."

Everyone looked at us. I knew what they were doing better than they did. They were wishing themselves back to a time before people like Tantie and I existed. They were hankering after the good old days before mongrel offspring and mouthy black women. They weren't interested in history, just in their version of it, the one that reassured them that even if today was farrago, right all snarled with wrong, things not wanting to stay where you put them, even if these days you couldn't be sure of anything, there was a time with a beginning and an end, there were lists, dates and numbers. They'd written that version so well they seemed to have forgotten it wasn't ever real; there were gaps you could fall down and never come out of again.

"You make me wonder, you do," I said and Colin turned, wary, "the all of you, you make me wonder how it can be we all people, all made up of the same things and the lot of us ain't got a thing in common. We as different as salt and sugar. And I look in the future and I see people like you, Colin, and you, Jenny Finch, and I tremble. I shake. Here we are, the century's dying, it's on its knees and the all of us should be glad to let it go, the shame it's seen, instead of which you're trying to prop it up." They could have gone through that door, let it swing shut behind them, left me talking to frescoes and men on horses and Tantie curled up like a hedgehog for a long winter. They didn't dare. They knew it like I knew it. I was coming up fast behind them. "Your time is over, you hear me, it's gone and I'm dancing on your coffin, baby, I'm driving in the nails with my hotstepping feet."

Colin gave a dry laugh. His hand was on the door.

"I want a vote," I said.

He stopped. "A what?"

"A vote. Jenny's idea or Mary's."

"Young lady," said Colin, "this isn't a democracy."

"Ain't no law 'gainst expressing an opinion."

I didn't know what I was doing, but I saw the way things were going and I saw Tantie and me were never going to win; whatever pride we had would have to be in the way and the fact of the fighting. And I saw Tantie there, all the sass and gas gone out of her, with slurs against her name and I looked round the room, did a quick head count and gambled on a moral win.

"Who votes for Mary?" I said. "Who votes for something new? Something make people sit up, take notice, something not been done before?" I stuck my hand straight up. "Well come on people I want to see some hands in the air!"

Slowly, hardly daring, Tantie's hand went up, then Helena's. Then Merg's.

Merg and Jenny stood across the table from each other; Jenny's mouth fell open in surprise, Merg blinking dry and hard. Something had broken between them in that moment. The rock on Jenny's finger, the B&B in Barnstaple; they'd pulled too hard on something that wasn't strong enough to bear it. It was clear as sunrise, Merg's shock at discovering that, for all her flesh and bosom, for all her milk and cream complexion, and her voice soft as ice-cream, Jenny was hard. She was granite. And it was bright as midday sun, Jenny's astonishment that beneath Merg's stiff, dry old grasshopper exterior, there was a beating heart that couldn't be tamed.

They looked at each other, and Jenny looked away first and Merg kept staring for a moment, his dry eyes filling up, and said, "The world isn't the place that it was, Jennifer, but what can you do but roll with it?"

Love will make you drink and gamble
Make you stay out all night long
Love will make you do things
That you know is wrong

Something like nothing

With ten days to go, after the worst row and the whole of it before the congregation, Mom encouraging them to take sides, and the choir giving a chorus of alleluias every time she hit a home run – Mom called the wedding off. If you ask me, it wasn't any of the vicar's business what Mom chose to wear, so long as she and Bob were happy, which they were, and no reverend had business excommunicating people left-right all because of a weakness for plunge neck. "Why did God give me them if he didn't want me to show them off?" Mom had said. "Forty years old and those things still getting her in trouble," Tantie had muttered. The happy couple had threatened eloping to St Lucia for a weddingmoon:

unlimited rum cocktails, all-you-can-eat buffets between the hours of noon and midnight and a Jacuzzi bath in the en-suite, but they'd settled for a civil do at the Town Hall after Bob's mom had refused to contemplate a twelve-hour flight.

In place of hen and stag dos and all that his-and-hers-ism, they'd called a BBQ at Bob's the night before, but a bad-tempered rain-shower (all grumbling thunder and sulky clouds – I ain't going to dignify it none by calling it a storm) had driven us indoors. It was the kind of a day that ought to be sunny but lay down and refused to try. Son Son, much recovered, Bo, Diddy, Tantie and Bob and Mom sat round Bob's kitchen table, picking at salad, listening to Lee Perry and arguing over the chances of the rain clearing and the temperature picking up. Even with an inch of rain laying in the back yard Mom was refusing to give up on the BBQ and use the electric grill; Bob looked mournfully at the trays of uncooked meat.

People started with a game of cards while Mom went up to pack for the honeymoon and I helped Bob with the dishes. Cody and Elise, his kids over for the night from their mom's, were running round, Bob and I were still dancing like cousins (manoeuvring clumsily, desperate not to tread on one another's toes and keener still not to get too close) around the fact that come another forty-eight hours he'd be my step-dad.

The last months over, as we'd got to see an off-stage Bob, an unscripted, un-black suited Bob, without lyrics crafted over the years by wise heads and wounded hearts, I'd found out he had been keeping a mighty big secret from his Blooz Hot colleagues all those years. You see, when he wasn't singing the sorest blues you could catch in our parts, Bob had a whole other nine-to-five identity. He was an accountant over at Price and Hart (Mom had been keeping that one quiet from Tantie) and besides that, he let the drawl (which always had caused me to wonder, since I knew where Bob grew up, and I don't think Essex is what they mean by Deep South) drop once he got a microphone out of his hand, and he spoke the Queen's best English, as proper as Jimmy ever was, all long vowels and consonants tighter than blue jeans on Brad Pitt.

While Bob put the girls in the bath, I went to help Mom. She'd laid out maybe a dozen bikinis on the bed and lingerie in varieties I think only came from a specialist store. Opened out on the bed was the blue jumbo case Bob had bought her. I watched her for a moment before she saw me. She looked up and smiled.

"You planning on taking any clothes?" I said.

"Clothes?" Mom laughed, her shoulders, her bosom rising up and down, "and for what?"

Bob's house, a three-bed new build, had as much soul to it as baked beans, but you know what? Mom loved it – loved its neat boxiness, the dado rail and the pile on the carpet, the roses trellising in the back garden, she told me, as she folded tissue paper between layers of lace and ribbon in the case. "All these things – him shaving in the morning while I'm taking a shower, or us washing our teeth together, spitting at the same time, you know, little things. But Lord, Georgie, it's fine. It's fine. He's fine." Then she said, "You can move in here, though, there's plenty room, and I run it by Bob and he says, well he says what I say: you don't need to be stopping with Tantie no more, unless –"

"I'm just fine with Tantie, Mom."

"But you ain't still –"

"No I ain't still."

"Mad at me?"

"No." I slipped behind her and wrapped my arms around her middle.

"I couldn't stand to go away with you mad at me. And I was thinking, this last month, even with Jimmy and all, I've felt so —" she balled her fist at her heart — "I don't know."

"Happy," I said. "It's called being happy. It's called love." I pinched a roll of fat on her waist, "It's called Bob."

"Sure some of it's Bob, but it ain't just Bob. That night in Paradise, it's like — you know?"

"Yes," I said, "I know."

"But I done wrong by you, I know that."

"What?"

"Your father."

I unpeeled myself from Mom and wrapped my arms around myself.

"But things is more complicated than you can imagine, you know it wasn't a matter of just giving you a name, there was — things were complicated. You think you're all grown up, I understand that, but to me, to me, Georgie —" Mom ran a finger up and down my arm. "That night with the doughnuts. You took me by surprise. I did what I always did do, I played dumb. And once I started not telling you, I couldn't stop, and the more you asked, it just got bigger and bigger until the truth didn't seem up to the job." Mom scooped up the rest of the pieces and dumped them in the case. She folded over the top of the case and sat down on the bed beside it. Through the wall I could hear Elise and Cody splashing in the bath.

"So –" Mom felt her way through the pause, "this thing with your father. Georgie, I can't give you a name –"

I shrugged, "It's OK – I thought it was something like –"

"It was something like nothing. Hear me out. It was something like nothing. I wasn't no margarine-legs like Mary." Mom played with the zip on her case. "I met him that first time down at Blue Hole. I used to go there mornings before Momma woke up and after Tantie got back from the bars. Felt like a place didn't belong to no one else so I made believe it belonged to me. Down at Blue Hole, if you got there chasing the sun, you could have the place to yourself. No one staring when you walked down the street. No trouble to be found. I'd kick off my shoes and sometimes, if the sun had been up long enough to warm the water, I'd swim a while. So one morning I went down and there he was, I caught him skimming stones across the pool, and I stood and watched him a while. He could send a stone a mighty long way across that water, and as I never could throw a ball nor a stone myself, it was kind of mesmerising."

"Was he at your school?"

Mom shook her head.

"Which school? We could find him!"

"He wasn't a kid, Georgie," Mom squinted at me, "He was maybe thirty. He was maybe forty."

Mom's hands were playing with the folds in her neck. "I didn't look fourteen, Georgie – hell I don't think I *ever* looked fourteen," she laughed. "Just went straight from nine to nineteen overnight."

"And he didn't ask?"

"No," Mom smiled. "He didn't ask me anything. And I didn't ask nothing of him. It happened, and after that morning it happened often times. Some mornings he'd be there and some mornings not and some mornings we'd skim stones across the pool, or swim, but we didn't talk. That's what I loved about Blue Hole: in that silence you could hear something you couldn't hear no place else. You could hear what you never would hear back in Georgetown with everyone whispering right behind your back and in your face too and under your nose. At Blue Hole I could hear myself think. And I could hear him think. And it was beautiful, Georgie, the first beautiful thing had happened to me, the sun on my skin and the blue of the water – Blue Hole they call it and it's so blue, doesn't look like water so much as – melted sky."

Mom sat on the bed, my head on her lap and her fingers twisting curls from my hair. "Then —" Mom sighed.

"He stopped coming?"

"He stopped coming."

I squeezed Mom's knee.

"I think someone saw us, is truth. Somebody who knew how old I was and how to cause a deal of trouble."

"What kind of trouble?"

"Police trouble. Worst kind of trouble. Do you know what they call it?"

"Call what?"

"Rape. Statutory rape. That's what the policeman said to me. The same policeman from when Daddy — it was the same policeman they sent over. Though it happened all the time. All the time. Rape — and it was the most beautiful thing I had. They didn't know nothing. Their laws don't mean nothing to me. Ain't nothing to do with the heart."

"Did they catch him?"

"I don't know. I guess not but — I never heard a word of him since."

Mom shook her head. She was quiet. I passed her a box of tissues, but she waved them away. There was still something I had to know, that shouldn't have mattered, but did. "Was he white?"

Mom lifted me up from her lap. She drew her shoulders up.

"It's OK if he is," I said, "I mean, I always figured he must be, what with, well, you looking like you and me looking like me."

"Lord, Georgetown, making a baby is not like mixing paint, you know."

"I know but –" I needed to know. "Mom?"

"Yes," she said. "Yes he was."

I took a tissue for myself then, blew my nose.

"You and me Georgie, sometimes we so different I catch my breath. You always wanting from the day you could speak to know why and I never saw that knowing why changed a thing: you believing in beginnings and endings and Br'er Rabbit morals to the story and in all my life I never knew one of them existed outside of a movie. I never yet came to the end of anything more than a bag of sugar; things run into one another. A thing picks up without another one running out."

I shook, with a chill in my gut, I was dizzy. I'd run to Texas and back again, held my head under the waters of the past too long. I looked at Mom, her smart hairdo, the new way she had of wearing her eyebrows. The past is there, solid as a wall, you can't get past it, through it, over it, under it and you'll run up against it over and over, give yourself concussion without ever making a mark on the thing. So what can you do but put your back to it, face out to the front? I'd been scared to turn my back to something when I didn't know what it was, but, Lord, I thought, scared of the future? What's to be scared of? It's what I'll make it. I might find my father, one day, who knew, but I was through with looking for him.

I got home after midnight, Bo walking me back from Mom's to Tantie's and the two of us saying a lengthy goodbye on the doorstep, which hadn't happened a long while. I snuck up the stairs to the flat, but the lights in the kitchen were on and Tantie was sat at the table, a mug of hot milk by her, and on the table a great big box, a wooden one, that I'd not seen before, spilling dust over all.

She didn't look up when I came in. She just sat, contemplating the box.

"What's this?" I said. I sniffed at the milk for brandy. "What's this, Mary?"

"Open it," she said.

"What is it?"

"Just open it."

The lid was stiff where the wood had warped. I had to jam the box between my knees and get my nails right underneath the lid to prise it off. Inside there were photographs, three, maybe four hundred of them, black and white and colour, Polaroids and pictures cut from newspapers, some of them clipped to little scraps of paper or folded or marked, and as soon as the lid was off they were sliding out of the box and onto my lap, these little snaps and mug shots spilled out onto my jeans, and I started. I looked at them, and they looked back at me; they were mug shots, all of them, of girls, little black girls, younger than me, but with years of living on me, every one of them. "Who are they?"

"Nina Ella. You want some milk?"

"No." I still had the Freixenet Son Son had brought bubbling in me.

"You think I gave up on her. You think the whole world's like you, heart on its sleeve, and if a body ain't weeping and wailing then it don't feel a thing. Let me tell you, there's things beyond talking about, there's tears that won't come. Georgie, there's pain like I hope you never know." Mary breathed in and breathed out like she was doing it for the world. "After I married Jimmy, I hired a PI, and when he didn't get lucky I hired me another and another. Six I got through, and three hundred seventy girls."

"And it's none of them?" I said.

"Not a one."

"You sure now?" It seemed to me that Tantie could buy a peace by adopting any one of these girls as her own, who surely needed a home as much as Tantie needed a stomach for those chitlins she'd been cooking, a mouth for those maws.

"Cheats, the lot of them. The PI's I'm meaning."

"And you still think –?"

She had set her heart on Aurelie. "I feel it when she's near," Tantie said, "and when she's far away."

I didn't make the obvious remark that half the town felt the same way or ask why she'd never mentioned this fact when Jimmy was alive. "Soon as I get Nina Ella back, this family can get back to normal."

I knew the opposite was true, for Aurelie had killed Jimmy, letting him play himself into his grave, and broken Sanderson where international legal systems couldn't. Wasn't a one of us would be the same since Aurelie. She brought our dead town to life and what was 'ready breathing, she damn near killed it.

Still, there was one thing Tantie seemed to have forgotten: if Aurelie was her daughter, then Sanderson Miller was the girl's father and things had come to pass between the two of them that shouldn't.

I took Tantie up to bed. Lit some incense to help get her off and checked she'd put the gas, the oven, the iron, everything off. Then I got my jacket and my keys, grabbed my phone, checked I had change and went back out into the night.

Crazy crazy

At Skinny Jack's, even if you weren't looking for trouble, you were pretty much sure to find it. You'd have more problems there with the kids and their knives than you ever would with the heavy-time gangsters had stopped by at Paradise. Aurelie could have sung anywhere. Ronnie Scott's would have taken her, the 100 Club, too, I bet, but in rough water, some people sink, and when Paradise shut, Aurelie came to Skinny Jack's, got up on stage seven nights a week, an hour before the dancers came on, and sang for nothing to men who listened with their eyes, their hands too, if she'd let them. It was a bilious place, an estate dive to the north of town tucked up in the gutter over a hairdresser's; it smelled of peroxide and Lynx.

It was early still when I stopped by, and I got the barman to fix me a white rum and lime. I went back to the sluice room, where someone had pasted a neon star on the door, and I watched Aurelie draw kohl above her eye. She saw me in the mirror and without turning round, without taking her hand from lining her lashes she said, "You know, we've got something, you and me. You looking for your father, me for my mother."

"We got nothing," I said.

Aurelie's dress hung on the doorback. A bowl of fruit balanced on a beer keg. Lilies sprang from the neck of a JD bottle, and there was patchouli smoking on a stack of chairs, but still, urine and bleach won through.

"So what is it then, Georgetown? What've you got that won't wait till morning 'cause you can trade with me anytime and I've a show to give and people waiting."

"Mary's in pieces," I said. I unpeeled gum.

"What you want me to do about it?"

I watched Aurelie arrange her hair, gathering snakes and binding them lifeless. I watched her cover the gloss of her skin with powder. "She's taken a notion to mind," I said.

Aurelie turned, dropped her hip. From the main room I could hear the bass growling louder. There was a hiss of the smoke machine and clouds of dirty vanilla crept under the door. "So?"

"So what are we, just fish in a bowl to you? Mary's in pieces. She had a baby," I said, hardening myself to it. "Back in New York. Twenty years ago. She didn't keep it."

Aurelie shook out a bottle of cocoa butter. "And?"

"And what do you think?" I said.

Aurelie rolled her eyes over me and laughed. She hitched up a skirt and stacked a stilletoed heel on the chair back and set to work the butter in.

"There's rumours about Arii Cook, you know that."

"There's enough rumours about Arii Cook to paper the moon. I didn't have you down for someone who believed in them."

"I don't. It's all flavours of crazy, but you've seen Mary, since Jimmy, you've seen her. And you come around here, stirring things all up together till people don't know, they just don't know what's likely from what's not, and what's worth dreaming – the woman took a notion, is all."

Aurelie stood straight again, wiped her hands on a rag. "What kind of a notion?"

"I'm just saying, if she comes here, shouting it loud, then you set her straight, you hear me Aurelie, 'cause fool she is won't believe it from no one else."

Aurelie looked at me, "Shouting what loud?"

"It was the same hospital, that's all. Arii Cook and Mary. The same hospital, the same month. So you see –"

Her lips fell open. She stood, one hand tight on the chair back, and she stared at me, her eyes all storm. The girl was shaking like she was caught in a monsoon and I went to her, my hands out before me, took her by the shoulders and felt a chill came off of her made me shiver, gave my eyes to smarting, my head to spinning like oxygen was going out of style. We were the same height, me and Aurelie, and I looked at her dead in the eye and I saw something felt like looking at my own soul. It wasn't that her eyes were like mine, or that her cheekbones curved the same way, 'cause they didn't, it was just that underneath the shell of the girl was something past description, something human for the first time, and I felt the possibility of loving this girl like a sister. She put her hand to my face like I was the most beautiful thing in the world, like she'd lived her life in a glass case and I was the first flesh and blood thing she'd held onto and I saw the possibility of a different kind of truth, of miracles and happy endings. But that was the problem, I thought, you hang around long enough with Aurelie and anything seems possible. And it ain't, the world just ain't like that. And then think of what we'd be risking, taking this stray in, not more used to people than a wild thing. What would it mean for Mom and Bob to have the girl rubbing up between the two of them, and where would I be, with this stranger calling my bed home; what would it do to Tantie, seeing her every day? She didn't think Aurelie would be anything more than pleased to see her, but did she think Aurelie was the kind of girl for whom forgiveness came like time of the month?

Oh, it might have seemed logical enough, the one of them crazy for a daughter, the other for a mother, the both of them missing a part of themselves; it might seem logical, Mary and Aurelie finding one another and thinking that they belonged together. You can't blame them for trying to fix a happy-ever-after ending, but things don't come because you call after them, and life got a logic beyond mathematics.

There was a knock on the door and a five-minute call for Aurelie. "There's things beyond rumour," I said, and I pulled away from her, left her holding her arms out empty, her fingers stretched.

"But maybe —" she said.

"There's DNA tests, there's —"

She dropped her eyes. Aurelie fished in her make-up bag, dived beneath the pots and pencils and took a picture out from somewhere, pinned it with one finger on the table in front of me, "I know who my mother is."

I looked at the photo. It was Arii all right but so alive I wouldn't have recognised her, her hair loose about her shoulders and a smile so wide it pulled her Cleopatra nose out of line. It beat the tight-assed beauty queen look and I came as close as I could to seeing her like Aurelie saw her. "There's things get carried on in the blood that you drink in with your milk," Aurelie said. "There's things you wouldn't understand."

People said Aurelie was crazy. Even before she'd come to town, there were stories of her running naked on the machair like a wild thing, rumours that her father had had to have doctors out to look at her. Then there was the way she looked, the way she carried on and the things she said, they were all half-crazy, but so was Billie, so was Nina half the time, it went with the territory, like that was just what you paid for a voice like that. But I heard her then talking about Arii and I saw that she wasn't wild crazy or drunk crazy or crazy in love, she was crazy crazy, didn't know who she was or what she was doing. And soon as I saw that I understood why she'd come back here. I looked in her eyes and saw the worst kind of nothing, a hole that couldn't be filled, that would eat you up from the inside.

"Don't sing tonight," I said.

"What do you care?"

"Sing, if you want to, then. And I'll wait. We'll go back together. We can go to Mary's and in the morning —"

"I got a room booked, Georgetown," Aurelie shrugged.

There was a banging on the door that shook the wall.

"Where?"

Aurelie smiled.

"Not The County. Aurelie, come stay at Mary's. Not The County, not tonight, this is —"

Someone shouted for her to get on stage, made a threat he wouldn't have been able to see through, wouldn't have dared to give if there hadn't been wood between him and her.

"Got to go," she said.

"Aurelie —"

"Go back to your aunt, Georgie. Go back to your mom. Tell Mary —" She checked herself. "Tell her I said she got it wrong."

I nodded. Mom and Bob, Jimmy, Tantie, the all of us, we were nothing to her, just something got caught up in the whirlwind of what the girl really had on her mind. I closed my eyes as she passed by, taking a last check in the mirror. From the next room I heard the shouts of approval, the whistles, as she took the mic. I could have stopped her. I was strong and she was tired, but I let her go. It seemed the shortest and only way to peace for us, and I stood there still in the shadows of backstage, and Aurelie sang like a nightingale does, right before it dies.

*Once we've accepted the theory of the perfect self, it is not
a huge leap to conceive of an individual who, if removed
from the contaminating effects of his or her society, could
achieve his or her perfect self.*

Jack Morea, *The Theory of Soul*

Something in the going

"Cake?" He wore a chewed pair of carpet slippers, a Monty Python T-shirt and held a plate of buttered fruit loaf out towards me. I stood on the doorstep. Jack Morea smelled of tobacco, hair pomade and Swarfega; his teeth were yellow and his eyes milky with age. There was flour in his hair and demerara on his trousers. A cat bowl lay upturned on the doorstep between us. I wish I could say that there was still a trace of something – charisma, genius, full-blown lunacy even – lingering like the smell of sulphur from a spent match, but really there was nothing but chicken liver, cake and *Life of Brian*.

He looked affronted. "What did you expect, hmm?" He left the door wide open on the machair and shuffled through to the back of the croft, "A beard? A white robe?" he mumbled to himself as he disappeared off the hallway. "Bloody Socrates?"

I waited a moment, then followed him through to a small, damp backroom crammed full of junk. A grandfather clock stood marooned in the middle of the room, and every surface battled with the chintzy, worn-out, hand-me-down feel of cheap antiques: gramophone players and cuckoo clocks, rows of soapstone elephants trumpeting along the bookcases, half-drunk cups of tea on the desk and another cat bowl beneath it. Jack Morea shuffled papers on his desk from one pile to another, his back to me. Beneath the liquorish tang of cake, below the mouldy reek of slowly rotting paper were eras of smell that told the story of his exile: the whiff of snuff that lingered, the savour of the leather chaise longue, the stale stench of cigars and brandy and the faint taint of treacle and ash from the sputtering fire. Everywhere, on all the walls, on every surface not covered in clutter, were photos of Aurelie. "I came –" I said.

"There's no need for formalities. Goodness, no." He turned, suddenly the host again, and waved me into a mossy armchair. "Let's skip straight to business, why don't we. You want me to explain the theory, or else you want to explain it to me, or maybe you just want to shake my hand and have your picture taken. I'm a bit like the Loch Ness monster, I gather; people want to see for themselves if I really exist. Well as you can see, I do, very much so, and I also make very good cakes. Excuse me," he heaved himself across the room to an old hi-fi in the corner where he fumbled a cassette into the slot and bathed the room in Viennese waltz. He smiled broadly, laced his fingers together and circled his thumbs round each other, contemplating the spooling tape.

"You get a lot of visitors then?" I said.

"A couple a month, perhaps. Americans mainly, you know how it is." He sat down then on the chair at his desk and leaned towards me confidentially, "Autographs are one and six, by the way, but I don't do photos." He winked, then leaned back. "Yes, it's worse than ever these days. Something called the internet, apparently. Whatever it is, brings them out like – well, like –"

"I'm sorry."

"Oh, you're all right, you're relatively sane. But you must eat your cake, and tell me, what do you think, too much cinnamon?"

I told him no, and he poured out tea in dinky cups and told me about the arthritis in his knee and how therapeutic baking was and asked if I'd visited the Hebrides before and wasn't surprised that I hadn't and then said, through a mouthful of cake (he was shaped like a barrel of port and gave off a curranty smell of his own), "The hermit business was a bad idea – Arii's of course, too many Garbo films – but what choice was there? I can't tell you, the seventies, you wouldn't believe it, after the book, I couldn't go anywhere. And I've always been keen on the sea, but as JD says, worst thing you can do, this hermit thing, for the fans I mean, reverse psychology or some such. Still there's the air. Marvellous air they get round here. And Strauss. But it's not all tea and cakes. I once had – you'll like this – a young man came. Norwegian, of all things, with a gun, can you imagine? More cake? No? I tell you what, I have a little, somewhere," and as I watched, a twenty-four-volume *Oxford English Dictionary* that had sat in an alcove by his desk became a drinks cabinet with a decanter and an assortment of glasses. Jack Morea tipped me a generous serving of ginger wine. "Where was I? The Norwegian, yes, with a revolver. And all for the theory."

There was a pause then, and he looked at me strangely, until I said, "What did you do?"

He nodded. "Oh I made up some old nonsense. I

usually do. Dropped in a bit of Wittgenstein, that always impresses."

It felt a bit tactless, after everything he'd said, to bring up the theory. Now that we'd had cake and tea and ginger wine, it seemed a bit cheap to bring up 1974, and I didn't care to be lumped in with the Norwegian assassin. So we talked about Arii Cook's fans, who he wouldn't open the door to, and about journalists from the Sundays who still turned up in silly season, and the call he'd had from Hollywood. After an hour of it, I said, "About the theory."

"You'd like me to explain it."

"I did wonder –"

"Of course you did, there's no need to be embarrassed. Of course you do." He smiled and shuffled forward in his seat, and I thought it crossed his mind to pat my knee, but he must have thought better of it, because he sat back in his chair and he said, "Everybody does."

"It's just such a good book," I said, coming over all groupie, practically drooling on his slippers, "I mean, since my parents died –" And that was it, the cork popped, and there I was drowning him in the Asti Spumante of grief, I told him all about Troy and Gag and about how until I'd read his book I'd never really thought about what I wanted, or who I was and more than that who I might have been, or believed there was anything more than luck to any of it and when I finally looked at him there he was impersonating indigestion, his face pulled tight, the palm of his hand held out towards me. "The thing you need to understand, my dear girl, the book."

"Yes, yes," I said.

"It isn't what you think it is," he said.

"It isn't?"

"It isn't the answer to all your problems."

I gave a little toss of my head as if I knew this all along, and swilled the last drops of tea round my mug.

"It isn't an answer at all," he said.

"Of course not." My voice like water down the plughole.

"It's a question mark."

I didn't say anything, and Jack twiddled his thumbs again, his head nodding along to Strauss, and he said with an air of great patience that I wanted no part in, "You write a book because, well because you want to ask a question, you want to have a conversation with the world. I didn't write *Theory of Soul* because I thought I knew it all. I mean, I'm not the Pope, I'm not, what do you call him, Dalai Lama. Who am I to be giving out answers?"

I shook my head. "But there's the equation. There's the bit where you say —"

"Oh, good grief." His fingers pushed crumbs around his plate, his hand shook, "It's only a book. One little book and the whole world goes crazy. You'd think people would get over it by now."

"Get over it? It changed my life, almost, at least it —"

"Only until the next fool comes along and changes it back again."

"It changed the world."

"Did it? Well, maybe, for a minute, I suppose that's what you want when you're young, change it before it changes you. Let me tell you, it's impossible. Life's a wheel, young lady, it spins, it turns, it comes round again and the only difference is you get dizzy. Nothing ever really changes."

He turned half round in his chair as he spoke, and he rearranged things on his desk, playing draughts with the old tea mugs and stationery, poking at piles of paper in an effort to give the place some kind of order, but it all looked wonderfully independent of him. His foot was tapping quickly now, and out of time. He didn't offer me another slice of cake.

"Perhaps you could explain it to me, this idea of the

perfect self, how to do it, you know, because like I said, since my parents –" Jack Morea had his back fully to me now, and was reading a water bill at his desk. "Without going into the details," I said, "I've felt as if my life, well, as if it doesn't fit. You know?" I tried again, "As if it's not big enough for me, and I'm trying to make it stretch when really, well, like I said, it's just not the right size."

There was a long pause. Then Jack put the water bill back in his pile of papers and said, "Everyone feels like that."

"Do they? I don't think so." Troy didn't feel like that, I was sure. I supposed Gag missed Paris, or the idea of it, like George missed the idea of her father, but I was the only one who felt quite like me.

"I can't help," he said. "I'd like to, but," he paused, as if coming to the punchline of his favourite joke, "I've forgotten." He threw his hands wide and brought them together, tucking them between his plump little thighs. He looked immensely pleased with himself and engrossed himself entirely with paperwork.

"Forgotten what?"

"All of it. The theory, the book. You assume the self is a continuous thing. That the 'I' of today is the same as the 'I' of yesterday, that memories are like marbles stored in a jar: jumbled, perhaps, but retrievable. But the Jack Morea of 1974 is a stranger to me as much as to you. You might as well ask me to dance the Twist as remember what I might have been meaning twenty-five years ago."

A cat came in at the door, gave a narrow-eyed look of boredom when it saw me then, tail in the air, turned and stalked away. What should I do now? What did *they* do, these other visitors? Did they believe him? The ginger wine and amnesia, it was a low trick. People had responsibilities, I wanted to tell him, you don't just write a book and then disappear off to the Hebrides without so much as an epilogue. You can't just say that you've discovered the secret of happiness and then refuse to elaborate. Getting people's hopes up, all this mumbo jumbo about self-determination and then... I didn't know what these other pilgrims thought, whether they just flung themselves off the cliffs at Tarbert, but I hadn't come there, caught the train, the plane, the ferry, driven a rusty Volkswagen across thirty miles of machair, hadn't come to the end of the earth to be told lies by a third-rate Mr Kipling. I watched him, his toes flexing in his slippers, looking quite relaxed at the end of another performance and I understood the Norwegian with the revolver, I wanted to get my hands on that Nobel Prize of his and beat him over the head, I wanted to shake him, pick him up, hold him by his ankles and shake until all these ideas fell out. "The reason I came —"

"Is no kind of reason at all." He spoke over his shoulder, drawling. I wanted to snatch his stapler and pin his fingers to his stupid desk. "Really, my dear girl, I don't want to hear it. If it wasn't me it would have been Freud. Him or Jesus. The usual suspects. So run along, if you've had your cake."

I put down my mug on a chess set; I pushed my plate, crumbs and all, away. I said, "I know where Aurelie is."

He looked at me then. Turned full round and forgot about bills and his eyes weren't so old any more and that back wasn't stooped and he said, "We all know where she is. You think I don't get papers? You think —" he waved his hand dismissively, the gesture ended limply, "How is she?"

I looked around the room at the pictures of her.

"Never mind," he said, "I know how she is. Homesick." He saw my face, "Oh not for here, for — well, she's another one wants answers. Everybody wants answers these days, nobody wants questions. What's coming to the world, I ask you?"

"What answers? About Arii Cook? About — what happened?"

"Did she send you here?" He was caught between hope and anger and I was surprised to see it, for the man Aurelie described to Mary was cold and hard, and yet here he was, his love flapping about in that room like a bird caught.

I shook my head. "But I can talk to her, I can tell her, if you want, if there's something you —"

He frowned, "There's nothing to say. Nothing I've to say that she'll pay any heed to, nothing she wants to hear that I'm willing to discuss. I ask you, what good will come of it? Who held her first, who found her in that hospital? I did. Held her in my hand like that, in my single hand." He reached out to the silver-framed photo that stood on his desk and he put his fingers up to the glass, "I held the world in my single hand and I saw, all this," he flung his hand at the shelves, "what a fool I'd been. I looked in her eyes, her tiny newborn eyes, like black holes opening up on the world, oh she could swallow you up with those eyes, and when she yawned, she could swallow continents, galaxies. I held her in my hand, fed her, changed her, those first months when all she wanted was — God, and I loved her, and I brought her here, away from the nonsense, the photographers, lies and gossip and all she's ever wanted, all she's ever really cared about, is her mother."

"Maybe if she had — some photos of her, something real, you know. I think she just —"

He rested his eye on the socket of his palm.

"You don't know what it's like out there," I said, "Like you said, about the gossip, people say things, even now, and what's Aurelie to think? If you don't tell her what really happened, what's she to believe?"

"She's not to believe anything at all."

"How's she to know what's true and what's not?"

"Truth?" he said. "Lies?" he said. "The world's not that simple. The truth is what happens when everybody's delusions coincide. My truth, your truth, these are only ever working hypotheses."

I recognised the quote. I knew it was wrong. I saw, for the first time, a glimpse of something poking through between his theory and the place we were.

Jack Morea put his fingers together in front of his nose. He was quiet for a long time, a long time. And then he sat himself up again, like a clockwork toy coming back to life and gave me the smile that he gave on the doorstep and he said, "Well, it's been most pleasant, but you really must be going. Last ferry is in half an hour and you won't have booked a hotel. They never do."

"But —"

"Oh, I'm an ogre, I know. And after you've come all this way." He was manoeuvring me out of the door.

"Please," I said, and I locked my arm across the door frame, in front of him and he turned to look at me. His face was right in mine and he said, loud and shrill, "Go home. Whatever you're looking for, it isn't here. It isn't here or within a hundred miles of this place."

"It has to be here," I said. I couldn't stand to go back. It would be unbearable to get on the ferry, to drive off, no wiser than when I landed, and worse, with the one hope that I'd had taken from me. To go back and watch Gag getting old and sick and dying, and Troy and me fighting, or worse, not fighting, not speaking at all and the museum not, after all, closing down, but going on and on all of it just like always, until I took up my place on the shelf beside the rest of them. I cried.

Jack Morea gave me a hankie. He leaned forward, his elbows on his knees, and he said, "Hundreds of people I've had here, over the years, hundreds; silly young girls like you, sillier boys, and I've fed them cake and made them tea and I've told them all, like I've said to you, that if you're looking to me for an answer, then I can't help you. But here's something, here's something that'll cheer you up."

I angled my chin so my tears would stay in my eyes instead of rolling down my face.

"Nobody's ever come back."

I blinked. "So?"

"So," he said, "think about it. They come all the way here, all that way, and flights aren't cheap, or ferries, and they go home disappointed, tears, some of them, just like you. But they never come back and here's my theory, the only theory you'll get from me. Are you listening? You'll go back, to wherever it is you come from, and nothing will have changed; your job and your boyfriend, your horrendous family, they'll all be just as terrible as ever. But you know what; they'll *seem* different." He smoothed his bristles with the flat of his hand. "Have you read Kierkegaard?"

I shook my head.

"No. Well. Never mind. My point is, there's something in the coming and going back. It changes things. There's something about coming, when all your friends told you not to, said you were mad, in taking the chance, in hoping," his voice deeper, a smile lurking round his face like a child in a sweetshop, "in believing, not in me, but in yourself, in the possibility of something you can hardly understand."

I dabbed at my nose with his handkerchief.

"There's something in the coming and going, there must be," he smiled. "Otherwise, you see, they'd come back."

Aurelie

For my last trick, ladies and gentlemen,
– pay attention at the back – I require
a knife, a box of matches, length of rope,
old newspaper and snakebite antidote.

This never to be repeated feat, (I'll be your headline of the week),
involves no sleight of hand, no puff of smoke,
no dry ice or loaded dice, no conjuring wand or alchemy.
There is nothing in my hands, my palms are empty as starvation.
See.

My grand finale's real flick of the wrist, knife to artery stuff,
no feint, no bluff
So take your places, no more bets.
Watch closely, please, mesdames messieurs.
Watch closely: there will be no encore.

We are, each of us, a mosaic. Unique only in as much as we represent a different patterning of the same tiny fragments. The myth of the twentieth century has been the myth of self-determination. All we can do, any of us, is rearrange the pieces we've been given.

Jack Morea, *The Theory of Soul*

What you remember

We'd decided to tackle the sections in order. We'd demolished roasting on Monday, the trivets were stacked, the smoke-jack dismantled and packed off to store, with dairy and baking finished that morning, leaving only the archives and preserving to clear, and then ourselves — Merg's retirement do at the Cathedral coffee shop kicked off at three and then I transferred to leisure services while the council considered its verdict.

The dust in the store room made Merg sneeze, and besides that he was jumpy, hoping that Jenny would call in to say goodbye before her coach at two, so I took the china and glass and left Merg with the copper pans, spoons and unbreakables.

"Are you making a speech?"

"When?"

"This afternoon, of course. They'll expect it, you know. You might get a pocket watch."

"Parker pen more like," Merg checked the spoon drawer was empty and swore, in his fashion, "This doesn't belong here; who's responsible for this?"

I looked over from beneath my fringe, unenthusiastic about another provenance debate.

Merg dangled a teaspoon between thumb and forefinger, "Eighteenth-century? What do you think, Helena?"

"I don't know. What's the hallmark?"

"I wouldn't have said it was older than me," Merg hoisted himself up in stages, back straight, one knee at a time. "Forties vintage, I'd say, Helena. They'll be putting me in a museum next."

"Merg," I said, "how old are you? I mean –"

"What kind of a question is that?"

"Do you remember the war?"

"The war? Merg blinked. "The *World* war?" He drew his lips together and straightened his spine, "How old do you take me for?" Then he caught me in the ribs with a clipboard. "I tell you what, some of those raids."

But the last thing I needed was more war stories. "Do you remember Gelda?" I said.

"Oh well," said Merg.

"Merg?"

"I was only six or seven."

"But you remember her."

"Of course." He shook his head, and I noticed how stiff he was these days, as if he was becoming a part of the place. "I tell you, Helena, skirts up to here and that hair! Nobody had hair that colour. Your Gelda would walk down the street and clocks would stop. I mean, there never was anybody like Gelda."

"So she wasn't in Paris," I said.

"Of course she was in Paris," said Merg. "I'm talking about when she came back."

I wrote out a tag for the blue ginger jar, copying out details from the red and black copybook onto the archive label. Merg kept watching me. "You know she was in Paris."

"I know she says she was." I held the jar up to the 90-watt. "This glaze has a chip in it, here, can you see? Did we know about that?"

Merg sat on the rung of the stepladder. The sole of his shoe was coming away from the leather above. He leaned in towards me. "What's this about, hey?" And then, before I could answer, he said, "If you think," Merg tasted his mouth, seemed to change his mind about something, "Whatever you think, you should speak to Gelda."

"Pass me the magnifier, will you?"

"Speak to her."

"I can't," I said "can I? She's in the flaming South Pacific dancing hula-hula."

I made a big show of checking the jar. It was one of Merg's favourites, a real antique that the V & A were having from us when the rest of the collection went to auction.

"All right," said Merg, with a tone of enforced reasonableness. "Was Gelda in Paris?"

"Merg —"

"If you're asking me, honestly, then I have to say, I don't know. Maybe she wasn't. Maybe it's the fluoride in the water talking."

I looked up at him.

"But I do know she came back swearing in French and with a pretty rosy photo collection too. And I know that Gelda says she was there. And that's good enough for me."

I lidded the crate with the ginger jar and pushed it over the floor to Merg, who lined up tacks and drove them in.

I crossed my legs beneath me and watched him, nails in mouth, missing his thumb with the hammer and missing the tack as well. "I just think, if everything was so great in Paris, you know, why did she come back? The way she speaks sometimes, you'd think she'd never gotten over it, as if the whole rest of it was some kind of great comedown, but she was the one who came back. It was her choice."

Crack! Hammer collided with thumb. Merg spat out the nails and looked almost relieved now that the inevitable was out of the way.

"I don't know who she is half the time, I mean the things she comes out with, they're ridiculous, even Troy catches her out sometimes with her contradictions. I mean everyone knows Marlene Dietrich wasn't –"

"Helena, Helena, listen to yourself. Does it matter? Whether she was or she wasn't. You're not in college now, you can give her her poetic –"

"It would just – it would just be nice, Merg, it would be nice to – I mean you knew Mum and Dad. And Granddad. Nobody's ever done anything, been anywhere."

"Troy and you might –"

"Troy can't work out his way from the duvet these days. We'll stay here, I bet, and it would compensate in some way if Gag at least, I mean if a minimum of one of us had once had the smallest bit of fun. And then – well, I don't know who she is, do I? What she's done. I don't know, I just want something real between the two of us instead of all this *'Allo 'Allo* business."

"Helena –" Merg was chuckling.

I drew my knees into my chest. "I mean she drinks her milk warm in the morning, likes her cheese soft and her beef half-raw but – you know I asked her once why she came back and you know what she said? She said gravity. What kind of an answer is that? She's not been further than Southend. She's no better than the rest of them. As Bohemian as –"

"Well now it was hardly her choice, was it?" Merg had the tone of one telling a well-worn truth. "Was it?" he said again, indignant.

I had to shrug.

Merg's eyes grew big as he took in my ignorance, and he pulled his neck back into his body, his features crumpling, wrinkles cascading down his face. "Her mother and father, your grand – no," he pushed his glasses back up his nose, "your *great*-grandparents," he said, "had strokes, both of them. Him first, then her. Terrible thing. This was winter '46, if I remember."

"And what happened?"

"Well, Maggie, your grandmother, she telegrammed to Gelda, to come home right away, I suppose. Anyway, wasn't more than a day after they went into the hospital but Gelda was back."

"I never knew."

"Well, why would you? What's any of that to do with you?"

"But why didn't she go back?"

"Oh, Maggie wouldn't have done with that. You have to remember she'd looked after them for years, all through the war and with your mother too. She had a time of it. Chalk and cheese those two, as they say; Maggie was born an old woman, and as for Gelda, well she was flighty, yes, flighty, oh, but she was alive-alive-o."

I shook my head.

"Maggie put her foot down and it wasn't the kind of foot you argued with."

"She was jealous."

"Well now, I couldn't –"

"Of course she was." I knew my grandmother from

a sepia photo in a Victorian frame, and I knew she was jealous of Gag and her Moulin Rouge tryout, of her romances, of red wine and cigarettes, accordion music and being alive. Who wouldn't be? "She could have gone back, though, couldn't she Merg? After her parents, I mean, after they'd died."

"But they didn't die, least not for a year or so. She was a marvel with them really, course they weren't what they'd been, your grandfather never spoke again, and your grandmother –" Merg caught my eye and cleared his throat.

"But even then –"

"A year's a year; she couldn't just go back and pick up where she'd left off."

"Why not? The war was over."

The lines on Merg's face sharpened into a frown.

"What?"

"Everybody knew Gelda had a fellow over there. When she first got back he used to send her chocolates. You'd see her hanging over the garden gate after the postman a quarter hour before he was due, and she used to wear, oh, only a cheap thing, a little cross on a chain that we knew was for his sake."

"And?"

"And she was nine months over here looking after her mother." Merg gave me a look like the moral was obvious. "The story I heard was – mind this was years later, the story was, that this fellow, he wouldn't have her. He'd married someone else, you see, while she'd been over here."

I worked at the tarnish on the copper without the slightest nostalgia. I was surprised, now that it was here, to find that I wouldn't miss any of it – coming home, my fingers stained with verdigris, my lungs heavy with dust. I was stepping away from a world of things with a specific purpose, a place, a value, a catalogue note into I didn't know what, and – damn the mortgage, the council pension scheme – I couldn't wait. I'd thought of myself, those last months, as the one that didn't belong, with my big ideas in a small town, the rogue Garibaldi in a pack of plain biscuits, but, after all, all the time there was Gag, a pink wafer in a world of digestives, and she didn't care who knew it. What did I want with philosophy when there was her?

"She should have said, she should have told me."

"Oh now, people don't go spilling their life stories without you asking them."

"Gag does," I said. I thought she did. But Gag's stories

were full of happiness, not heartbreak and as for him, this Jean, this Pierre, whoever he was, she'd never even said his name.

Merg brewed up some tea and pulled out two slices of Battenburg from somewhere. "You're upset."

"It's a sad story."

"But romantic, don't you think?"

"What's romantic about it?"

"Oh, people say things are romantic because what else should they say?" Merg smiled. "You remember the good stuff. My mother had a saying, in the war, she said, if the bombers took your leccy out, you were to say, isn't candle-light romantic. If you were out of candles you said, ain't the stars spread out nice tonight. You make it romantic. You remember the good things. And Gelda's the best at that."

I licked my finger and picked up cake crumbs.

"So," he said, "this new place, this museum of whatever they decide to do with it in the end."

"What about it?"

"Great opportunity."

"For what?" I snorted.

"For you. Why not? I'll write the reference. You could run that place on your head, without me to – keep an eye on."

"Oh Merg — I —" I stopped. Merg had a definite daughter-I-never-had look in his eye. "I don't know," I said. "I just — I mean." I didn't want a life like Merg's, to turn slowly into a relic myself. I didn't want to be surrounded day after day by death, these *memento mori*, scornful, all of them, that whilst we came and went they went on regardless. I didn't want things; I wanted people. I wanted, today and tomorrow and the day after, to clear my lungs of dust and breathe in the whole world.

"You could do what you liked," Merg was saying. "School visits, hands-on displays."

"History isn't dates and times and places. It isn't objects gathering dust. It's you, Merg, and Gelda and me. It's not what's in museums, is it? It's what you remember, what you don't even know you know but you carry it round with you because it's in your blood."

Merg smiled, "Listen. About Gelda."

"I've been an idiot."

"Now," said Merg, "we've all been fools on occasion."

But I knew I'd been the worst kind of fool and for a very long time, and as soon as I could I left Merg to finish the boxing and labelling and headed over to the Clays to Troy's. I had an apology for him, the first apology either of us had ever made to the other without Mum standing over us with a metaphorical rolling pin or a plate of peanut cookies. I also had, which I thought Troy would appreciate possibly more, a raisin, lemon and chocolate king-size cheesecake I'd picked up from the new New York Cheesecake Store where the wool shop had been.

I cut through the town square. There was a crowd gathered at the foot of the clock tower, and three or four ambulances. I looked away, my arms goose-bumping; another suicide, I thought. They happened round this time of year: exams. They ought to knock the thing down. It was cursed. Even the guy who'd built it was in on the trend: Godfrey Churton spent twenty-five years architecturing the thing and as soon as the ribbon was cut flung himself off.

I rang the bell at number twenty-seven and Boz, Troy's pink-haired housemate, opened the door. He stared at the cheesecake.

"Is Troy in?"

"Troy," said Boz, the name ringing distant bells, his eyes still on dessert. I wondered briefly whether it would be an act of citizenship to tell the university authorities, before they awarded Boz his third-class medical degree, about his collection of pot plants. "He's at – no wait, he's in hospital."

"What?" I said.

"Yeah."

"Which is it? In it or at it?"

"In it," Boz said, suddenly definite once given a multiple choice. "Overdose. I tried to call. Are you taking that cheesecake?"

Go as you know how to go, Go now!

I walk up on the air like getting out of bed.

I don't need no wings

no strings to bear my heavy heart when I rise up,

riding the wind, black

against the black sky

bright before the moon.

My mother's daughter's free,

a pearl no longer bound

in gold's cold clasp

nor strung in ropes of ornament.

I open my eyes to a crystalline ocean.

Coral reefs fill amniotic seas

and skin divers search for *Te Ufi*.

I see the island shores approaching,

feel wet sand moulding to my shape and all is once more

Haere Maru, Oa Oa,

there is sunrise for every sunset, a tide in for every tide out.

I will sing myself hoarse and bathe in the silence.

I will go where the black sand and the white sand

sit striped together

like truth and lies, lies and truth.

What you do with it

Even with tubes sticking out of him and puke on his hair, Troy looked like a Calvin Klein ad. The doctors said he was going to be fine. What they meant was, he wasn't going to die, but there's a long way between breathing and feeling good about it. I sat with him till the sun started showing over the outbuildings, then wandered out along the gardens where Troy used to sneak for a fag while Mum slept, round to the main reception, thumbing a pound coin in my pocket. There was a queue at the soup machine. An old man was having trouble with the wrist action. He put a coin in the slot, stooped a moment later to retrieve it when the machine spat it out, stood up again and repeated the process. I went to help. I knew the hospital front to back, every relatives' room, every corridor, the peculiarities of vending machines. "Do you want a hand?"

The man picked up the coin again, dropped it in the slot once more; there was a second's pause and the clunk of the return.

I put my hand over the coin slot. The man turned to look at me. It wasn't until we were face to face that I recognised Jack Morea. "Aurelie," he said.

I shook my head.

"All my fault," he said.

I thought, *the clock tower. It was her*.

"Here," I took his shilling from him, my hands and voice both shaky, and plunged my pound in. "What do you want?"

He shrugged. I hit tomato. "Is she –?"

"Intensive care."

"But she's –?"

"You know what they'll write," he turned his shilling over. "Like mother like daughter."

"I'm really sorry."

"Like mother like daughter. But what if it wasn't the genes? What if it was me?"

"Aurelie was unhappy, for a long time, for as long as –"

"What if it's my fault?"

"OK," I'd gotten this often enough, taking a breather in the relatives' room, or at the soup machine; the Vendex was always good for deep and meaningfuls. I'd lost count of the confessions I'd heard over the years from next of kins and estranged spouses, people always felt better when there was someone to blame, even if it was themselves. What they couldn't cope with was not knowing, was chance, was the way life is. "One person jumped, Jack, and it wasn't you."

"But, you see, if I'd talked to her."

"People don't get made like gingerbread men. They make choices, they —" Jack Morea had spent a quarter century persuading the world to give up on perfection, but he couldn't convince himself. "You still believe in it, don't you?"

"I don't believe in anything."

"*The Theory of Soul*; you still think life's logical and there's someone to point the finger at, but you know —"

"If I'd spoken to her, told her about Arii."

"Then she might still have jumped." He was still engrossed in his shilling, "Drink your soup," I said. "Let's get some air."

We walked along Spinal and out into the little rose

garden by Oncology. The bushes were past their best, browning at the edges, but the lavender was blooming, and the fuschias, and children played in the rainbow that sprinklers misted over the path. We sat on a bench and watched the sky.

"You know, I always thought it was the parents did the teaching. Before Aurelie I had a theory, I had hundreds of them. I had sequels planned, I had – never mind." He smiled as a little girl shyly presented him with a daisy. "It seems like somebody else's life, when I look back on it, and I have to remind myself that the mad hermit I read about in the papers, and the fool who came up with that book, that was me."

"Jack," I said.

"What?"

"You should be with her."

"Yes." He looked at his soup.

"Talk to her."

"About Arii?"

"It's a start."

"You're right." He frowned at the bubbles on his soup.

"How much worse can things get, Jack?" I said.

He smiled.

"Sometimes you need to take a chance."

He stood up and walked towards Aurelie's room.

I took a sip of the soup; it was luke-warm. I watched the kids chasing water and the patients watching them and I walked back towards Troy's room, and as I came to the payphone, where the corridor split in two, there was Gag, standing with her suitcase behind her, sunburned and sober, silhouetted against the afternoon sun. I'd been waiting for fifteen hours for somebody to come and put their arms around me. I wrapped her up in a hug, held her as she deserved to be held onto. "Stupid fool," she said, and I didn't know which one of us she meant. "You should have called me, you should have –"

I told Gag that he was still sleeping it off; that the doctors had wanted to wait till she got there, that they'd told me nothing. We were used to doctors.

Gag took the cold soup. I took her suitcase. We went through to his room and stood by the window, whispering into the silence.

"But why, Helena? Why this? I thought he was –"

"Ever since Mum. Ever since then he's been impossible."

"Of course he has," Gag said simply. "He feels guilty."

"Guilty? For what?"

"'For what?' she says," Gag shook her eyes like dice. "For all the things you think he should feel guilty about – the car, the cigarettes, the girls."

"That's not it."

"He told me."

I had difficulty imagining Troy admitting to any feelings that weren't biological urges.

Gag blinked. She said, "You're lucky, Helena. You can look back, and there's nothing on your conscience. You did your best. As for Troy, you think you're the only one noticed that he screwed up back there? What's he to do; he can't turn the clock back, and besides that's the person he is, *c'est la etcetera*, so what is he to do, you tell me? What do you do with the past, hey, and what are you going to let it do to you?"

I sat there. Trust Troy to luck out with a window room. The sky always looked big from this part of town: no high rises to break it up, no hills to cut it short; it stretched inarguably as far as you could see and further. If we were still here in a couplefew hours there'd be a sunset worth seeing and after that some mean stars. Gag rustled a sweetie wrapper. My hands had swollen up with the stress and my wristwatch was biting into my skin. My hair felt greasy; there'd been no time to wash it.

Here I was again. So many years I'd spent in little rooms dreaming of big skies. Gag was staring at me. "What did you miss? Really though, Helena – drinking sweet cider along the river bank, snogging spotty boys in grotty bedsits? If you wanted to, you could do it tomorrow. As for Troy, what he missed out on there's no substituting for."

We sat then for a long time, till my heart synched in with the beep of Troy's monitor, trying to compose my first words for him, knowing we were running out of chances, and then, just after ten, when all three of us were breathing at once, Troy opened his eyes. He looked straight at me and shut them again. "Bollocks," he said then, quite loudly.

"How do you feel?" Gag said.

"Like a beer." Troy opened his eyes again and looked at us both. "Seriously," he said, "I feel like shit."

Then I started crying and Troy just stared at me and Gag went to look out of the window. I said that I was sorry, that I hadn't known he was feeling so bad and that I felt just lousy about the stupid row. Mum wouldn't want him to feel guilty about anything. We loved her, we all did and we'd get through this; there was only the three of us now in the whole world, there was us three and if we didn't stick together –

Troy looked at the place on his wrist where the drip went in. Gag looked at me. Troy pointed at the drip and grinned at Gelda, "Cool!"

A nurse came in with a glass of water for Troy. He gave her the old once over, I saw she wiggled her behind on the way out, and a smile spread over her like butter.

"I want you to know you can talk to me, Troy," I said. "This, what's happened, it can be – we can start over, can't we?"

Troy said, "I took a bad E, H. It's not like some sign of some deep spiritual malaise. It's not a sign of anything. It just, I dunno, happened."

Gag narrowed her eyes at me, "You said it was an overdose."

"H!" Troy had a look of moral outrage.

"I just thought –" I said, "I mean – Boz said."

"Boz?" said Troy and Gelda together. "What about the doctors?"

"I don't know." The whole idea seemed suddenly a bad one. Troy refused to contemplate death until there was metaphysical proof of the existence of Pot Noodle in the afterlife. Besides, hardly anything that Troy had done had really been on purpose.

"But why would you even think?" said Troy. "Shit."

"When did you learn the word 'malaise'?" I said.

I sent Gag home, confiscating the Thomas Cook brochure from her duty-free bag. A consultant came round with a clipboard and ran through a quarter-hearted lecture about drugs awareness, they changed Troy's drip, they brought in a menu choices form for the next day, and between all of this we shifted, we manoeuvred the conversation round, poking and prodding at the silences, moving in incremental stages round to the topic of Mum and Dad. The whole thing was like playing Ker-plunk, trying to pull the right sticks out, knowing that any sudden move would send the whole lot down.

Troy picked at a scab on his elbow. "I'm sorry," he said.

"For what?"

He looked up at me through his fringe. "You want a list?"

"Forget lists," I said. "I want a signed affidavit."

Troy lay back and looked up at the ceiling. "OK. I'm sorry for you having to, you know, for having to make up for me. To Mum and Dad. I'm sorry you had to be the sensible one. I'm sorry, OK?"

I looked at Troy. His surfer's suntan was paling and, lying down, he looked much smaller than usual, and I noticed for the first time the mole he had, a small one, just left of centre on his top lip. How long had he had that? How long had I had mine? "I wanted to do it," I said. "Well, not exactly wanted to, but –" but given the range of options, I'd rather have these regrets than the other kind and maybe it was me owed the apology, not him.

Troy and me, we'd always thought of ourselves in this way, defining ourselves in opposition to each other. I was the smart one, so Troy was the dumb one. Troy was the wild child where I was sensible. I ate my courgettes; Troy fed them to the cat when he thought Mum wasn't looking. But we didn't have to do that. We could both be the smart ones or we could both be dumb; the possibility was caught for a moment, like a butterfly under a glass. We could be whoever we wanted to be.

"There's something we need to do when you get out," I said.

"Agatha's wedding."

"There's something else. We need to bury Mum and Dad."

"Didn't we do that already? I mean, there was a

funeral, H, I remember a poached salmon."

"Yes," I said, "OK, but we need to – scatter the ashes or something."

"Oh." He didn't say anything for a while.

"I can't stand it any more, Troy. Them being there all the time and it's not like I don't miss them, because I do, all the time. It's just – them being there, I mean on the freaking shelf, Troy, when I'm having my dinner, when I get in, when I get up. You can't keep your parents on the shelf, Troy. It's not normal. We have to let them go because –"

"OK, OK," Troy said. "We'll do it. Soon as I get out, we'll just, we'll go to the park and we'll –"

"Are you sure though?"

"Yeah. It's cool, sis."

"It is?"

"Yeah. It's all good, H. Everything's cool."

And we sat there together – or I sat and Troy lay – with the same genes, near as you can get, and same upbringing but different as two people could be, and who would ever really know why, so we'll just have to put it down to that one percent, those things that can't be accounted for. Those things that people call soul.

It's just skin between me and
dissolving,
dispersing like salt.

My blood's flowing thick
and slow with the water
thick and slow and I do not know
if I open my eyes can I see?
If I open my mouth can I speak?
Is the blackness only in my head? And the pounding?

She bubbles about me
breaks on my skin

Aurelieaurelieaurelie

she says

come in, pulls

with the tide, surfs and breaks

about me in a roar

I bob for a moment giddy as cork then

fall down to where dark waters

fold about me, roll over and hold me below in the cold.

Then another voice, distant from the shore:

"They called her the Tahitian pearl. Not all Tahitian pearls are black, of course; they come in blue and green, in gold and silver and in aubergine, but she understands from the name they give her what they mean her to understand: she is exotic, and beautiful, and black, and for sale."

It's him, the fisherman come

to poach me from my ocean.

A two-legger, no merman, he

would cut my tail from me, keep me

on dry land where the air's dead and too clouded for visions

and love shrivels. I won't take the bait

swim deeper down

to where her voice echoes

like sea in a shell

and I chase it

escape him

my shins scraping coral my fingers

tangling seaweed

"In the evening, she would dance the *tamure* in perfumed leis, and they would buy shell necklaces to take home to their wives. Those days were the happiest, when the dance still meant nothing more to her than the steps she had memorised and everything was *Haere Maru*, *Oa Oa*, and there was a sunrise for every sunset and a tide in for every tide out.

"In 1962 the dancing stopped. Arii was twelve. The same year, they opened the first oyster farm: 5,000 pipis were strung up, ten to a rope and caged in chicken wire, starved until they wept pure pearl. Three long years they waited for the harvest, the oysters growing fat and Arii growing breasts that rounded out in front of her, hips that swayed like palm trees ripe with fruit and a mind grown fat with stories of faraway lands."

Not everyone is born on an island, Daddy, not everyone

can draw a shoreline, a tidemark

between one thing and another. Some people

live in swamps, never knowing what will take their weight,

when they are better to swim,

when to make a stand.

Some of us are merpeople

caught between the elements.

And I float,

him above me on the shore, her below on the ocean floor,

And I listen to her

Aurelieaurelieaurelie

calling me back to her

and I listen to him:

"By the time I found her, she was washed up. Wrung out. Fame had taken what it could and left. It was Christmas Eve, the trash cans and taxi cabs, the hobos, all beneath a crisp four inches, and she was stuck in a rehearsal hall off-off-Broadway, looping over and over the key change, trying to nail the intonation. Arii watched me, this old man, take a front row seat, brushing the flakes from my overcoat, shaking my hat.

'I think it's still snowing out there then,' she says.

'Yes, rather heavily I'm afraid,' I say.

'You're English!' She throws her hands together, for the English, she believed, are a step nearer God and civilisation than Americans. 'Have you been here long?'

'I just landed. Conference in Cornell after New Year. Interesting interpretation by the way.'

'Are you a critic?' Her smile fades and she reaches for her shoulder strap, wrapping her arms around her breasts.

I smile reassurance, 'No.'

'What then?' She is heading for the wings; she is scanning the lightbox to see if she is alone.

'A philosopher,' I stand up; there is a stiffness as I bow.

She stops. Opens her mouth in a slow revelation of ecstasy. 'Really? A philosopher in America, that is an unusual thing, you know. Here, I think they are getting their philosophy most of all from bus tickets and, what do you call them, the crackers in the Chinese restaurant.'

'Fortune cookies.'

We laugh.

'So you are a fan of the theatre?' She changes her clothes. She does it easily, except, to save my blushes, she turns her back. As she wriggles out of the red silk I see the curve of her breast, understand her nakedness, that skin, like a solar eclipse, like oil over my soul. When she turns back to me, in jeans and black polo-neck, ready to be taken for coffee and discuss Sartre and Wittgenstein with this genteel Englishman, I cannot look her in the eye, don't understand where the show stops and the real woman begins. I never did learn.

"I buy her a coffee, black and four sugars, we talk about Sartre (her English does not extend to philosophical terms; I do not speak French so we discuss the love affair with Beauvoir and who was the genius, who the lunatic), we watch the snow settle in drifts, the young couples lugging Christmas trees along the streets and finally, when she has sunk enough caffeine to make another woman tremble, the snow stops and the whiteness turns to sludge, like regret, like hangover. Then, I ask her to marry me.

"It was a long distance love affair, our passion divided by the cold Atlantic waves, the soulless fish, the grey unending sky. I couldn't work in New York. The skyscrapers, I told her, stood between me and God, the smell of used banknotes made writing impossible. I left her to her soft-shoe shuffle and red velvet curtains and our love crackled and hissed on a transatlantic telephone call. We made our declarations in *The New York Times* and *The Telegraph*. We called it a whirlwind romance, and she believed it. I'd been in love with her for years. Anyway, the wedding was tasteful. She wore white, and after we were done, she released twenty-four doves into the crisp London air. She looked like Audrey Hepburn."

It's greenish black and thick
with cold. It's shipwreck land, old bones and gold
down here and everything forgotten
Aurelieaurelieaurelie
Take a breath, she says

"Aurelie, there will always be remnants. You cannot gather up every last crumb of your past and roll it into something new. There will always be a grain you will miss, like sand between your toes, a speck in the crevices. Don't look at her mistakes and call it your destiny. You have her eyes, Aurelie, and her walk, but that's all, and you're mine as much as hers and more than that, you're your own person. And I'll tell you something else: Arii couldn't hold a note. Her voice was thin and dry and out of tune most times I heard it. No one gave you that voice. The world might look at you and see Arii, but when you sing, it's you they listen to. It's you they hear, Aurelie. Those fans of yours, down at that club, they're not applauding Arii Cook. They forgot all about her soon as you opened your mouth. So talk to me Aurelie, talk to me, please."

> I look up to where the sunlight
> meets the water, staining it
> turquoise, gold, cerise.
> I kick my legs against the tide.
> I swim up
> up to the sky to the warm air
> and my father.
>
> Is it Aurelie she's calling anyway, or Arii?
> Is it her own name she's left repeating
> tide in, tide out, eddying about
> her voice distorting on the waves?
>
> I don't look back.

My father weeps. I open my eyes; hold out my hand

to him. I know my mother. I am her daughter. But I am not her. I am not her.

All those things at once

The sun, for the first time in weeks, had lifted himself up into the sky. He sat there knowing he had something to prove; he'd been gone so long, we'd all but given up believing. He chased the clouds away till blue sky showed through, cooked the air up nice and hot and people put their summer demeanour on – slapped on suncream, slipped on summer clothes and laid back on their lawns and terraces, taking in the day. Seemed the whole world had been building to an impro right in time for Mom and Bob's wedding, even if it was only the kind of day they deserved, and Mom was forty-eight miles past capable of being impressed by the British weather.

We waited outside the registrar's office in the Town

Hall. There were frescoes above us of fat gods and pink babies; on either side there was lists of war dead. The party of us was impervious to the all of it. Mom wore a sheath dress in burgundy shimmer and in her hair, kinkless as the Nile, a gerbera. Bob had gone for the Cuban pimp look in his black button-down shirt and pants, spats and his black hat with its white band, his skinny white tie showing off the bulk of the rest of him. There was something more solid about the two of them there as a couple than the pairs of teens and twenty-somethings waiting their turn in the foyer. Mom and Tantie, when it hit them, both had a way of being happy others didn't, I guess because it came unpractised.

"I'm hungry; anybody here hungry?" Diddy said.

"I could eat a good meal, starving so," Bo said and winked at me.

"I don't know about anybody else, but I had myself a sausage roll on the way over," Bob said. "I hear the food at this wedding, it ain't up to much."

"Bloody hilarious," I said, best English. I'd been up since six, four hours in Tantie's kitchen in my Pink Panther nightshirt, Bebe's straightening lotion on my hair and up to my elbows in pork. Taken all up with the worry of whether my mother would get her size fourteen dress to zip up, and whether Bob would have a last minute change of heart, I rubbed salt into skin and cursed Tantie, who hadn't left me anything useful, like a recipe, a menu, an instruction on temperature or utensils. She'd left me ten pounds of raw meat, a ragbag of vegetables, and a feeling that whatever it was I was supposed to be doing I should have started three hours ago. Cooking should have come natural to me as bleeding, but it wouldn't. Sure I could peel a potato or mince meat, but introduce heat into the equation and I was lost. Tantie said I think too much about it. When she caught me with my face in a recipe book or counting out teaspoons of spice and seasoning, she'd say, "Can't cook a chicken leg by thinking about it and can't skin it neither. Cooking ain't something goes on in here," she'd tap her temple with her forefinger, "it's something happens out here," and she made a gesture took in the world. "You got to disengage the brain, see. Got to let everything move just howsoever it likes."

"Yes," I'd say, "but can you just tell me if I can use fennel seed if we out of caraway?"

"What I'm saying, Georgie, is cooking is a function of the unconscious mind."

Helena waved from across the foyer. I snuck over

to her, before Mom could ask me to check her teeth for lipstick, her hemline for petticoat, her breath for garlic, for the eighteenth time that day. "Well?" I said.

She grinned, "I got it."

"You did?" I said. "Well, let's see."

"What's this?" Diddy said, turning round. "An airplane ticket?" Helena handed him the wallet. "What's in Costa Rica?"

"Snakes mostly, where we're going, which I can't stand, and some great surf, whatever that means. I can't wait."

I gave her a hug.

"Gag thinks we're mad," Helena said. "But where's Mary?"

I linked my arm through hers and waltzed her over to the window; I pushed my finger up against the glass. All Helena could say was, "Christ."

Tantie was at the Town Hall too, see, but with a banner, not a bouquet, in her hands and on the outside. Facing up to what happened, it had stitched up something been leaking out of Mom, but it had punctured Tantie, that and Jimmy, and left her with no way back to herself. She'd found out that week that the museum was becoming a mobile phone shop. After having to give up on Aurelie, she'd taken it bad; she'd been those few days marching back and forwards over the town square and she wasn't about to stop for something as politically insignificant as her sister's wedding.

I'd spent twenty minutes going back between the two of them, pleading with Tantie to see sense, pleading with Mom to make her see it. "Go and ask her," I said.

"I asked her already. She got an invite like the rest of y'all."

"Ask again," I said. "She's proud."

"Hmph," says Mom, "and I ain't?"

I'd begged Bo and the guys to hustle my aunt in there, but there wasn't one of them man enough to make the attempt.

When the registrar asked us to come in, Mom gave a grim smile, punched her bouquet at Bob, turned on her three inchers and, fists pumping, bottom grinding, stormed across the hall. We all trailed after her. "We'll be back," I said to the registrar who looked just thrilled at the idea.

With a single throw of her shoulder, Mom dislocated the oak door, "You waiting for a personal invitation?" she hollered across the courtyard. It was Saturday and the square was full of shoppers, lugging home bags with the weekly shop and kids jumping skateboard along the sides of the fountains. There were buses stacking up like empties in the bays, the couple previous posing for photos and a bratty pageboy kicking pigeons. Everyone looked at my mom.

"I'm busy." Tantie shook it out and let it settle back again, but she didn't stop marching and she hoisted that banner another foot in the air.

"Busy making a fool of yourself and myself. It's my wedding!"

Tantie threw her head in a half-circle. "Life don't stop, you know. The rest of the world don't stop just 'cause you got a flower in your buttonhole."

"The rest of the world keep spinning without you pushing it for one day, you know that?" Mom said.

But Tantie knew no such thing. Tantie knew soon as her back was turned people were chopping down trees and putting lions in cages and oppressing the peasant women of Bangladesh. Being Tantie was a 24-7 occupation with no breaks for sugared almonds and confetti. Even on her own wedding day she had, in place of a just married sign on the back of the cab, a notice read *Free Nelson Mandela*. She knew, the way the world was going, she was all between it and the apocalypse.

"Ladies, ladiez, laydeeeez," Diddy says, pushing himself forward. "Ain't we all adults here? Don't we all understand the principle of compromise?"

"Compromise?" Mom and Tantie almost found themselves in a moment of agreement on the stupidity of that idea. Years of growing up had taught them that when one sister got, the other one didn't. There is no such thing as compromise in families; you keep count, you know the score, and little families is the worst: in a little family, everything is magnified. Lord knows there is no such thing as small stuff for us; every batted eyelid, every sucked tooth made waves.

I looked over at Bob, who rearranged his feet on the pavement.

Tantie's bottom lip was shaking. Her eyes rolled 'round the crowd as she looked for that killer argument. In the end she said, "Didn't they do that dress in your size?"

Mom, who really was busting out all over, did a brief impression of speechlessness (she always did like a crowd, and she could work them in a way Tantie couldn't). "If you got it," she said.

Tantie held more cards than she knew. Mom's passport was in her married name: there was coconut cocktails waiting for her, there was candlelit dinner on the beach, all she had to do was swallow some pride and get the hell on. But Mom cared more for face than freebies, and in the end it was Mary, the big sister, who said, through her teeth, and hands on hips but with a lift of her chin hinted that she might yet accept a total surrender graciously. "So it's some kind of big deal to you, is *that* what you're saying?"

"A big," Mom sounded the word out slow, "deal, you might say it that way."

Some of us held onto our tongues, others couldn't help but let a curse escape or mutter a prayer; our heads were going one side to the other like it was the Williams sisters not the Easys we were watching.

"So how come then, how come −" For the first time now Tantie stopped marching, she let the banner down. "Tell me, 'cause I want to know," she said. "Why you never asked me to be your bridesmaid? Hmmm?"

"Well," Mom shifted her weight from one hip to the other. This was something, what Tantie was saying, that she might even consider the thing. Tantie in white or lace and giving out bonbons, Tantie walking three paces behind my mom, Tantie putting aside about a hundred and seventeen of her principles (even if she did have principles to spare). Everyone looked at Mom. Bob and Diddy clutched each other by the elbow, the two of them miming an enthusiastic nod. Mom put her hands over her eyes. "No, no, no, Mary Hosannah Easy, I ain't having you as no bridesmaid of mine. No way."

At some point in this disputation, an old white couple had sat themselves down on one of the benches in the square, eating cheese and onion crisps and watching my family like a movie show. At Mom's answer they let out a groan. Everybody likes a happy ending.

"That's to say," Mom hitched at her dress, a blink above a nipple, "who else I got to give me away?"

That did it. For the first time that anyone could remember (and wouldn't you know it ain't been seen since), Tantie was unable to speak, she could only flap her hand about her bosom and raise her eyebrows and try and keep her lip from shaking. And then the official wedding photographer, if he, that is Diddy, had not been picking chewing gum from the sole of his shoe, might have caught a moment when Mom and Tantie collapsed into each other and held onto each other because – even today being the day it was – what else was there to hold onto?

Then Bob checked his watch and decided to take

charge, now that nobody else was trying to. He grabbed my mom, flashed her a smile and pulled her, sandals clacking on the cobbles, bosoms making a run for it, inside. We – Tantie followed by me and Bo and Diddy and Helena and Troy and Gelda and Son Son and all the rest of them – in a line, ran after them.

After the big I do's we stood in the square, Cody and Elise collecting confetti in champagne glasses as Diddy choreographed my parents and Tantie prepared her speech. She'd had Diddy make her a stage from two MDF MFI wardrobes and borrowed the sound system from the club. At three o'clock she was launching her protest rally. "I'm going to say my piece, and they going to hear it," she said, jabbing her finger at the microphone, jerking her head at the office windows. It was a sad thing: her usual gang of protesters were double-booked, picketing a Chunky Chicken factory in Hereford.

Bo walked over, all faking nonchalant, but the brother looked fine and knew it in that old pink shirt always was a favourite of mine. "Well?" I said, pretending all interest in my buttonhole.

"Licence came through this afternoon."

"So," I said, "What's the plan?"

He said, "Oh you know, bring things up to speed some."

"With what?"

"A little hip-hop, a little garage, you know."

"And old skool?" I said. "And funk?"

Bo scratched his head and smiled the goofiest smile.

"You'll never get Mom and Tantie in," I said. "Not with music like that."

Bo smiled, "That's too bad, Georgie, really," and as Tantie waved him over and he took my empty glass from me he let his hand stay a little longer on mine than it needed. "You're seeming more yourself," he said.

"More myself than what?"

He laughed, "You got me in knots, sister. In knots, you hear." Then he called over my head, "Mary, let's test the bass on this thing, yeah?"

You reach a point beyond facts, when dates and times and names and places become insubstantial as smoke. All of us, Texan or Tahitian, are separated, oceans across oceans, skins shading through space and time like sugar cooking, by a percentage point which is nothing, and, at the same time, all. That 1 percent is the kink in my hair and the kick in my stride, the swing of my hips and the hang of my waist, that 1 percent is what makes it worth being alive. Wasn't Mom or Sanderson, Tantie or Helena could tell me who I was, and the answer wouldn't be found in Texas, Tahiti, or Tarbert, nor at the bottom of a bowl of sugar doughnuts. So I considered my fathers, Sanderson, Jimmy and Bob, all three of them, and did not try to cling to the idea of one of them lest the others wriggle past my grasp, for ain't one of us can claim an independence of what links us all, not blood but soul, not words, but music.

The truth's like climbing mountains, and soon as you reach one, you see a bigger one up ahead. As Mom would say, weaving a blanket of aphorisms to wrap me in and hold me tight, a girl could spend her life climbing, growing dizzy at high altitude. You want to try and answer one question without finding another hanging on its tail like a flea on a dog? You might as well try finding a fish without a bone, try finding a peach without a stone, try living your life alone. No matter how many questions you ask, or how far back you go, there will always be dry desert plains and oases; miracles remain.

"Girl!" Tantie was waving her arm at me, not being one to respect a moment of silence, "Stop staring and get your ass over here and fix my – Lord!"

"Fix your pardon me?" Diddy said. But Tantie was

near hysterical, poking in her handbag for her lipstick and rolling her eyes at a TV crew crossing the road towards the town hall.

"You put a photo-call out, Mary?" Bo said.

"You brung the TV to my wedding?" Mom was winding up the voltage.

"Word gets around," Tantie said, layering lipstick. Wouldn't you know she had a vanity natural to every woman. She clambered up onto her stage, Bo lifting her by the armpit, Diddy using a well-placed hand on her behind. She stood there, mic in hand, stuck out her chest, pulled up her spine and placed her feet in a neat T, like she told me she did the days she practised for Miss Texas. The crew came towards Tantie, brushed straight past her and set up to the far side of the square, their lenses pointed at the Royal County, waiting for Jack Morea to show.

Tantie fiddled with the microphone. I saw her wipe away a tear.

"Look," I said out of nowhere and pointed right at my aunt with a look of ecstasy on my face. "It's Maya Angelou!"

"Maya Angelou?" said the man on the park bench with the fish paste sandwiches.

"That's right," said Bob, in his best stage voice, "Doctor Maya Angelou."

Mom pretended to swoon into his arms.

The TV crew looked at Tantie, who smiled like there wasn't a thing on her conscience, and reversed manoeuvres, scuttling back in our direction. The producer got his mobile out. The boom-operator asked Dr Angelou (who looked like she was born for this kind of adoration) for her autograph. Mary Easy smiled sweetly at them and began, once the lighting was right and the film was rolling, "John Henrik Clare," she said, "wrote that to control a people you must first control what they think about themselves and how they regard their history and culture." Tantie read from the 5 x 3s I'd printed in thick felt tip. She leaned into the mic, "When your conqueror makes you ashamed of your culture and your history, he needs no prison walls and no chains to hold you."

Tantie stopped and looked around. Now, you might disagree with my aunt, and you might think her mistaken, or a museum a small thing to get worked up over but we all reach a place where we need to draw a line. Some people are halfway to the devil before they find something worth arguing over, but Tantie fought every metre of ground and if St Peter didn't recognise her by her onion hands, he'd have turned her over and identified her by the *100% genuine* stamp on her American ass. The only thing bogus about Tantie, I thought, as I stood there, was this protest. And the bogus thing was, it played by the rules. You wouldn't have found Tantie with a stage at Greenham Common or at Newbury with a two-tone A5 flyer. I hoped that Tantie was not growing too respectable on us.

Just then a smile spread fatly through her, her breasts rising, her spine twisting, her hips shaking. She raised her hands as if to run them through her hair and she stopped like that. Then I heard a rumble, a tremor through the ground must have measured on the Richter scale, and it wasn't something you heard with your ears so much as felt with your bones and it bottle-stopped every mouth into a hiccough of silence and into that silence slid a note so golden it can't have been heard on this earth these two thousand years, not since angels was last around and it hung honeyed on the air and it fluttered warm against your skin, rippled up and down, whipping up the air like egg-white, buoying us up on its sweet, thick feel. And maybe two heartbeats after that note was a thrum kicked a throaty kind of a thing that throbbed along and filled out and gave out. I tried to turn my head around (but I told you, that air was thick, opening your eyes was like diving in treacle) to look for Aurelie but then I saw it wasn't Aurelie responsible, it was Tantie and in that single-second upbeat (and she hadn't even started to sing yet) she held that crowd like a mother a newborn, all helpless and precious at once in her arms. And then she began,

I ain't good looking,

The line lashed out, cut right across that quadrant trailing a rainbow in its wake and stinging whoever got in its way. She stopped then sang again,

And my hair ain't curls

And this time a voice answered it,

I ain't good looking,
and my hair ain't curls

It was Mom, and following her, voice came in upon voice and before I could make up my mind to join in I was singing and when I sang, instead of the hollowed-out sound of trains on the underground there was feelings, all manner of them, layering on top of one another, filling each other out, smoothing each other down. There was a top-note of sadness that carried across that square and came back to me sweeter, like a dove set free, and the key-note was swelled ripe with pride and there in the bass sat – yes – sat happiness. There was all those things at once and we sang,

But my momma, she gave me something
It's going to carry me through this world.

PERMISSIONS